I0678796

# Unwavering Hope

## Pam Kumpe

*Pam Kumpe*

Photo on Cover: Pam Kumpe

ISBN- 978-0692894699

## DEDICATION

To the Lord
Thank you for saving me!

To Cindy Ross
When God made you, He used guitar strings.
When God molded your heart, He used musical notes.
When God gave you breath, He sang a song.

*Pam Kumpe*

Your eyes saw my unformed substance;
in your book were written, every one of them, the days that
were formed for me, when as yet there was none of them.
How precious to me are your thoughts, O God! How vast is
the sum of them! If I could count them, they are more than the
sand. I awake, and I am still with you.
Psalm 139:16-18 NIV

# DISCLAIMER

This is a work of fiction. Names, characters, businesses, places, events and incidents are either the products of the author's imagination or used in a fictitious manner. Any resemblance to actual persons, living or dead, or actual events is purely coincidental. Although, there are many historical events that ring of truth in these pages.

*Pam Kumpe*

Memphis, Tennessee

## Closet Dreams

Even if Ms. Susan and Mr. Boyd shower me with frilly dresses, with ugly porcelain dolls, or with special outings across the street to the library to read the poetry books, I'm not staying in Jefferson, Texas. I'm not meant to live in a frame house with a picket fence unless it's Beech Street Manor back in Texarkana. I'm meant for the railroad tracks. For the rock and bump of the boxcar. For the rail.

The only reason I've stayed this long, crying in this closet after midnight, sitting with my satchel packed with sardines and crackers, while wiping away the heartbreak of the last two years is because of Lizzy Beth.

*Creak!* The wooden slats ached with the settling of the May night's air, with the heaviness of another day with people who act like they want me, but want me to leave.

"I best be quiet, Lizzy Beth's asleep under the quilt over there." I peeked through the cracked closet door at the Choctaw hair of my baby sister, who's nearly five now, who's nestled in her contentment and security of having a ma and pa, even if she's adopted.

I pulled on the knob, leaving a sliver of an opening to let the light in, but not to let the world inside with me. My fingers slid through my soft blonde ponytail. "I'm twelve and my hair's golden like burnt butter, not pretty and shiny. Just yellowish. The dress on the hanger has less dots than I have freckles."

Sighing, I crossed my legs, leaning against the back wall of the bunker-closet. "This must be how Molasses Jones felt when going to the Proving Grounds in Washington. A

hideaway, a place to dream and a place where nightmares
remind you of the hurt, the sorrow, and the loss." The lacy
Sunday dresses and day dresses of cotton danced from the
hangers above my head, with Lizzy Beth's matching dresses
on one end, mine on the other. "Dresses. Yuck. Pretty on
Lizzy Beth. Like sackcloth on me." I swished my hand along
the hems, causing them to sway like the rhythm of a boxcar
bouncing down the tracks.

"I've never worn so many dresses. A dress to church. A
dress to the library. A dress to the café to help Ms. Susan. A
dress to visit the boy's orphanage. A dress to go to the store."

*Shacuff... Shacuff... Creak!*

A small face stuck her head into my bunker. "What's my
big sister sitting in the closet for?" The door widened, and the
words of a pintsize sleepy-eyed reminder of Tin Can Mahlee
stood before me. Her face a younger version of her real mama,
a reminder of death for me. "My bed is lonely. I woke up.
You were gone."

"I'm thinking. This is my thinking place. I write poems in
here, dream about my daddy, and ... I'll be there soon." I
coughed. "I was thinking about our real daddy, Sidecar Ace."

Lizzy Beth pointed to the hallway. "Daddy Boyd is our
daddy. He loves us."

"Well, he doesn't love me. He bosses me. He gives me
evil glances at the supper table. He snaps at me and I've seen
his switch in the corner by his big chair in the parlor. The one
from the bushes out our window."

I wiggled to the corner as if I moved away from life, but
there was no escape from the pain, only a deep shadow of
loneliness hovering over me like a canopy of dresses. "Lizzy
Beth, why have you colored the walls in here with
dreamcatchers? I've never seen these many circles. Mama

Susan is going to spank you for using your crayons on the walls, again."

Sitting next to me, facing me like she might give advice, Lizzy Beth leaned in with her nose touching mine. "I love to color. These happened when you're in school. I dream of you. Of playing with you."

I ran my fingers through her hair. "Silly little girl. You'll be five this October, and I've been here almost a year. I still can't believe how Mr. Marion Kane pretended you were sick to trick me into coming back to Jefferson."

"I glad. I glad you come back." She kissed my nose. "I love you, Annie Grace."

Kissing her cheek. "Call me Shoelace. I like it better."

"Then call me Memphis Belle. Mr. Boyd calls me that when he's going to read to me." She yawned, stretching her arms, causing our dresses to sway above our heads.

"He does talk sweet to you. He agreed to take me in when Mr. Marion told him I was alone without … without family. He feels sorry for me."

"I am your sister. We be family."

"Yes, sweet beautiful Memphis Belle. You are the bestest thing to happen to me since I tasted the sweet syrup at the café."

Yawning, Lizzy Beth curled up next to me. "I sleep here, if you not come to bed."

I pulled her gown over her legs, her small toes curled under the hem, and she dozed off in seconds. I found myself touching the dreamcatcher sketched on the wall, remembering how I first saw Lizzy Beth at Wheelock Academy and how she never spoke. How she slept under a dreamcatcher and gave it to me. How I lost it somewhere.

When Lizzy Beth moved in with Ms. Susan and Mr. Boyd, she discovered her voice, rattling with chatter at sunrise until late into the night. She asks too many questions, and can already read like a third grader. Even at four and a half. She follows me, bumps into me, tugs on me, and hugs me.

Wiping a tear from my eye, I choked on leftover saliva stuck in my throat, and talked to the spotted dress hanging right above my head, to the spotted mouse twitching his nose on the top of the wooden hanger on the sleeve of the ruffle. I whispered to my mouse, the one once belonging to Silas Jones in Washington. "Powder, I can't stay. I must go. I have to know."

Lizzy Beth wiggled. "Night, night. I have to know what?"

"Never mind, go to sleep."

"Okay, I not know what I don't know."

"You're talking in your sleep." I cradled Lizzy Beth in my arms, steadying myself by scrunching a bunch of dresses into a wad on one end of the rack. "Come on. Let me put you back in bed."

"Okay. I love you, Sister. Tell Powder goodnight."

"I will. He loves to show himself to you. Too bad Mr. Boyd can't see him. He thinks I'm fibbing about having a mouse, but we know Powder is real. He's just shy." Kissing her hair, I tucked her in the bed, and sat on my knees watching Lizzy Beth sleep. "A year. I've been here almost a year. A birthday for Lizzy Beth last October. A birthday for me this past January. A reminder of Grandma Elsie's dying in January last year, too.

Taddy's birthday has come and gone in February, and the jonquils have bloomed and wilted. The anniversary of Pastor Cody dying in the fire in Washington, Arkansas, has slipped by with not a person speaking of it. And the only mama I knew, Tin Can Mahlee died at the hands of her own brothers while she tried to save my life.

Wiping a wild piece of hair from Lizzy Beth's cheeks. "Poor baby sister, you have no idea about Tin Can Mahlee being your real mama. She loved you so much she gave you away. She saved you, too."

Sobbing, I curled up in the bed, not sure how to tell Lizzy Beth goodbye, but I must go back to the life I know, the one riding in boxcars, where life click-clacks and curves with untold mysteries, where mamas die, and pastors cry, and little girls go to die.

**

"Be careful what you say, Boyd. She's having trouble being in the family. Give her some time." Ms. Susan whispered, a firm order as if she was about to explode with more words.

I scooted from the bed across the floor in my sock feet, my gown flowing with my wobbling jerks like a flag whipping in the wind. Leaning close to the door leading from our bedroom, I absorbed the words coming from the parlor.

"Honey, you see her. She's disobedient. She skips school. She doesn't do her chores, and I find her out by the shack where the Crush boys once lived. She sits in the tree by the window at the bayou, and stares into the woods like an owl awake but not alive, stuck and not sure how to fly."

"It's only been a year. She's bound to be excited when we tell her. When we share the good news. After all, we're adding to the family. This will be great for all of us. And since your eyes cleared up and you got your sight back, we're whole. We're going to be a complete and a perfect family. May 1948 is our fresh start."

I leaned my ear close to the door leading from our bedroom. I whispered under my breath, "Is Ms. Susan having a baby? No way. Not a baby. Why would she think this is good news?"

I crumpled to the floor like a rag, wrinkled in pain, broken in sorrow, lost in the past two years, and wondering if tomorrow was the day I might catch the train to nowhere, to somewhere, to a life waiting to give me a reason to live.

Inhaling, I got lost in the plans of my escape, stood to my feet, and moved the curtain to peek into the shadows of the late night. To the world awaiting my departure from this town. I caught sight of a shadow-body. "Who else stays up this late and why is he crouched by the fence in our yard?"

## Late Night Troubles

Storming from my bedroom, sliding across the floor and tumbling forward, I bounced off the side cushion of the arm chair, barreling across Mama Susan's lap. "Someone's in the yard. Outside. I saw them in the window." I choked on the letters flying from my mouth as the fear cut off my breathing.

Holding my neck, I watched pieces of paper, those Mr. Boyd and Ms. Susan were looking at, float to the hardwood floor at my feet.

Mr. Boyd rose like a commander, his brow wrinkled, his head shaking. "Shoelace, what now? Between your nightmares and midnight fears, you haven't slept an entire night since you joined us. Come over and sit next to me on the sofa."

"No! There's a person crouching outside my window. I saw him. I saw the man."

Ms. Susan gathered me up from the floor, sat me in her big chair and held both my shoulders in place, keeping my shivering from tossing me back to the floor. "Honey, we've talked about this. You have those nightmares. You wake up and it's like you're seeing the Phantom Killer from Texarkana. Well, you're safe. He's long gone. You're here with us."

By now, Mr. Boyd held me from the side, a fatherly attempt to hug me, but his hairy arms, his bushy eyebrows, and those bugged eyes caused more shaking and shivering.

I looked up at him. "I promise. I'm not making this up. I promise. I'm telling the truth. Get your gun. It's in the drawer. I know where you keep it. It's loaded, too."

Mr. Boyd stepped to face me. "Now, we've talked about the gun, too. I keep the pistol there to protect my family. But, it's not to be touched by you or by Lizzy Beth. Hands off. Besides, it's not loaded. I keep the bullets put up high on the mantle by the fireplace."

"It is loaded. I put bullets in there myself, for nights when my nightmares become real. And tonight, they rose from the cemetery. I saw a man by the fence, stooping and snooping."

From across the room, the pad-pad of soft footsteps called to the three of us between my sobs, between Mr. Boyd's stern gaze and correction, and between Ms. Susan holding me close to her thin, but strong body, saying sweet things in my ear.

Lizzy Beth whined, "What's wrong? I woke up, again. Everyone is yelling. I not like yelling. I scared. I was alone. Not like being alone. Shoelace, come tuck me in." She wiped her nose with the back of her hand.

"I'll be there in a second. Oh, baby girl, stop crying."

Mr. Boyd brought out his deep voice. "That's it, Shoelace. You keep us up every night. You won't stay in bed. You get at least five drinks of water. You go the bathroom and dilly-dally, and then you sit in the closet in your bedroom until the wee hours. No wonder, you can't get up for school. You're exhausted. Now, get to bed. The both of you. I've had it." His hands planted themselves on his hips, and the loose trousers hung like curtains around his waist, and his chin quivered.

"Darling, no need to raise your voice." Ms. Susan tromped over next to Mr. Boyd, her robe dragging the floor as it slid from one shoulder, the belt untying and dropping like a snake to the floor. Those papers floated around like butterflies from the coffee table.

Mr. Boyd smiled a crooked grin. "I'm tuckered out from these shenanigans. Quiet. Everyone be quiet. I need some quiet."

14

I jumped to my feet, as the shadowy silhouette swooped across the parlor window. "There! He's on the porch!" I pointed at the picture window, to the wall by the front door, near the spot with the gun in the drawer in the table holding the phone captive on the crocheted dolly.

Sniffing, Lizzy Beth darted from the parlor to our bedroom and slammed the door, disappearing from the scolding. I expected Mr. Boyd to unleash my punishment, something I received regular. He thinks I overreact, and he reacts louder than my reactions.

I storm in circles. He storms with harsh words. He can't control me. And I can't control myself. I'm miserable. I shouldn't be, but my family is gone, except Lizzy Beth, but family isn't family until you know you are loved. I'm extra baggage, like a satchel weighed down with rocks of despair. So far, I haven't given Mr. Boyd or Ms. Susan much to love. I'm the reason for the yelling. And the crying. It happens almost every night.

I vouched for myself. "I'm telling the truth. There's someone on the porch." Charging to the drawer, I yanked on the handle, and grabbed the pistol with my right hand, trembling as I turned the door knob.

Ms. Susan sobbed behind me, her screams louder than Mr. Boyd's hollering, although his words landed in my ears one letter at a time. "Shoelace, put the gun down. I've told you it's not loaded, and you're the last person who needs to have a gun in her hand." His fingers reached my shoulder, squeezing with a firmness and I swung around, only to point the gun at his chest. He slapped my hand away. "What are you doing?"

I hollered at him. "Stop touching me. I don't like touching."

"I don't like a gun sticking me in the ribs, either." Yanking the pistol from my grasp, Mr. Boyd held the gun to his side, and we both saw the motion through the window. The silhouette was joined with another silhouette, and Mr. Boyd shoved me aside. "Move. Let me see who's out there."

I ran to the big armed chair where Ms. Susan wept as she held a stack of those papers that I'd stirred into a whirlwind to the floor. I touched her face. "I'm sorry. I get caught in dark thoughts. I saw something. I did. I'm sorry. I get scared. I do. I'm sorry."

She pulled me to her lap, as she placed the papers on the coffee table, and we both swung our gaze to the front door where Mr. Boyd straddled the entrance. "What in the world? Archie? Crush? Do you two know what time it is? It's after midnight."

I uncurled myself from Ms. Susan's lap, and heard the door creaking to my right. "Lizzy Beth, it's not bad men. It's just Crush and Archie. Go back to bed."

"Mama Susan. I not like scary nights. I like sleepy nights."

Ms. Susan hurried over to pick Lizzy Beth up and she carried her back to the bedroom, shutting the door.

I watched across the room as Mr. Boyd motioned the two figures into the front room. "Tell me, Crush. Does Marion Kane know you're out this late? You're not much older than Shoelace, and she's not allowed out this late." He turned to Archie, my handkerchief-carrying friend whom I first met on the train in Millerton, Oklahoma, when Grandma Elsie died. "So, what is a grown man doing wandering around my house with a teenager?"

Coughing, Archie explained, "I was walking by when I saw someone crouching by your shrubs. I called to him, and found out it was Crush."

"Walking by at this hour?"

"Yes, I've got the late shift at the desk at the Jefferson Hotel. It's a new job. I'm not used to working inside. It'll take some getting used to, but it'll get me some groceries."

I took over, "Crush, what were you thinking? I made a bet with you, and you lost. You were to trim the shrubs tomorrow in the daylight, before school. You lost the bet. You've got to do my chores for a week. Why would you come this late?" I circled Crush, pouring my questions at him like invisible bullets.

Crush sighed. "I wasn't going to have time to finish it tomorrow. And I know you. You'd retaliate if I didn't get it done. I'd gone to bed, when I jerked awake from a nightmare. And you were in it, holding the pruning shears at my neck. Shaking your fist at me."

"I would never hurt you, I'm your friend, mostly."

Mr. Boyd gained control. "Crush, stop betting with this child. You keep losing. She needs to carry her own weight around here."

"Yes, sir. She's so … so hard to not argue with, and then the next thing, I'm making wagers." Crush wiped his sweaty palms on his legs, and moved toward the opened door. "Please, don't tell Mr. Marion. If you do, I'll have more chores than just doing Shoelace's chores."

I inched toward my bedroom, ready to disappear, hoping to miss out on the wrath ready to spew from Mr. Boyd. While scooting away, Archie apologized for the bother too, and left. Then Crush rushed from the house like a wild dog set loose from its leash. Mr. Boyd called to me, "Sit. Over there. On the sofa. Now." He motioned with his free hand like a sergeant in the Army giving orders.

I obeyed with fear, as if he was holding the gun on me. "I'm sorry. I saw the shadow. I got scared." Plopping to the cushion, I caused yet another whirlwind of air, and tried to stop the papers from flying to the floor.

"Leave those. We need to talk."

I scuttled to my knees. "I can help. Let me pick up these papers."

"No. Leave them. You don't need to see those just yet."

"See them? Why not?"

"Not tonight. We're going to tell you, just not right this second."

"Tell me what?"

Mr. Boyd seized the sheets from my hands, crumbling them into a wad, shoving them to the other side of the table away from me. "We need to talk." He placed the pistol on top of the papers, realizing he still had it in his grip.

"What? Talk about what?"

Mr. Boyd sat next me, turning toward me some. "We got off to a bit of a hard start. I met you first, when my eyes were healing. When you were running away from everyone. And I struggled with not having children after we couldn't have our own. Then we heard of Lizzy Beth, my precious little Memphis Belle who found her way from Memphis to Wheelock Academy in Oklahoma. We had a picture and we knew she was ours!" He smiled like he loved her, like she was his own daughter.

"But then you got me." I smarted off. "I know you don't want me. I don't want you, either." I turned my anger at him as if hurting him might make my heart less vulnerable. Of course, I was wrong. The spouting of my unhappiness always singes like hot charcoal. Like striking a match in my throat.

Mr. Boyd placed his hand on my knee. "I see you. Before you cut me off, I was going to say how much we love you, too. I know it's been rough for you, and you're healing. I see

18

how wounded you are from all the death and hurt, and ugliness you've witnessed. I want to start over. Can we be friends? Can we start there? And see how friendship works?"

I swallowed hard, the sticky stuff from my nose draining backwards, and the goo clogged my throat. I grabbed my neck. "I feel like no one will ever want me. Not really. I feel like I'm always the extra one. The one no one knows what to do with, or how to care for, or where to keep."

"Well, we're keeping you. We need to find some peace with each other. I'll watch how I speak to you, if you'll try to watch how you react to me. Is it a deal?"

I rose from the couch, ready to listen, but not ready to deal. "But what are these papers for? Is Ms. Susan pregnant? You said she can't have children. But I heard you talking. I heard you earlier." I picked up the pistol, waving it, and grabbed some sheets of paper, wadding them in my grasp. "What is this? Doctor's notes about your new baby?"

"Shoelace." Mr. Boyd circled the coffee table as I moved away from him. "Give me the gun. This is not working. You won't listen."

"I am listening. You think I can't hear you and Ms. Susan talking about me. I heard how you complain about me." I waved the gun like all-control left my arm. "

*Creeeeekkkkk!*

"What are you doing, Shoelace? Put the gun down. You're going to have a chore list longer than you can finish. I've gotten your sister to sleep, but your constant selfishness must stop. It's been a year! You are our child. We've adopted you. We're not giving up on you." Ms. Susan bent in half, her hands crossing in front of her belly.

Mr. Boyd ran to her. "Honey, come with me. You are exhausted." He glanced at me. "Put the gun down. Do it now. Or else."

I welled up with anxious thoughts traveling like spider webs in my head, thoughts of running to the closet. Of hiding in there forever. I heard myself answer in a small voice. "Yes, sir. I'm sorry." And I put the gun on the table.

They rushed from the room and down the hallway to their bedroom, and I fell back to the sofa, noticing the scattered sheets of paper littered on the floor. "I need to clean this up. I need to go to bed. I need to leave this room. I need to get to bed. I need help. I don't know how to live or love or laugh anymore." My tears landed on the paper like giant raindrops of sadness, as if the drops were like acid ready to burn up the hope.

Unfolding a sheet of paper, I read the words across the top. It was a letter from an attorney in Memphis to Mr. Boyd and Ms. Susan. I grabbed another one. Another letter. Each paper was more letter writing, some to them, some from them.

From the down the hall, Mr. Boyd called to his wife, "Honey, let me get Shoelace to bed. We all need sleep. Rest. We'll see clearly in the morning. The light of a new day brings clarity. And perspective." Mr. Boyd padded my way, and I shoved some of the papers under a cushion to read later, stacking the rest on the table.

I hurried from the room to the kitchen, darting the other way through the dining room, my sock feet slipping with each glide. I had to move. I had to flee.

"Shoelace, get yourself in here right now. I said, come here."

I shuffled back into the parlor. "Yes, sir."

"Where's the gun? I asked you to put it up. Where is it? I checked the drawer. It's not there, or on the table. What have you done with it?"

20

I spun in a circle, noticing the door to my and Lizzy Beth's room wide open. "Mr. Boyd. Lizzy Beth!" I charged to my bedroom. "Where are you, Lizzy Beth?"

Mr. Boyd bumped into me from behind. "Where is she? She doesn't have the gun, does she?"

"I don't know. I left it on the coffee table."

A squeaky sound rose from inside the closet. "I'm in here. I have the gun. No more fighting. The gun makes everybody fight. I no like fights."

I stuck my head into the dark closet, and from behind me the light switch lit up the room as Mr. Boyd must have turned it on. "Why do you have the gun? Give it to me, Sister." I reached for it, and she held the pistol next to her chest. "Hand, it to me."

Mr. Boyd shoved me aside. "Memphis Belle, let me have the gun."

"Will you stop fighting with Shoelace? I no like fighting."

"Yes, let me have the gun. We need to put it up."

I crawled between Mr. Boyd's legs. "I'll get the gun. She'll give it to me."

*Screech!*

Ms. Susan's high-pitched holler startled all of us. She shouted, "What is going on? What is wrong with my family?" Ms. Susan's hollow sounds echoed like death in the bayou after a flood.

The four of us found ourselves in the closet, the crayon-world of dreamcatchers catching all the ugly inside our hearts, the words jumping from me, from Lizzy Beth, and from Mr. Boyd and Ms. Susan, all at once.

I found myself holding the gun, jumping from the maze of dresses wrapped around my head. "I have the gun. I have it. Lizzy Beth is fine. She's fine." I twirled, stumbled and toppled to the mattress, bouncing with my excitement at saving my sister. Then, as I balanced myself, and as if my fingers latched onto the trigger, I heard the zing. *Pffft! Pffft!*

I clutched the pistol in my hand, and my fingers burned with the 'why' of how I even snatched it from Lizzy Beth. The reality of firing the gun made me shake with fear and a trembling rattled my body. I collapsed sideways, falling to the floor, dropping the pistol. *Kaplud!* Then I heard the thud of another falling person, and found myself next to him on the floor.

*Unwavering Hope*

## When Bullets Fly

Forced to sit on the sofa, after the screaming and the ambulance, after the scolding and Mr. Boyd's sermon; I'm biting my lip from the horror, and swallowing the pain of what Lizzy Beth witnessed.

One week of school left. One week until summer. One week until I could hide from the school kids. Hide from the other people in town. Hide at our frame house in the middle of the block. The house close to the old Jewish synagogue. The house across from where I hid one night in the loft of the library, last year. The house where my little sister loves having a family, and now I'm the one who's torn the hope from the walls like peeling paint.

Some days I want to live here, but then I do things and cause a stir, and unravel the hem from this family. I'm torn and ripped and wrinkled and unsure where I belong, but Ms. Susan prayed with me at church last Sunday. She's leaning on God for me to trust Him. But when the sky gets dark at night, my world takes on the shadows of losing my daddy and my mama, of losing Tin Can Mahlee, and Pastor Cody.

If I disappear, no one else gets hurt or dies.

Wiping my eyes, my near swollen lids burned, and I curled my legs under my body. My gown hung like wrinkled old leaves, like dead grass. I could sleep now, the ache in my bones throbbing with a heartbeat.

The sunrise broke through the darkness and lit up the sadness an hour ago, and the daylight's uglier than the shadow of nightfall. No one will talk to me. No one will look at me. I've left a mark of sorrow in my bedroom, along with the blood and the broken glass on the floor. The red is splattered like spilled tomato juice on the wooden floor.

I tilted my head onto the arm of the sofa, watching the policeman take notes on a small pad of paper, as he spoke to Mr. Marion Kane, my friend who probably will disown me now. He came by fifteen minutes ago, hurried, flustered and frowning.

I wiggled to get comfortable, whispering to the air, hoping for God to hear me. "I've disappointed them. Ms. Susan has Lizzy Beth tucked away in her bedroom. She's furious with me. Mr. Boyd keeps pacing on the porch. He just wiped his brow and shook his head, again. God, I'm sorry. I don't belong here. I don't."

*Tap-a-dap. Tap-a-dap.*

The sound of shoes beating on the steps of the porch meant someone else was arriving, and the front door swung open. In flew the trousers and jacket, and he flew right by Mr. Boyd who peered at me through the window pane.

Archie announced himself, "I heard there was a shooting. I saw Marion at the café earlier, and Susan wasn't there serving me coffee, and smiling. I knew something was wrong."

I nodded. "I made the wrong. I'm no good."

Archie held his fedora in one hand, and waved his other like he was writing on a chalk board. He spoke to the room, and zeroed in on Marion Kane and the cop. "What happened here?"

I didn't wait for them to answer. "It was me. I didn't mean to shoot the gun. I fell, it went off, and then …"

Archie placed his hat on the coffee table. "Shoelace, you have a future with Susan and Boyd, a chance at having a family. We're working on making this family complete. Now what have you done? It can't be too bad." Handing me a handkerchief, he patted my arm as if he were saying goodbye to a good friend.

Sitting up, I moved to the edge of the cushion, my socked feet stuck like glue to the sorrow. Folding my hands together between my knees, with the handkerchief between them, I rocked. "I'm sorry, Archie. I can't get this right. I'm not meant for this family. And now I've gone and done it. Will I go to jail?"

"Jail? Why would you go to jail?"

"You said it yourself. You heard of the shooting."

"I did hear of the shooting."

Marion Kane interjected a flat tone. "The boys' orphanage was ransacked last night. Tak was shot by the intruder, and the thief got away. Seems the boys saw a shadow run to the tracks. Two other places were broken into on our road."

I sighed. "No way! Tak's hurt?"

Archie pursed his lips. "Yes, Tak's asking for you. He wants the girl who's brave to help him be strong. He sent me, I'm here to get you. I ran to the hospital when I found out about the awful night, and I hopped a ride with Old Man Dunn to Marshall. I've been there most of the morning."

"No, not little Tak. Shot? Where did he get shot?"

"He caught a bullet in his arm. Near the bone. Doc got it out, but he's pretty shaken up."

Marion Kane fidgeted, and returned to finish his talking with the cop, and I jumped to my feet, running to my bedroom. I toddled through the not-so-dry blood on the floor, and tossed my gown over my head. Pulling a blue shirt over my head, I slipped on my Saturday overalls even though it was Thursday. Digging for my red PF Flyers in the closet, I touched a dreamcatcher circle, and wished for do overs.

A hand on my shoulder spun me around like a top twirling, and the face of the cop drilled me, his wart wiggling on his eyelid. "Shoelace, you need to stay out of this room. This is an investigation. You're lucky the bullets only put holes in the wall. This is the fifth time in six months I've been called to this house for a disturbance or domestic trouble. I'm watching you."

I wiggled from his touch. "Wait! Last night, I shot Crush! I saw him fall. I saw the blood. I saw him on the floor. I saw him frozen. He didn't move."

Marion joined the conversation. "Shoelace, he came over here to do your chores after making some sort of wager with you at school. He has his own chores, and it seems he forgot about the strawberries. He had placed them on the ground by the fence, and in the commotion forgot them, and forgot the pruning shears on the porch."

I shook my head faster than a bullet flying from a pistol. "No," I glanced to the floor. "Look at this blood. It's everywhere."

The cop bent down. "These are strawberries. Smashed and squished. Not blood."

"But, Crush was out cold on the floor."

"I've talked to the boy. When he heard the yelling, he barreled into the house, and the noise of the gun firing sent him ducking. He tumbled backwards by the bed, hit his head on the dresser, knocked over some of those porcelain dolls and got knocked cold."

"No way. I didn't shoot Crush?"

Mr. Boyd slipped in behind the cop and Archie. "No, but you could have, and Lizzy Beth could have gotten hurt, too. The chaos you bring gets worse with each episode we endure. I'm not sure what is next for us."

Shaking my head, my thoughts jumbled into a bunch of crisscrossing of questions. "What? You're not sure what's next?" My throat quivered when I heard his words, which sounded in my ears like a wish for me to run away.

Archie must have read my mind. "Come with me. I'll run you to the hospital. I've borrowed Marion's old truck. Tak needs to see you."

Marion Kane embraced me, moving toward the doorway to the front room. "Put your shoes on. I'll be right there myself. I'm finishing up with the officer about our break-in last night, about Crush being here. Ms. Ginny is with the children. They're all pretty shaken up. I'm about to head back to see Tak, and to check on Crush. Thankfully all he has is a concussion."

I replayed the night's incident over and over, again. No matter how it went, I was in trouble with Mr. Boyd and Ms. Susan. And the policeman is tired of me, too!

Archie reached for his hat, and I grabbed his arm. "What did you mean when you said we're working on making this family complete?"

"Nothing my dear. Hurry along. Tie those shoelaces. I'll wait in the truck."

I sat on the sofa, clutching the handkerchief, and my shoes. Watching my lanky friend who dances when he walks, who smiles like an angel, who calms me with his presence, I couldn't help but remember how every time someone needs to wipe a tear, Archie appears.

He's there when you need him. He's there when you don't. He's there in the boxcar. He's there on the road. He's there in Millerton, Oklahoma. He shows up in Washington, Arkansas. He's there at the cemetery in Texarkana. He's everywhere.

Bending down to tie my shoes, the crunch of paper under the cushion made crackling noises. I reached for them, tucking a few of those attorney letters into my pockets. Maybe an answer. Maybe a clue. Maybe I'll see what Ms. Susan is up to.

What Mr. Boyd is hiding with their secret talks after we go to bed. Is there a baby? Or is it me? Could they be planning to get rid of me?

"Shoelace, hurry outside. Archie is waiting." Mr. Boyd stormed into the room, his eyes red, his hair wild. "Go be with your friend, Tak. And stop in on Crush. You need to make amends with him, too. I'll come for you later."

I scooted to Mr. Boyd. "I'm sorry. I cause pain. I wish it weren't so. I didn't mean to do all of this."

He reached for my head, and hugged me with a soft touch. "I wish it were easy. I wish it were …" His words faded, his tears fell, and I ran from his side knowing I'd made a grown man sad, and ruined my chances of making a go of it. Even though, most days I don't try so hard at being a daughter to anyone.

Stomping down the three steps, I ran through the picket fence gate, ready to race to the tracks. I had to leave. I couldn't stay. I had to see Tak. I needed to tell Crush I'm sorry. My heart beat for the rail. My heart was broken in a hundred pieces as if the stains of last night would change where I sleep and where I go.

Archie called to me, "Come along. Time's a wasting."

## Unmovable Mountains

The heavy door to the truck clanked with a bang when I yanked on it, and I sighed a deep breath of worn-out sorrow. Nothing was "well with my soul," and I leaned back in the seat as the old jalopy bounced down the road toward Marshall, toward the only hospital in the county.

Archie, with his long fingers, wrapped around the steering wheel, hummed. His joy crept into the cab like a melody of hope, and he broke into a song as if the world was at peace. Had he forgotten the turmoil I'd caused? How I'd had a part in hurting Crush? Did he forget Tak was suffering from a gunshot wound?

He rocked, and chimed in with, "When peace, like a river, attendeth my way, when sorrow like sea billows roll." He tapped the steering wheel with the beat of the hymn. "Whatever my lot, thou has taught me to say, it is well, it is well with my soul."

I tugged on his sleeve, waving my arm, knocking his Fedora into the floorboard. "Sorry, I didn't mean to knock your hat off."

Humming his answer, Archie rocked his head sideways as if he was lost in the words of the song, and he nodded, adding, "It is well with my soul. It's a hat, not so important. Not so important as you, my little Shoelace."

Reaching, I placed the hat in the seat next to us. "I'm not important to anyone. No one wants me. Not really. Even Mr. Boyd's giving up on me. He's tired of my hurt and my sorrow. I can't get anything right. I'm making Lizzy Beth cry now, too."

"You, my little one, are too busy falling into your past. Too caught up in reliving your wishing and wanting. You need to trust God for the 'even if,' even if you don't have the answers, you have a God who can make it well with your soul."

Shaking my head, his riddles confused me, leaving me with more questions, and lots of reasons to quiz him. "So how come you show up wherever I go?"

"I go wherever the tracks lead. I'm a wandering soul, a wandering messenger who looks for the 'one' who needs hope." He grinned as if he was pleased with his answer.

"You were riding in a passenger car when I met you back in Millerton." I cleared my throat. "On the day my grandma died from a broken heart. I'm the reason she died. I caused her heartache. I caused her too much pain."

Archie patted my knee. "Your grandma's heart gave out, this is true. But from what I've heard, it's your daddy who broke her heart. He did take you from her. He stole you from her grasp when you were just starting school."

Arguing, I curled my leg under me and turned to face him in the seat. "What are you saying? You don't even know my daddy. Stop talking about him. You don't know how much he loved me."

"I might know more than you know. I might know more than you want me to know. In time, in time, you will see. Your grandma's heart was never the same after he took you, after he carried you to Georgia Tann in Memphis, Tennessee."

"What? Who is Georgia Tann? I don't know her. I've never heard of her." I swallowed hard. "I don't care who she is, and I don't want to know." I folded my arms, angry at Archie, furious at the world.

Archie began singing again, "I know you're able, Lord. You save through the fire, through the death, and through the hurts. Move this mountain of hate from Shoelace. But if you leave the mountain in place, give her the strength to sing, it is well with her soul."

Scowling, I whined under my breath at the man who was now singing words I'd never heard, words I hated. "I'm broken beyond repair, unless I wake up to find these last seven years were a nightmare. God, I need to cling to you, and I know everyone says you're able, but I'm not so sure I'm able. I've hurt Crush. And poor Tak, he's only a little older than Lizzy Beth. Who shoots a little boy?"

Apparently, Archie can hear and sing at the same time, and he answered me, "Rumor has it the person who broke into the orphanage was looking for food, and Tak had gone into the kitchen for a drink. He startled the intruder, and got in the way, and ran from him."

"So, the man got away?"

"Yes, he did. But Tak told them he was a man with brown curly hair, with eyes of marble blue. He said he favored Archie, but younger."

"How could he see his eyes. Wasn't it dark in the house?"

"Tak turned on the light when he came into the kitchen, and the man was in the ice box digging for food. That's how he saw him. It was probably someone riding through town. Probably came from the tracks in front of the orphanage."

"I know. I remember when I first rode into Jefferson, before I knew Ms. Susan or Mr. Boyd, or anyone in this town, how the house was empty and abandoned. The windows were broken out, and now it's a place for the Crush Boys. For other orphan boys, thanks to Marion Kane."

Wiping tears from my eyes, I couldn't help but think of the "what if" of accidently shooting the gun. Of how close I came to becoming a murderer myself. I blasted my thoughts, letting them explode. "It's Crush who shouldn't have come. He needs to win a bet sometime. And strawberries? He brought them to me too, even after the way I treat him at school."

"I've heard he's taking a liking to you."

"Nobody likes me. They just put up with me."

"I like you. You're a challenge."

"I can be." I swung my foot from under me, to let the blood come back into my leg. "I could have killed Crush. Timmons and Tak are his baby brothers. I would have died myself if I'd done such a thing. And to think, a thief could have killed Tak, and poor Timmons who's barely eight wouldn't have had any family left."

Archie disagreed. "Theodore, Thomas and the triplets might as well be their brothers. Those eight boys have gone through so much together. Crush took them in and he grew up fast."

My brain processed what Archie told me. "Wait? How do you know what they've gone through? Those five boys lost their parents in the flood here a few years ago, and so did … so did Crush, Timmons and Tak."

My chest throbbed with pain, and I knew my hope in Jesus should rise from all those Sunday school teachings. The ones Ms. Susan insisted I attend, but my sadness was consuming me instead.

I picked up Archie's hat and scooted close to him. "Why do you know so much about all of us?"

"I wander for God, and look for those who need to know it can be well with their soul. I knew their families. I knew them well. I left from the bayou many years back and spent most of my twenties in Memphis. I got lost myself for a time, but then

I came to my senses and now I travel for God. I go where He sends me."

Shocked, I choked on the words unfolding in the cab of the truck. "You didn't lose family in the flood, did you?"

"I did. I lost an aunt, and three brothers. They were caught in the rush of water when it rose over the banks. I got word much later after it was over, but 1945 left a loss in my family, too. We all suffer, we all know about hurt, and we all find our ride in life to be filled with unmovable mountains." He swiped his cheek with his hand, wiping the leaking tears from his face. "But, I can say it is well with my soul. So now I'm helping you. I'm going to help you find …"

"Helping me? Why me? What do you know about me, that I don't?"

"More than you know. More than I can say. More than I pray. But we are sorting it through, me and Mr. Boyd, and Ms. Susan, too."

I shook my head. "I don't understand."

"I've said too much. Things are not as they seem. Faith, have a little faith. It will carry you. Just have faith."

*Chug-a-lug. Chug-a-lug.*

"Faith. I don't know how. I don't know how." Archie parked the truck, handing me two handkerchiefs. "Give one to Crush. And give the other one to Tak. Show kindness. Do what your Grandma Elsie would do. Do it for her. And do it for God. It's time for you to become who you were born to be."

Shaking, my body lost all control, and I fell into Archie's embrace. "But, I don't know how. I don't know what to do with all of this brokenness."

"God will show you. He will hold you. He will use you."

"Me? I'm not so sure He trusts me."

"Then trust Him. He's your strength."

I stepped from the truck. "Aren't you coming?"

"No, you need to become a little messenger of hope."

"What? Me?" I held the door to the truck open, seeing the pieces of paper I'd stuck into my pockets crumpled on the floorboard. Grabbing them, I stuck them back inside my overalls pockets, as Archie glared at me like he wanted to quiz me, but I interrupted his chance. "Will you be here when I come back?"

"I sure will. It's a long walk back to Jefferson. I won't leave you."

I clutched the handkerchiefs, and my PF Flyers felt like rocks, and my stomach heaved with fear, and burning in my throat flew into my mouth. I thought I might throw up. "I'll go find Crush first. Then Tak."

Archie's nod brought him back to his singing, his opened truck window let his voice capture a harmony like a chorus of angels were singing with him. "It's is well with my soul. It is well with my soul."

I moved to open the door to the hospital. "It's not well with my soul. I'm held to the flame. This is no game. And I'm the one to blame."

## Making Amends Again

The nurse sent me to this door, but I'm struggling to enter, afraid to go inside. I twirled around, and plastered myself right into the brown suit, and the skinny fingers reached over my shoulders. "I best open the door for you. I had a feeling you'd need a little company to make this walk."

"Archie? I don't know how to tell Crush how I made this mess."

"I expect he knows. He's seen you in action before last night."

Sighing, I pushed the door. "I'm getting so much wrong these days. All the screaming and fighting feels as if I'm choking on bad sardines left out in the sun. Even a salty cracker can't fix the taste."

He spun me around, and swung the door to give me enough room to squeeze into the dimly lit room. I inched to the bed, and Archie didn't follow me.

The sheets covered Crush to his chest, and his eyes were closed. The blinds were pulled, the room shadowy. His breathing came with a rush of air releasing, and sucking in a breath. Like a fan circulating air, and moving around the dust.

Looking back to tell Archie we should leave, since Crush was asleep, I found myself alone with my own breaths. They rattled like a tornado, whirling and whizzing, and consuming me with more questions. With more regret than twenty boxcars falling from the tracks into the river.

I faced my freckled friend, a teen who gave me more attention than I deserved, who argued with me like a big brother. Who drove for Mr. Marion Kane now. Who gave me rides to Taddy's house at the Clementine Plantation west of town, so I could watch for him, in case he came outside.

Taddy and me, we've been best friends for two years. But since Tin Can Mahlee's death, and all the horrible shootings and escapes, he's just another ratty boy. And now that the plantation was left to Taddy's mama, Priscilla, they moved to Jefferson last fall. Which was about the time I moved here too, after the terrible and awful things happened in Arkansas.

I cradled my knees on the floor, talking to no one but pretending the gnat whizzing by my head was listening. "Taddy hasn't come out to play with me yet. He's convinced I'm more trouble than those stinky skunks in the woods. He's become one of those kids at school who laughs at me. And I'm confused."

Sighing, Crush took a deep breath. I looked to see if he was waking up, but he got still again.

I continued my whining, "I had to find her when she ran off to Washington, Arkansas. Taddy's sure I had something to do with Pastor Cody's death and Mahlee's death." I sobbed, "And he's right. I'm no good. I'm horrible."

I used the handkerchiefs in my hand, blowing my nose. "I'm so mixed up, God. I know I've hurt people. Why am I here? What is wrong with me? I don't understand how my broken heart can be a part of a bigger plan. I don't understand."

I coughed from the sadness clogging my throat. "I need to make sense of this. I need to figure out what to do. I know you're God, and I'm not. But this is too much." I got on my knees and lifted my hands to the ceiling. "God, I know you see me. I know everyone says you have big plans for me, too. So, can you help me? I don't know how to be me."

*Sha-luffle. Sha-luffle.*

The bed creaked, and Crush turned his head sideways, his words slipping from his groggy self. "Shoelace, is that you? What are you doing, sitting on the floor?"

I jumped to my feet. "Crush, I'm so sorry. I won't make any bets with you anymore. You don't have to do my chores, either." My words poured out like hot tea in a cup. "I had no idea you'd come into the house. I lost my balance, and the gun went off. I thought … I thought you were dead."

He mustered up some strength, grimacing. "Marion told me. He's so mad at me for going out so late. He also blames me for not being at the orphanage when Tak got shot."

"Blames you? But you would have been asleep."

No, I probably wouldn't have, since Timmons and Tak won't sleep in their room. They crawl in bed with me every night. It's crowded, but they're all I've got. I've got to look out for them. If Tak had gotten up, I would have known."

Sighing, I whimpered from my leftover sobbing, "I don't think Mr. Boyd is going to keep me. I think he's going to get rid of me now." I sat on the edge of the bed. "I also think Ms. Susan is pregnant. If she has another baby, then I'm the last person she'll want around her baby."

Crush tried to sit up a little, and I stuffed his pillow behind his head. "Thanks, my head's a throbbing. I may need more aspirin."

"Do you want me to get the nurse?"

"No, stay. I'm glad you're here."

I touched his arm. "I am sorry." I blinked, and a fresh new set of tears streamed down my face. "Thank you for the strawberries, too. Not that I've gotten to eat them. They're kind of smeared in my room on the waxed floor. Ms. Susan's not happy about the mess."

Crush giggled, "I don't know what I was thinking. I came back for Marion's shears, and I was leaving them on the porch when I heard the screaming along with muzzled sounds of Ms. Susan hollering. I had stumbled upon the basket of berries too, and planned to leave them on the porch." He grabbed his head as if talking made the pounding worse.

"I'm sorry. I wish we could go back."

"It's going to be fine. I just have a bad headache."

Smiling, I responded with, "I think I'm your bad headache."

"We already know you cause me nightmares. You may be right." He reached for the back of his head again. "Maybe I need the nurse."

"I'll get her. But I had to tell you first. I'm sorry, Crush. I'm really sorry." I handed him a handkerchief, the one with plenty of snot.

"Yuck! This is used."

"I know. It's broken in for you."

He laughed, a Crush chuckle, one that made me know we were friends even with the history of pain I inflict.

I ran to the door. "I'm glad you're alive."

"Me, too."

"I'll get the nurse. I'm going to see Tak now."

"Hug him for me."

"I will. Thanks for forgiving me."

"I may need some chores done for me until I get better."

Smiling, I nodded. "It's the least I can do."

Crush grabbed his head. "I know."

**

Staring loneliness in the face, I ran my fingers through Tak's yellow hair. His room dark, the blinds pulled, the shadows thick. I leaned over him. The crack from the hallway door allowed a bit of light, enough to see the freckles and the pudgy nose. "I love you, my little Tak. I'm sad. I will get the person who shot you. I would take a bullet for you."

Tak winced, and his jerky movements told me he was in pain. He seemed medicated with something to make him sleep, and when I touched him, he calmed down, and rested. When I moved my hand, he wiggled, and gurgled little cries.

"Papa Marion. Where's my Crush?" His words rippled with a slow slur, and he dozed back off.

Crawling into the hospital bed, I curled up next to him, on his good side, and snuggled with Tak. My lack of sleep made my head heavy, and my body sluggish. I felt myself leaving and disappearing as if I was falling through the mattress.

I hugged him with a half-embrace. "Poor little thing. No parents. And your big brother almost got killed by me. I'm the worst at being a friend."

"That's so right. You are having bouts of trouble at making Jefferson fit your life, aren't you?"

I fell from the bed, to my feet, and my legs wobbled. "Who's there? What are you doing sitting in the dark?"

Toby stood from sitting the chair. "I was here first. So, let me ask you. What are you doing here?"

I moved around the bed. "Toby? Why aren't you at school?"

"Why aren't you?" He came into the dim stream of light on my side of the room.

"Haven't you heard?"

"Heard what?"

"What I did to Crush?"

"What did you do?"

"I'm sure you know. You're just trying to get me to admit it."

"Admit what?"

"Toby Raike." I shouted, realizing how loud I sounded, and glanced at Tak who didn't move. "You're practicing your preacher talk with me. We're the same age, and you're not a preacher, yet."

"I will be. I'm on my way to living behind the pulpit."

"So, you do know?"

"Know what?"

I stomped my feet. "You know, Crush snuck out, and came over to do my chores, and he brought me strawberries from your garden."

He put his hands on his hips. "I do know. Your life is one big second chance of second chances. You're like a cat with nine lives, but you've used them all up. Now, you're living on the good graces of God. I guess, He must have something big for you in this life. I mean, you're being attacked by the devil. He wants to steal and destroy your life."

Shaking my finger at Toby, I yelled, "Don't be preaching to me, Toby." I looked around the room, and twirled in a circle. "I don't see no devil."

"He's a prowling in your life, and meddling with your destiny. Don't give in. Run your race. Live your life for Him."

Swallowing my anger, I pressed my finger in Toby's chest. "You. You need to leave me be. I am running. And it's out of this town, I'm sure."

"That's what's wrong. You're running the wrong way. You need to run to Jesus."

"He doesn't like me. I keep causing too much trouble."

"He does like you. He loves you, Shoelace."

When Toby spoke the word 'love' I melted from exhaustion, and collapsed to my knees, holding the clean handkerchief Archie had given me. I blew my nose, and wept like a puppy lost from its mama, sobbing from too many nightmares, and all those nights sitting in the closet with my satchel.

Toby knelt beside me. "Let me pray for you."

I nodded, not having any strength left to argue with Toby.

"I know you keep calling and calling on God."

"How do you know?"

"I've watched you at church. You look up and whisper, and I can read your lips."

"So, you're spying on my prayers?"

"I am. I pray them with you. I figure you could use extra prayer."

"I hoped Taddy would forgive me for Pastor Cody's and for Tin Can Mahlee's deaths. I can't carry that weight much longer. My heart can't beat with the pain anymore. I know he went into that church in Washington to save me, but I wasn't even inside. I also know Mahlee sacrificed herself for me on that balcony with her mean brothers. But I feel like I've destroyed too many things."

"You are right where you need to be. Right here. This is your place in our world. God's coming to your rescue, to save you, to redeem these no-good bad seasons."

I glanced into the brown eyes of a boy my age who talked like a grown-up preacher. "I have no one to turn to, and my worst fears have come true. People I love, die."

"They do. We all lose people. Even I live with my grandpa."

"That's true. Mr. Marion Kane is the bestest grandpa."

Toby placed his hand on my shoulder. "Dear God, if then was now, and Shoelace could have her family back, I pray that she'd trust you and love you. But she's feeling alone, and I ask you to give her memories of her past that make her smile. Help her remember her daddy's love for her. Help her see how Tin Can Mahlee did her best, even if her best was awful. And let her know that you heal the broken, and you can heal her heart, too. Amen."

I added another part to the prayer. "God. Tin Can Mahlee wasn't always awful. Oh, I pray for Taddy too. I need him to be my friend. And if Boyd and Susan send me away, show me where to go before they send me to a mean family."

"They're not sending you away."

*Achooo. Achooo.*

Tak sneezed, screaming. "Crush, get me. Save me."

Toby held Tak like a preacher would, not like a preacher-in-training. "Tak, it's Toby. I'm here with you. It's me. Calm down. Your stitches hurt, I'm sure."

I wandered from the room, grasping the handkerchief, and crunched the papers into my pocket. Sitting on the floor outside of Tak's room, I wondered if the pain would ever stop pressing my chest like a stone on my body. I wondered if I could do something that doesn't cause problems.

One of the papers toppled from my pocket. "What are these? What were Mr. Boyd and Ms. Susan talking about?"

Unfolding the crumpled paper, I read part of the attorney letter aloud, "I've found Lizzy Beth's birth certificate records." Tossing that paper down, I unfolded another sheet from inside my pocket. "Archie is right. She's a twin. Lizzy Beth has a brother."

I wrinkled my face into a contortion. The announcement knocked a blow to my heart, and the whizzing sound made me feel dizzy. I wiped my face, feeling numb. The final letter couldn't get yanked from my pocket fast enough. I looked at the words, reading most to myself. Then I saw a name I'd just heard earlier, and I bellowed from the hospital floor. "And Georgia Tann could be responsible for the boy's disappearance. We're searching for him."

## Hidden Truths

Storming like a wild horse, I raced down the hallway, around the nurse's station, and right out the front door. I was suffocating. Suffocating from the hidden lies. The not knowing. From what I just read. And from wondering if the letters were true.

I careened through the doors of the hospital, the word "twin" circling my head like a cloud. I ran in circles, stopped, peered up to the sky, looked to my left, then my right. I forgot who I was, forgot why I was alive, and forgot to move as the silver Oldsmobile edged closer.

All I could do was stand frozen like a weed in front of the bumper, ready for the car to mow me down. Then the pain would stop. And the lies. And the hidden truths.

*Honk! Honk!*

Startled, I jumped, choked on my tightening throat, and placed my hands high into the air. Not like a girl praising God, but out of fear of being alone when Mr. Boyd sends me away.

I frowned at the driver, and slammed my hands on her car. "I'm not afraid of you. Run me over," I shouted at the driver, a small woman, too old to drive, too short to see over her steering wheel.

Slamming my fist on the hood, I pounded the car. "You have no idea who you're dealing with, old lady." I stood with both hands on my hips, shouting words at her. My ugliness poured into the dust of the dirt below my feet, and I moved to her driver's side door, shaking my fist at her.

*Creak.*

Her door opened, the car idled, and the wrinkled and round woman wearing a cotton gray dress stepped from her car, and now she shook her fist at me. "I lost my husband minutes ago. Do you hear me? I don't have time for little girls like you. How dare you shout your bad words as if you have a right to speak to me with hate."

The granny-type woman moved closer than I wanted, getting inches from my face, and I could see her red eyes. The trembling way her voice cracked made me regret hollering at her. I hung my head. "I'm sorry." I bent in half, folding into a ball and sat right down, in the dirt, rocking. I held my ears, unable to think, unable to know what to do, unable to get up.

The woman parked herself on the ground with me, crossing her legs behind her, and she wrapped her sagging skin around my neck, holding me close. "I'm sorry. I never yell. Today I needed to scream though, because I wasn't ready to say goodbye to my husband. But his heart stopped. He couldn't hang on."

"My grandma's heart gave out, too. My daddy died in a river. My pastor died in a church fire. My Tin Can Mahlee saved me before she died. Everyone I touch dies!"

"Oh, baby girl. I'm sorry. You must have loved them. My husband smelled of fish from the pond. He wore a nasty old straw hat. He never put his shoes up. But he made my coffee every morning. He loved me, and I loved him." Her scrambled sentences wrapped sadness around my heart as if the grayness from the clouds rolling in over our heads might drop black rain from them.

Nodding, I wept, wiping my own tears. "Grandma Elsie made me chocolate cake. She made my clothes smell good. She let me drink sweet tea with her on the porch at the manor.

She was the bestest person I've ever known. She loved me, too."

The granny-woman touched my face. Her soft fingers felt like Grandma Elsie's kindness, as if heaven were in her fingertips. "Come now, child. We can't stay here sitting in the dirt. I've got to plan a funeral. I've got to say goodbye to him. I've got to go. I can't stay here. I'm … sitting on the ground acting like a blubbering old woman."

I ignored her, and snot poured from my nose. "No one thinks I'm special. I'm always in someone's way. I'm the girl who landed here like a weed in the garden."

"Honey … honey … We must get up. This ground is hard. There's a storm coming in from the west." The gust of sandy wind cut across the parking lot, and the swirl of dirt picked up my ponytail, whipping it across my face.

I moved my hair, shaking my head, shouting inside with thoughts of running away today, of doing it now. I got on my knees. "I'll leave this old town. I'll say goodbye to the Crush Boys. I'll go to Taddy's house and wave, even though he won't come outside. I'll kiss …" I choked on the word kiss. "I'll kiss Lizzy Beth goodbye."

Screaming at the gust of wind barreling at us. "And Archie! I trusted him! And now he's betrayed me!"

I hollered over the wind at the old woman who was reminiscing of her marriage while I talked to her and anyone who might listen. "I'm sorry. I don't know what to do. I get in the way without trying. I must go. I must leave. I can't stay!"

She mustered up words to comfort me. "I hope you find hope. And share hope. My husband would want us to do that, to honor God with our lives."

Sobbing, I wanted to care about her loss, but my pain and confusion required all my attention. I sniffled, my hair snapping back and forth, my eyes burning from the dust cutting my skin, and I stood up. "I'm sorry. My ride's over there. I don't plan on being so mean. We have to leave, this storm is on top of us" I pointed to Archie who slept like a baby in the truck, who was seconds from facing an onslaught of my questions.

"Baby girl, help me from the ground. I'm getting too old. Going down is easy. It's the getting up."

I reached for her hand, and she wobbled to her feet. I whispered. "I'm sorry I screamed at you. I've had a bad couple of years."

"Me too, sweetie. Me, too. When a heart dies, it leaves behind a trail of sadness. Or maybe ..." She gazed at the sky. "Maybe it leaves behind a trail of destruction from the tornado that blows in on you. We best get out of this weather."

I charged toward Archie, and glanced over my shoulder to watch the old woman drive away as a blanket of rain showered down on us. Charging between the trucks and cars, the pelting rain soaked my shirt and my overalls, and I jerked on Archie's door. He jolted awake, barking at me. "What are you doing? I nearly fell from the truck." His eyes glassy from his nap, he snapped, "Shut that door, and get inside. It's pouring down. I'm getting wet."

I drilled Archie, standing like a wet puppy. "I don't care if you get wet. What do you know? When did you learn Lizzy Beth was a twin? Why didn't you tell me? Why won't anyone tell me anything?"

Archie motioned to me, "Get in. No need to soak the both of us."

I raised my voice, the rain landing on my tongue like sour lemons. "And where is he? Does he know about Lizzy Beth? Or is that a secret, too? Is any of this true?"

Archie cut himself from his seat, reaching for me. "I think you need to talk to Mr. Boyd. I'm not the person to ask, and how did you find out about your brother?"

"My brother? It's not true. It can't be. If you knew anything, you'd know that Mahlee gave Lizzy Beth up when she was born. A girl. One baby. She saw her, and everything."

Archie's hair drooped like cooked noodles, and his jacket became a soaked cloak. "I know you need to know more than you know. Just know this, someone took the boy. There was another baby!"

I marched to the passenger seat, climbing inside, wringing my pants leg on the floorboard. "Take me home. Take me home now. I can't trust you. I can't trust anyone."

Archie wrung himself out in the seat, slamming his door. "Let Mr. Boyd and Ms. Susan tell you what you don't know. I've said too much."

"Too much? You kept secrets. You hide things from me." I cried like the rain was inside of the truck. "Mr. Boyd doesn't want me. Now I know why. They're searching for a son. A boy. A brother for Lizzy Beth. So they can send me away."

Cranking the truck, Archie argued with me. "You have this mixed up in your mind. It's not what you see, or what you think. It's what is true."

"What? Talking in circles won't fix this."

"I'm helping. I want to save a life."

"Save a life? You're ruining my life."

"Not true. You don't know what I know."

"I know they don't like me. I'm not the perfect daughter, because I'm not *their* daughter. I'm nobody!" My voice punctured the air like a knife, as if the tornado of my heart might explode. "I can't believe you're sneaking around with them. I thought you were my friend."

"Shoelace, you're jumping to conclusions based on what you don't know. There's more to this story, and more to learn. Give your parents a chance to tell you."

"They're not my parents!" I folded my arms, moving as far away from Archie as possible, and I hung onto the door. Staring out the window, I counted the rain drops, too many to keep up, but if I looked at Archie one more time, I might hit him.

Archie maneuvered the pickup to the highway, the cab full of lost questions and no answers, and the tires slapped in the puddles of broken hearts and broken dreams. I was filled with conflict, one second glad to have a brother, but torn at no one telling me I might have a brother. I became invisible and allowed the walls of discord to surround my entire being.

The drive went silent except for the pounding of rain beating on the truck. Except for the snapping of trees to our left. Except for the squeal of the gusts blowing around the truck. The dirt road became a lake as we headed back to Jefferson. My thoughts consumed me, and turned into a disgusting and detestable mesh of stormy words, those I'd not say out loud.

Archie broke the silence after more than a half hour, as we rounded the road and crossed the bridge over the bayou. "Shoelace, in the book of Isaiah, the Bible tells us..." He paused, sighing. "I'm sorry this is happening. But God has so much to say to you."

"Don't do that. Don't keep saying stuff about God. Do you really think He's working this out for me?"

"Yes, absolutely! I was going to tell you what Isaiah 41:10 says, and how it encourages us not to fear, for God is with us. That He strengthens us and helps us. He also upholds us."

"I hope he's ready to hold me, because where I'm going, I'm going to need His strength. As for being afraid, I'm not. I am not afraid. I don't need anyone."

"Shoelace, I'm going inside with you. We need to talk with Mr. Boyd and Ms. Susan. This is great news. You'll see."

"Great news for them! You'll see. They don't care about me." I argued like I was in charge, like I knew what I was talking about, and yet, I knew that all I wanted was to crawl into a hole and hide until I turned into a grownup.

Archie parked the truck and we slithered from our seats like wet rags, and I forced myself in front of him as I propelled myself to the porch. The wall of distrust grew into a wedge as wide as a lake, and I stormed into the house. I grabbed the wet letters from my pockets, ready to scream, ready to drill my adoptive parents.

But then I saw Ms. Susan holding a three-layer platter of chocolate cake! And Lizzy Beth ran to me holding a photo. "My brother! I have a brother!"

## Back in the Closet

How one day started like an avalanche of pain, and how the day ended with a storm and me standing soaked in the living room with chocolate cake feels like a memory I'll keep for the rest of my life.

Holding the photograph, I clicked the flashlight on. "Yep, the little boy in the picture is an identical face to Lizzy Beth."

*Click.*

The closet went dark, my breath the only noise inside the hole where I hid at night, when sleep falls for everyone but me.

*Click.*

Staring at the paper photo, I glued my eyes on the image. "Yes, those eyes. He's got the same deep charcoal eyes as Lizzy Beth. And the same face. Same Choctaw bones."

*Click.*

Thinking in the dark is one thing I get right, but I must do it aloud. "That was the best cake today. I can't believe Ms. Susan allowed us to eat the cake in the parlor on the coffee table. We never eat there, and Powder, my little mouse who hides from Ms. Susan, he showed himself today. We had too many crumbs! And he nibbled on them too close to her foot."

Ha-ha! Ha-ha!

*Click.*

I gazed at the dresses now hanging back in the proper place in the closet. All facing the same direction. All in order like Ms. Susan likes them. "Powder, where are you? I'm sorry she stomped her shoe and scared you. You'll need to watch out for her after I'm gone."

*Click.*

Sighing, I closed my eyes, even though I was sitting in the darkness of the closet at midnight, with my satchel on my shoulder, with my PF Flyers on, wearing my overalls and my denim shirt.

*Click.*

I wiggled my toes. "These are getting smaller or I'm getting bigger feet." My toes pushed at the end of the shoes, but for now, I can run faster than most boys, except for Crush. I'm not sure how Crush will feel when I'm gone. I think he's close to becoming a good friend.

*Click.*

My eyes watered from the memories of the past year with Ms. Susan and Mr. Boyd. I'm a part of the fabric of this home, even if I've flushed towels down the toilet to get attention. Even if I emptied the vacuum in the kitchen. Even if I spilled the powder detergent onto the basket of clean clothes. Even if I give them reason to send me away.

*Click.*

Sobbing, I shook my head, staring at the photograph of my half brother and wondering if he was alive. Could he be Lizzy Beth's real brother? Archie's not talking, and didn't stay for cake. He figured the family needed to spend the day being honest with each other. And I tried to listen to them for the first time since I can't remember.

No one's telling me how Lizzy Beth ended up away from him. But from what I can tell, she doesn't know him. She's thrilled to have a brother, but doesn't understand that he's lost out there—somewhere in Memphis, Tennessee.

That attorney is searching for him, but it seems to me, he writes mostly letters about it. I'm a much better 'vestigator, and I must go. I must go find this little boy, especially if I'm his big sister.

*Click.*

Darkness is my best place to think, my best place to plan, my best place to disappear from the daylight before anyone misses me.

*Creeeaaak.*

I pushed the door open, tiptoeing toward the door, moving to the foot of the bed where Lizzy Beth slept. The dim light from the window gave me shadows of orange in the room, and now my dolls, alongside Lizzy Beth's were gone. Well, except for the one glued together, the one with gold hair. She was missing most of her backside and left ear. The one dressed in overalls with red shoes.

Running the tip of my finger across the base of the doll, I remembered how Lizzy Beth snuck Ms. Susan's red nail polish and colored the once black shoes, red. I took the paddling for her, since it was my idea.

Whispering, I knelt beside the bed, gazing into my sweet little sister's face. "Baby sister, I've only known one other person who loved me like you, and that's our Grandma Elsie. You would have loved her." Wiping the flood of tears from my cheeks, I put my chin right on the edge of the mattress, memorizing Lizzy Beth's face.

I kissed my fingers and put them on her nose. "See you soon." I paused. "I hope."

Rising to my feet, I inhaled the memories of spending every day and night with Lizzy Beth, of having Ms. Susan greet me with, "Good morning, this is the day the Lord has made, let's rejoice and be glad in it."

Gargling from the extra saliva forming faster than I could swallow, I didn't even realize how nice Ms. Susan was, until right at this moment.

Now, Mr. Boyd's continued scolding isn't his fault. I was guilty every time. I pushed him. I pressed him. I forced him to respond to my disobedience. It's not like I gave him a reason to like me, let alone love me.

Turning the doorknob, I stepped from my bedroom, and as I pulled the door closed, I spoke so low I barely heard myself. "Goodbye, Lizzy Beth. I'm going to save our brother. I'm going to Memphis to find him."

I froze like a statue in the parlor, and moved to the small table with the pistol. The not-loaded gun Mr. Boyd emphasized I leave alone called to me, even though he warned me to never touch the gun again.

Sliding the drawer open, I touched it one more time, just because I could. Giggling, I knew my mean streak was anything but over, and yet, I shut the drawer leaving the gun in its place.

With our house, a few blocks from the tracks, I'll wave goodbye to the boys' orphanage on Soda Street, and catch the next train as it leaves town. This will take me through Texarkana, and I'll need to be sure and hop the right train toward Memphis. I'll find White Beard or maybe Peg Leg back at the hobo camps. It's near a cemetery, so I'll find them. I'll get their help, and we'll find my brother!

Not much money on me, but with my nickels from taking soda pop bottles to the store, my pockets are packed.

Opening the front door, I looked back into the parlor, remembering the laughter and the chocolate cake. I remembered how Ms. Susan and Mr. Boyd hesitated to tell me of the other twin, until I showed them the letters in my pockets. I also won't forget how I received the first slice of cake, and how Lizzy Beth giggled and sat by me on the sofa. How she hummed a no-song tune and made up her own noises, and we all clapped.

"I should stay. Lizzy Beth won't understand. Neither will my adoptive mama and daddy. I promised them today I'd make good choices and make better decisions. I guess I lied, a little. Although this is a good choice as far as I can see."

Boy, today, for a few minutes I felt like I belonged—but I can't let our brother not have cake. He needs to know us. I must go find him. He needs me. He needs Lizzy Beth. And somehow, I know I'll need him, too! That is, if he's alive. And if he's really our brother!

The long walk to the street, a mere six feet or so felt like a mile, and I opened the picket fence gate, and left, not looking back—afraid I'd change my mind.

The boxcar called, the hum of the rail roared—and I ran like a lion in the circus to devour the person or persons responsible for separating Lizzy Beth from—Willie!

I shouted in the wind. "Willie, here I come. Willie, I will find you! Geronimo!"

## The Bridge to the Cemetery

Two weeks of digging through the trash for food, and begging for pennies from ladies wearing frilly hats, while using my sad face, left me with four cents and a dime.

Putting smudges of dirt on my face, ratting my hair with my hands, and holding my belly worked great when I was smaller. But being twelve and taller, brought second glances from store owners when I stood at their windows too long. And those ladies lifted their noses higher than their hats most of the time.

One man shooed me off with a broom. Another old geezer handed me an orange and a banana, and slipped a dime into my hand. He warned me to get moving, to not be out after dark in this part of town, because I'd come up missing.

I couldn't figure out how I'd be missing if I knew where I was, I never get lost. So, I left on the next train out of town, and found myself headed north. I didn't know it at first, but then the sun swung to the west later that day.

Making up time, I had to jump, catch another train and find one headed east.

Five times! I can't believe I keep getting mixed up in my directions. I've never had trouble before with catching the wrong train. I'm rusty. Out of practice. I'm not counting how Tin Can Mahlee kept us moving down trails, to train depots. She always knew where we were and where we were headed.

Earlier, I jumped into a boxcar with this teenage boy. He was wearing a brown vest and dark green slacks. He cut his eyes at me, watching me from the end of the boxcar.

Rocking back and forth, listening to the hum of the wheels clacking toward Tennessee, his green eyes pierced my entire being. My blue ones cut him in half.

He never spoke to me, until right before he hopped from the train in the last town. "Kid, you better wise up if you're gonna make it. The railroad cops are gonna get you. You'll see."

"Don't think I don't know when to get off."

He jumped, and I peeked from the opened boxcar, only to see a cop pulling the boy by the collar. I'd rolled down the hill like a ball, like a circus performer, and hid in the tall grass until it was quiet.

Now, I'm riding in a boxcar with four men, and one woman whose teeth are missing, whose wrinkles hang over her collar. Her gum-smile makes me gag. I better quit staring at her, because she is rubbing her hands together, and her eyes are glued on my satchel.

Hugging my belongings, I leaned on the boxcar wall. The way I was forced to keep from tumbling to my right, I knew we were climbing a hill. With the low light changing from bright to gray, I also knew sundown and darkness lingered within the hour. Nights in a boxcar creak louder than sleep and without Mahlee or my daddy, riding the rail isn't the same when you're alone.

I considered getting out of this boxcar when the five sloppy and slobbering people piled in, but the train picked up speed too fast at the last town. Now I'm stuck with this crew until morning, most likely.

The woman gained her footing, pressing her hand on the wall of the boxcar, kicking some straw. "Girl, you got any food? What's in the bag?"

"Just my clothes."

"You a runaway?"

"No, I'm looking for someone."

"Me, too." She licked her lips. "I'm searching, too."

I mouthed, "Searching for what?"

"For me some supper. It's been two days since I ate. Two days. My guys lost their last two dollars in a card game. They can't keep their money, and they lose it faster than they earn it."

The one with a piece of straw in his mouth kicked the woman. "Work? I don't need to work. I can play me some poker in one night and make more than if I worked a week."

She kicked him back. "Not if you keep losing."

I interrupted them. "I'm hungry, too. I don't have anything you can eat." I shuffled backwards on my bottom.

The fat man with the short legs popped up like a bottle cap flying from a soda pop. "Leave her alone. She's a kid. Don't you see you scare her?"

The other three men offered me their crooked and lopsided smiles. It seemed like they were used to grinning together.

The woman hopped from one foot to the other, wobbling and jumping. "I don't scare nobody. I can't bite you, girl. I don't have all my teeth. I can barely see you, but my right eye knows you're there. My left sees you like a shadow. A scrawny one." She turned to the man to her side. "I mean no harm. I'm just talking to her."

Mr. Pop-up pulled on the woman's pant leg. "Be quiet. Get over here and sit down. We've a got a long night ahead. Memphis is ahead, but we might need to jump at some of them smaller train depots. So, you keep watch. The rail cops are about these parts like a pack of wolves."

The woman stuck her tongue at me. "I'm not gonna hurt you, girl." She twirled with the bump of the boxcar. "Being alone all these years, you lose who you used to be, who you wished to be, and become who you forgot you was and you lose yourself."

Shaking my head, her words rattled in my brain, and the roar of the wheels creaked louder than a crazy woman shouting in the night. I shifted all the way to the corner of the boxcar, near some old boxes, ready to jump if needed, ready to run if the rail cops come at me. And ready to clobber the toothless woman if she came over to my side of the boxcar.

**

*Swalap!*
"Ouch! What in the world?"

The flapping lips of the woman hollered like a sick rooster. "We have to get off. The train's a slowing. On the other side of the river is Memphis, Tennessee. There's some flashing lights up ahead. Might be trouble. We best get off now."

I twirled around on my knees, unraveling from sleeping in a ball in the corner. "Hey, that's my satchel."

The woman fumbled the bag in her hands as the train jerked. "I was gonna hand it to ya."

Pursing my lips, I hollered, "Sure you were. You were hoping to get off before I saw you."

"I wouldn't have shaken you awake if that were true." She threw the satchel at me. "There! Little runaways get caught. They don't grow up to be anything but crazy old women nobody wants, nobody knows, and nobody misses."

She hung on the opened boxcar door, and in one lunge she tossed herself to the bushes out the door, into the morning sunlight where anything could happen, where the unknown awaited.

I glanced around the boxcar, sitting there alone, for the other four men were gone, too "What did she mean? Flashing lights?"

Holding on, I twisted my head out of the boxcar door. The clunk-clack of the train inched slower and slower, inching like a snail. "What's going on? There's a few cars on the road, and the police are searching them. Oh no! Rail cops! The ones with the sticks. They're looking inside the boxcars on top of a bridge. This must be bad. Cars stopped and a train. Who are they looking for?"

Wrapping my satchel over my shoulder, I dove to the ground with a tuck, landing in a pile of loose dirt that felt like a mattress. Dusting myself off, I slid down the side of the tracks toward a patch of wood, hiding in the brush, hoping for the commotion to end.

Whispering to myself, "I bet they're searching for a criminal. Bet it was that woman and four boyfriends. Or maybe it was that boy from yesterday." You never know what kind of folks you'll run into on the tracks or riding in a boxcar.

A memory of sleeping in the soft bed with Lizzy Beth crept into my head and I shook at hearing my thoughts remind me of what I left behind in Jefferson. I wondered if those cops were looking for me. I am a runaway, sort of.

I slapped my face like I was splashing water on my skin. "Get yourself together. You must find Willie. You can do this, don't get scared now."

I sat on a stump, and waited, swinging my feet, and rocking with the rays of sun glistening through the top of the whistling trees. The sun moved high into the sky, and my feet tingled from dangling. "What are they doing? Who could they be searching for?"

I stepped on the vines shooting around my feet, and I peeked into the clearing, for the sixth time. "Yep, they're out there. The train's not even moving now."

*Scuffle-shad-cuff. Scuffle-shad-cuff.*

"Who's there?" I climbed back onto the stump to see over the bushes, wiping the sweat from my forehead. I peered for anything or anyone who moved. "Who's there?"

"It's me, just another friend from the rail."

"A friend? I don't know your voice. Show yourself." I ordered the person to come closer, unsure why I sounded brave when my gut quivered with fear like a worm.

From behind a patch of trees, a man with blue-marbled eyes offered me his smile. "Hi, Missy." He tipped his hat. "Sorry to scare you. I was riding the train, hiding out in a car behind you. I saw the others jump, and figured they was your family."

"My family? I don't even know them. They were in my boxcar. I'm headed to Memphis. Where are you headed?" I noticed his duffel bag dragging behind him, overstuffed and heavy. Not waiting for him to answer, I quizzed the man who was a good ten years older than me. "What's weighing you down? You're traveling with a big load."

"Oh this, it's packed with all I have. I lost everything in a fire, got out with a few keepsakes of my mama's. God rest her soul." He put his hand to his heart. "I'm headed to … headed to …" He ran his fingers through his waving hair, his lip quivering. "Where did you say, you're going?"

I pointed in the direction of the Mississippi River. "I'm going across the Harahan Bridge …" I choked on the word Harahan, remembering the night in the coal car when Daddy fell, when life turned dark, when the river swallowed up my daddy. The night I got my hobo name. The night I lost myself.

A shove on my shoulder brought me back to reality. "Girl, you went away. You were dreaming and got stuck in a nightmare. Your eyes went dark."

Clearing my throat, I jumped from the stump, making up a fib. "I'm headed to my auntie's house. I'm going to stay with her for the summer. See, I lost my train ticket, so I hopped in a boxcar."

"So you say. Somehow, you don't look like a girl with a home, you look like a girl without a place to sleep. And like a story with broken pieces and with lies." He grabbed my collar. "What's in your satchel? Got any keepsakes?"

Screaming, I yelled like a little girl who needed her daddy, who prayed he'd come from the river like a ghost and save her. "Stop yanking on me. I don't have anything you want. I'm … I'm a hobo girl. Just got one change of clothes. That's all."

*Slam-bop!*

From behind me, a bunch of legs and arms rushed by, as I toppled to the ground like a rope lassoing the weeds. The voices of the crew hollered, and the one making the most noise, the toothless woman shouted at the man who let me go. "Leave my girl alone. She's not for the taking. She belongs to us. She's ours." I gazed up at the skin bouncing on the woman's face, and she socked the man with the gorgeous eyes. "Leave her be."

Stumbling backwards, he howled, "I'll be on my way. On my way, you hear?"

Another rustling came with clinking noises up on the tracks, along with pounding on boxcars. Whispering, I hung onto the woman's hand. "We're going to jail, aren't we?"

She smiled, her gums red and her eyes sparkled, and she spoke with a low sneaky voice. "You aren't, and I'm not. My friends aren't either, as you see they're already hiding." She yanked on my arm, and I crumbled into a wad of smallness, and we hid in the thicket near a bunch of dead trees. "*Shhh! Be as quiet as a mouse.*"

I nodded, knowing exactly how to act like Powder, my mouse, when he didn't want to show himself.

A man's voice came from the tracks like a cannon of noise. "I know you're in there. Come out. We've followed you. You've stolen from every house in East Texas, and West Arkansas, but you're not getting away with it anymore."

Glancing for the peddler with the duffel bag, I muttered, "Where is he hiding? The cops want him. I'm sure of it."

Then a deep and firm voice came through the trees like hope to my ears. A voice I knew. A voice that shows up more often than others. A voice I was grateful to hear.

But this time, his voice cracked, "Buster! We know you're hiding in there." His panicked scream sent the birds flying. The flutter felt like a tragedy awaited, like past hurts were bleeding with pain. "Buster, I know you're in these woods. You need to give yourself up. You must surrender, or the cops will shoot you. You have nowhere to run."

## Brother with Bad Blood

"Archie? Is that you? How in the heck did you get here?"

"Shoelace? Remain calm. I've come for my brother."

"Brother? You have a brother?"

"Yes! We received a tip that he was on this train. And I saw him myself when he ran from around the boxcar, lugging his duffel bag. I'm here to help him surrender, so he can keep himself from being killed. I know he's a runner."

Buster hollered, interrupting our yelling match in the woods. "I'm not giving up. I've told you how this is the way it is for me. I steal. I run. I hide. You abide. You're the good son." The peddler gave himself away from behind the trees, and he was too close for me to sneak off.

*Crack. Crunch. Crack.*

Stepping into the small clearing, Archie gave his location away too, by perching himself in the sunny spot by the stump. His face lit up from the glare of light streaking like lightning from above the trees, and he squinted, "Buster. It's over. You've got the entire state of Arkansas after you, and now the Shelby County police. They've tracked you from Jefferson, to Texarkana, and up and down the Arkansas rail. You're cornered. Give yourself up."

Before I moved from my safety, I screamed, "Archie, he was in Jefferson?"

"Yes, the night … the night Tak was shot!"

I lost my breath. "Did your brother shoot my little Tak?"

"It seems he did, and we're finding out he shot a few other folks, too. "

The old woman crouched beside me, whose fat wobbled from her arms like pudding, and she nudged me. "What did you say? Do you know the man they're after?"

"I know the man who is the brother to the one they're after, not that I knew he had a brother." Shaking my head, I popped to my feet, but before I could yell for Archie or let him see me, a thud made me jump. A long breath like the exhaling of life blew against my head, and I twirled around to see the woman crumbling to the ground. "What?"

A gun pointed at my face. "Don't move. Don't yell. And stop all that talking."

Standing face to face with Archie's brother, facing a killer and a peddler, my hand went to my mouth to keep in my scream. The flabby woman lay between us on the loose dirt and weeds, gushing with blood from her nose and ear.

Buster whispered, "You're my ticket out of this place."

"What? I don't have any pull with the cops. I'm wanted myself."

"Sure you are kid."

I held my satchel on my shoulder, while he clinched the wrist of my left arm. "Let go of me."

"Not yet. Your tears will keep me safe. I'll let you go when we get across the river."

"What? I'm not going anywhere with you."

"Yes, you are. Or you'll end up like her." He pointed with the pistol, only to flip it right into my side.

I spouted off, "Her gang will get you. There's four of them. You'll see."

He smirked. "I don't think so. They ran off down the dirt road back there by the old tractor. They deserted her. And you."

I wiggled, trying to get my arm loose. "I'm not with them anyway. I'm with … with myself."

"I know. Which means no one cares if you die or not."

Scowling, I kicked the man. "Let me go. Archie will save me. He's my friend."

"Archie? You know my Archie?" The peddler laughed under his breath.

"He is … we've been friends for a long time."

"Well, I've known him longer than you have, especially since he's my big brother."

"He's never told me about you."

Branches behind me snapped with a wisp. "Buster, let the girl go." Archie's order sent me spinning as Buster put my back in front of his chest, and placed the gun at my head.

I cringed, since I stepped on the woman's hair, getting blood on my shoes. "Archie. What's going on?"

Archie kept his distance, watching his brother, and glancing at me. And shaking his head when he saw the body lifeless at our feet. "Buster, this doesn't need to go down this way."

"Go down this way? I'm the one with a gun. She's walking across the Harahan Bridge with me. A mile to my freedom. A mile until I can disappear. She's going with me to guarantee my safety."

*Chug-a-lug. Chug-a lug.*

Archie argued, "There's a handful of policemen waiting for you on the other side of the tracks. I told them I'd bring you out and you'd turn yourself in."

"No. I've stolen a few trinkets, nothing to cause such a ruckus."

"Ruckus? You shot a little boy in Jefferson, a six-year-old. And a man back at a bakery in Little Rock. I can't believe you've taken this route. Ma and Pa would be so disappointed in you."

"They would, but they're not here to see me. They're gone, remember?"

"But you can make this right."

I nodded, "Make it right, Buster. Archie knows good comes from bad things. I've heard him say so."

*Swalap!*

"Ouch! You didn't have to slap me."

Archie marched a few feet closer. "Hurt the girl, and I'll take you out myself. This is over, and it's over today." The sun no longer offered a glow of hope, instead the sweat from my forehead burned my eyes.

Buster began his bargaining. "I'll make you a deal. And she can live."

Archie rubbed his hands together, his brown shirt showing the wet under his arms too, and his deep breaths made me worry.

I peered up at the peddler. "Mr. Buster, let me go. I never did nothing to you."

Archie questioned his brother. "So, if we let you cross the river, you'll leave Arkansas and never return? And you'll never come back to Texas, either? You'll stay in Tennessee?"

"I'll never come back your way. You'll never see me again."

I wrinkled my nose, wondering why Archie offered his brother a deal he couldn't keep, and then Buster called him on it. "You need to get rid of the rail cops and the officers. You have five minutes. If not, I'll shoot her."

"You don't want to hurt anyone else, Buster. This has to stop."

"Stop? I came to you in Jefferson to borrow money. To help me out with a loan. But you sent me away. Told me to get out of town."

"You come when you're in trouble. You take advantage of me. If I give you money, you drain me dry. I can't loan you money every few months. I have to let you find your way out of your swamp of deceit."

"Deceit? You've brainwashed this little girl. She thinks you're her friend. She has no idea how you've helped Georgia Tann make money off them babies. How she paid you to drive her around Memphis and drop off babies to new parents, stealing them from single mothers and poor folks."

Archie made a fist, shaking his hand at Buster. "That's not the whole story, and you know it. Don't muddy the water."

"I didn't muddy it, you're the one acting like an honorable man, but your secrets of deceit are right across the Mississippi River. And you know it."

I swallowed my spit. "Archie? What is he saying?"

Archie's nostrils widened, his skinny body looking like a limb ready to break. "Don't listen to him."

Buster continued, "You drove Ms. Georgia around in her black limousine, and she dressed you up in those suits. I only needed a little cash to get a fresh start. Talk about a swamp of deceit."

My ears burned, the ugly about Archie pierced my heart like a million bee stings. "Archie, what's he talking about? Did you help get rid of babies? What about Willie? Does this have anything to do with him?"

Archie shushed me. "He's got his facts mixed up. Let's get you out of this fix first" He looked up the trail leading back to the tracks. "Let me talk to the police, Buster. I'll make them think you rushed off with some of the others who jumped off the train. Give me a minute. And don't hurt my Shoelace."

Mocking Archie, I repeated some of his words. "I'm not so sure I'm your Shoelace. Or anyone's Shoelace."

Buster's arm tightened around my chest, slipping closer to my neck. "Hurry, big brother. I need to get across that bridge. That's our deal."

Archie ran up the hill, disappearing behind the shadow of the trees. I wiggled, and Buster shoved me. "Go sit down on that stump. And don't move."

*Chug-a-lug. Chug-a-lug. Choo. Choo. Choo.*

I whispered, "The train's moving. They've finished the search. They must be leaving."

"Be quiet. Sit."

I acted like I didn't understand. "Over where?"

"On the stump in the clearing. You can see it, right?" And don't try and run." He pointed the pistol at my face, laughing. "I'm a pretty good shot."

"Sure, you are. You hit a kid in a house and barely grazed his arm."

"I didn't want to shoot him, but he was running for help."

"Some man you are. Shooting little boys."

"Shut up!" Buster turned his back to me, as if I reminded him of what a terrible-bad man he'd become. Then the woman started groaning. She wasn't dead!

"Help me. I need someone to fix my head, it's ... it's throbbing."

I stood to my feet. "Help her. You can't just let her die."

"I can. And I will."

"You are horrible. Archie doesn't deserve you. Oh wait, he's probably as bad as you, but acting ... what did you say?"

Snickering, Buster answered, "Honorable. He is just like me. You'll see. He may not have a gun, but he's been a part of letting babies be sold to families who can't have kids, but if they get sick, watch out—they come up missing."

Buster's joy at making fun of Archie made my stomach sour, and I gagged. "I'm gonna throw up."

"Go ahead, this is the woods."

I ran at Buster, and my stomach unloaded. *Barfffffff!*

"Oh my! Girl, you are vomiting on me!" He shoved me backwards, his hands covered in green icky liquid, even his gun dripped with my barf.

I barreled up the hill, branches of twigs slapping me in the face, and I rushed to the tracks. This was my chance to get away, so I jumped between the now wide-open tracks and charged across the Harahan Bridge. My legs wobbled, the water below an invitation to certain death, but I was convinced Buster might be on my heels. If so, the cops would see him and arrest him.

After running for at least three boxcar lengths, with the bridge branching out like a clothesline over the river, I stopped and peeked behind me, huffing with a nasty vomit taste lingering in my mouth. "Where did he go? He must be chasing me. And where is Archie? Where are the police?"

The air felt like a wave of ocean water caving over me, heavy with fear like sharks were attacking. The bridge for the cars was built on the side of the railroad bridge and ran next to the tracks, but lower. I peered up and down the tracks and the road. A couple of cars were up ahead driving into Memphis.

The train had disappeared over the mighty Mississippi River, long gone. "Where is everyone?" Then I felt the sting. "Ouch! My ankle!" I gazed down. "What? Oh my, I've been shot!?"

## The Harahan Takes Another Life

I touched my leg, the blood oozing, but only a trickle. "Thank goodness, Buster's a horrible shot."

"Stop! Girl, you stop now, or you'll die in the river." Buster was charging at me, but his duffel bag, the one loaded with stolen goods, was attached to his arm. He wasn't letting it go, and his gait became slower than molasses dripping down the side of a syrup jar. Which gave me added running steps to run ahead of him over the bridge.

Archie rode up beside us in what looked like Marion Kane's old truck. I couldn't see him so good since the road was lower than the bridge. The car-bridge part hung on the side of the iron tracks like a ledge. And every little bit, I caught a glimpse of the truck, but the more I ran, the windier it got, and the wobblier I felt. And the less I saw of Archie.

My leg ached and the blood seeped through my sock, redder now, like a river of sorrow releasing from my skin. To catch my breath, I bent over and rubbed my ankle, and a flood of memories the night Daddy fell to the river below consumed me. I could barely move—stuck in the past, hurting from his falling, lost in the goodbye of never seeing him again.

Then Buster marched at me. He'd left his bag on the side of the tracks on a rafter, and waved his pistol. "Stop there. Stop now."

My bad attitude leaked on him. "I'm already stopped. Why shoot me? It's not like you're getting away with your crimes. You're trapped in the pain already. It's like vomit to you, or you wouldn't be running." I spouted at him, handing out wisdom from somewhere deep inside my gut, words I didn't know existed.

"Shut up!" He pointed the gun at me, seizing me once again, jerking me to his chest, putting me between anyone who came at us.

Since I was trapped, I blurted, "Why are you a criminal?"

"Hush it up."

"No! Why do your steal? Why don't you get a job? Don't you see how you're not just stealing to eat? Now, you're killing people. People who never did you wrong."

Buster flew into a rage, shoving me to the bridge tracks, and my head bounced off the rail. "You just can't help yourself. Can you?" He pointed the gun at my head.

Crying, I shouted at *my daddy*, "If you'd gotten a real job. If you'd stayed in Texarkana and worked with Grandpa. If you'd been my daddy and loved me. If you'd helped Grandma. If you'd cared for me." I hollered and bellowed and shouted and pulled every part of losing my daddy from the pit of my stomach, like vomit.

I released the pain and the horror of losing my daddy into this river, on these tracks, on Thanksgiving Day two years ago. Seems my daddy might have escaped from the Memphis cops himself, which is why we were really leaving. He was just pretending to take me to Grandma Elsie's for Christmas.

Shaking, I curled into a ball, wishing for the next train to rumble over me. "Daddy! I loved you! But you never loved me enough to stay sober! Or to give me a home!"

Buster moved toward me, kicking my side. "Get up. No time for little girl tantrums."

I stared at him from the tracks, not moving, not unfolding, not obeying. "Just shoot me. That's what you do. You shoot kids now." I hollered, "You have no idea who I am. Or what I will do. Or where I come from. Or if I'm nobody. Or somebody."

Buster knelt as if he were consoling me. "Shut your trap, little girl. We're moving across the river, and we're going now." He yanked on my arm, plucking me to my feet, but I went limp causing him to stumble on the railroad ties. His gun fell from his grasp. "No! Not my pistol!" The gun drifted downward, falling and falling, until it became a small dot, and then the gun plunged into the water.

I hurled myself to my feet, and charged toward Tennessee, running and galloping like a wild horse. I felt dizzy from the wind, and from the height of the bridge of the river. My knees shook, my body cramped, and I kept telling myself not to glance down.

I wondered why Buster hadn't snatched me or chased me, so I glanced backwards. "What?" He'd returned to get his duffel bag, and was no longer following me, but faced west toward Arkansas, frozen between the tracks.

I hadn't noticed how his build was lean and strong like my daddy. I hadn't noticed how his hair was black like my daddy. I hadn't noticed how his slacks were almost like the same ones my daddy wore on poker nights. But what I did notice, it seemed death had caught up with Buster because another train rumbled our way.

I spun around in a complete circle, after seeing what he saw, and tried to decide how close I was to land on the Tennessee side. My thoughts jumbled, and I screamed, shouting to the bridge. "I want to live. I need to find my brother. I need to save his life. I can't die in the river like my daddy. I need to do this. I can do this. I need a reason to do good with my life. And this is it."

Seconds later, I saw the end of the bridge, and I was close to the Indian burial grounds where my daddy fell. But I wasn't going to fall. I was going to live. "God, please carry me. I'm bleeding way too much to finish this on my own." My plea with God wasn't so much about my ankle and the blood, but more about my bleeding heart and that last two years of death and scars, of hurts and loss.

*Choo-choo! Choo-choo!*

The whistle of the train behind me left me with instant sorrow—for I knew that Archie's brother was gone, probably a mere spec in the Mississippi River, a life gone that should be here—like my daddy's life.

"If I don't hurry, I'm next. "God, please … please let my legs run like a deer. Or use an angel to get me there."

I charged and galloped, and barreled with leaps, and hurled over the railroad ties, and my right ankle throbbed like my heart had fallen into my foot. I limped. The weak leg trailed like dead weight. My head throbbed from hitting the track, and suddenly—like a burst from somewhere behind me, I gave a final jump to the side, leaving the tracks.

Rolling down the hill, with my satchel bouncing in flip-flops, I landed on the bluffs below the bridge—at the very spot where Tin Can Mahlee gave me my hobo name. Where she changed my name from Annie Grace Kree, to Shoelace. To the very spot where I'd found my daddy's satchel, the one looped around my neck, choking me.

"Ouch! My head has a heartbeat now, too. And my ankle is aching like a knife jabbed me." I felt of my wet hair. "More blood?" Sighing, I felt weak, and the sun hung like a spotlight right above me, warm and hot, but I was alive.

I wobbled and lost myself, disappearing to a place where everything switched to a cold and pitch-black sinkhole. And I was falling into the hidden abyss alone!

*Pam Kumpe*

## Madame Jolene's Softness in Red

How did I get on this giant marshmallow of sweetness? Sniffing, I inhaled the particles of goodness floating up my nose, and the shadows broke off like splintered glass, turning invisible behind my eyelids. Blinking, I focused on the nothing and with each breath the nothings formed into somethings.

I cuddled in the softness below me, taking in the weight of the fabric covering my body. My head rested on its own marshmallow, and my ears tingled with the sounds coming from around me, below me, and over me.

"Shoelace? Are you waking up, my dear?" A call to my heart brought beauty to my ears. "Welcome back, precious daughter of the grand and famous Sidecar Ace."

Wiggling and stirring, I cradled my body into the cushion of the coffin. I must be dead. It's too peaceful. Nice. Warm. And safe.

A pushing on my arm from above the coffin came with, "Darling, you've had a long few days. Your fever is gone, and your leg is healing, but the concussion you received sent you to the depth of sorrow for the last three days. The bullet grazed you, but you're all stitched up now. I'm thrilled to see your face and those eyes. They remind me of your father." The song of words sounded like an angel called to me, but I was trapped inside the coffin, ready to leave, and ready to go to heaven.

*Swoosh! Swoosh!*

The layer of fabric flew off me, like covers being moved, and light blasted like a lightning strike into my face. I widened my eyes, and they stung as the brightness woke them up. "Where … where am I? And who are you?"

"I'm Madame Jolene. You're at my place."

"And where is your place?"

"The Crystal Palace. I run the restaurant downstairs and live on the second floor. I serve oysters from New Orleans to my guests."

"Oysters? Sounds horrible, crusty shells with slimy stuff. I couldn't eat those."

Sitting up, my senses of living and remembering swam before my eyes. I saw the tracks, the train, and Buster skidding down the rail. I remembered running and falling, and going into a dark hole. "Where's Archie? Where ... where is he? And how did you get me? I don't know you."

I rolled to the other side of the bed; the red bedspread blended with the red curtains on the four slender windows, draping the wall like rippled blood.

The woman with whiter than normal skin, red cheeks, long eyelashes, and a mop of dangling blonde curls reached for me. "Archie brought you here after the incident."

"The incident? So, I'm not dead?"

"No, my dear. You're alive. Maybe a little scarred, and maybe a little exhausted. But I have some biscuits for you, and homemade strawberry jam."

*Clunk. Clunk. Clunk.*

A noise like giant rats stomping in the attic made both of us look at the ceiling. "What is that?"

Ms. Jolene's fingers danced in the air. "Oh, nothing. My cook and his family live up on the third floor. Probably one of his boys. One boy is five. The other is about eleven. They won't bother you. Their mammie keeps them in line."

I ignored most of what she said about her cook, but the word *strawberry* zapped me to reality, and to worrying if Crush was better, and if Tak was home from the hospital.

I remembered why I left Jefferson, why I ran, and why I found myself in the path of another killer. I paused my thoughts to keep from losing my breath. "Ms. Lady? Did Buster die on the bridge?"

"Call me, Madame Jolene. I like the sound of my name. It's speaks of royalty. Not that I am royalty. But it has a nice sound." She shook her head, coming back to my question. "I'm sorry to say, he lost his life in the river. Archie's torn up about it, and can't keep from searching for his body at the river. But so far, there's no sign."

She patted the red sheets. "Come over here. Let's take a look at your leg. I may need to change your bandage."

Grimacing, I jerked my leg. "It's fine. I don't know you. I need my clothes." Glancing down, I saw the red slinky pajama bottoms, and the red top. "Where are my overalls?"

"I'll get them. But no need to dress. You can come join me at the window in the parlor. I have a table set for two. I used my good plates just for you."

"I might be a little hungry."

I took in the room, and the dresser by the wall held porcelain china dolls on top, too many to count. Above the dresser, the strokes of color captured Ms. Jolene's elegance in the painting. She was slim and beautiful, sitting in a high-back chair with a slit in her dress that showed most of her leg.

A tug on my hand made me topple over. "Now, come on, sweetie. Let's get to know each other. I always wanted to know about Sidecar Ace's life. He kept so many secrets. But he did tell of you, at times."

"Tell of me? How do you know my daddy? And no one calls him that, except his bestest friends."

"I was one of his …" she put her hand to neck. "Well, let's just say, I knew him well."

"What does that mean? How could you know him? I was with him all the time. I was his girl. He took grand care of me. We slept on purple sheets. And we have flashy curtains at our house. And we ate shrimp. Not oysters. You don't know anything about my daddy."

"I'm sorry. I didn't mean to upset you. You were his girl. There's no doubt about it. He loved you so much. That's why he came for you when you were five. He missed you so much."

"You know he came for me?"

"I did know him, my dear. We were good friends."

I swung my legs around. My right ankle throbbed a teeny bit, but not enough to miss breakfast. The old wooden slats of the floor felt slick, like polished glass beneath my bare feet. "Madame Jolene, I need to use the bathroom first."

"Come with me. It's the door just outside this bedroom, on the left. Then you can come into the parlor." She floated across the floor like royalty with a walk I've never seen before, one of graceful movement. Her swaying in her day dress of red polka dots caused her round rear to wiggle.

Mocking her, I swayed my boney rear to the bathroom, and inside, the toilet was wrapped in red fur, and the rug by the bear-claw tub was red, too. I popped my head from the bathroom, not sure why no one had contacted Ms. Susan, so she could fetch me. I must not be wanted by her after all.

But this Madame Jolene, she knew my daddy and that made me feel close to him. Even if I was never seeing him again. I frolicked into the parlor, acting a little prissy and feeling rather mouthy. That was a good sign, because now I'm sure I'm not dead. I'm alive, and Willie is out there somewhere. Maybe this Madame could help me. But I'm not sure I trust her yet.

"Come sit with me. I poured you some hot English tea in the cup. I poured a spot of cream, and dropped a sugar cube in it, too. It's should be scrumptious."

I sat in the chair at the small round table with two chairs, with two over-easy eggs looking at me, and the brownest biscuits lathered in butter. They called to be eaten. "This looks grand. Are you a good cook? My grandma Elsie was great at baking."

"I do good with most foods. I love the kitchen. It's the place to create masterpieces and where food touches the belly, it pleases the taste buds and makes people smile."

Grinning, I agreed, and smacked on a biscuit after Madame Jolene lathered it with jam. I slurped the gooey yellow of the eggs right down my throat in one swallow. Wiping my lips with a cloth napkin, my quizzing resumed. "Thank you for breakfast. So where is Archie now? And is Ms. Susan coming for me? Or is Mr. Boyd?"

She placed her teacup in the saucer. "Ms. Susan? Mr. Boyd? Who might they be?"

Scooting my metal chair back across the floor, I jumped to my feet, and dropped my biscuit in my plate. The screeching of metal on wood joined in with my yell. "So, you don't really know me?"

Madam Jolene clanked her fork, dropping it to her plate. "I know a little about you. Not much. I told Archie I would keep an eye on you, and the doctor came to see you and he's the one who stitched you up. I'm not much on this mothering thing. I have no children. I'm just helping out an old friend."

I waved my arms like a wild bird. "Well, Ms. Susan adopted me. And she adopted Lizzy Beth. And Mr. Boyd is my adoptive dad. Why haven't you called them?"

"I don't know them … but who is Lizzy Beth?"

"She's my baby sister. She's five." And why do you care? I figured someone would call them since I got shot. But you haven't, have you? You don't know who I am! You're lying. You've stolen me from Archie! Where are my clothes? I'm leaving. I've got to go. I have to find my brother!"

"Trust me. Archie's mourning his brother's tragic death. He hasn't filled me in yet. I'm just babysitting you."

"I don't need a babysitter. I'm leaving here, and I'm leaving now."

Charging to the red room filled with the color of blood, I pulled open a drawer, searching for my overalls. A little porcelain china doll tumbled to the floor, splintering into a mess of white glass specs.

From behind me, the embrace of the woman enveloped me. "I'm sorry this is happening to you. I know your life has been hard. Your daddy used to tell me of how he stroked your blonde hair at night, how he counted your freckles.

I turned, falling into her arms. "He did count them. He thought they gave me character."

The lady who loved red whispered, "They do. Let me get your clothes from the closet."

I sat on the edge of the bed, careful to miss the glass on the floor. Madame Jolene swung open the closet door, and my shirt hung on a hanger, alongside my overalls. My PF Flyers were on the floor in the closet, next to … next to a small pair of brown loafers and next to a pair of black PF Flyers.

She wiggled toward me. "Here's your clothes. Let's go find Archie and piece this all together. I mean you no harm."

I clutched my overalls. "Madam Jolene?"

"Yes," she swayed my way.

"I thought you said you didn't have any children. Aren't those loafer and PF Flyers a little small for you?"

Madame Jolene rushed from the bedroom, slamming the door. "Get dressed. Wait here." She hollered through the keyhole as she locked the door, trapping me inside the red coffin room. "I'll be right back. You'll see."

I screamed at her, "Let me out! You don't even know Archie, do you?"

## Escape to Elmwood Cemetery

Peering under the bed, I hollered, "Where is my satchel? It's my daddy's satchel. I need it. It has my dime, and my clothes. And the picture of Willie."

I tore the red sheets from the mattress, pulling the pillow cases from the pillow, and the floor turned red like blood. The ripples of the sheets caught the air and waved at me, and I moved to the bottom of the bed, careful not to step on the broken china doll.

Spinning around in a circle, the room appeared to tighten around my neck like a noose, and my breathing shortened. I swung the closet door open, and moved the hanging clothes aside, and there, in the back, a shelf protected my satchel. It sat next to a red purse. Some white gloves. And three blonde wigs. One long and straight. The other short like a bowl cut. And the other with tight curls as if the bobby pins had been left in too long.

Slinging my satchel on my shoulder, I climbed into my overalls and buttoned my shirt, then clasped my bib to each buckle.

I shook the door knob, the rattle of the door loose but locked. "Let me out! I have no idea who you are, but when Archie finds out you stole me, he's gonna have your hide."

My screams fell like pieces of china doll glass into the sinkhole of lost cries, to a place where no one cares, or comes. "Ms. Susan! I can't believe you didn't come for me!"

I felt my heart fading into cold heartbeats where nothing could hurt, where nothing could pierce, and my heart felt only the darkness of living in fear. Like no one would hear my cry—ever.

Sitting with my back to the barrier of a door, I sobbed, letting off the steam of my own engine that seemed stuck on the track, the one of utter loneliness. "God, my heart is full of broken dreams. Everything is gone, and once again I'm full of pain. The arms of those I want relief from, are nowhere. So, are you there? Will you carry me out of here? Or do I need to jump from the window and leave life behind?"

My words wandered like the rippled sheets floating on the floor of the tomb I found myself sitting in, and I prayed for real, "Where are you now, God? Are you searching for me?"

I got on my knees, my ankle stinging at the pull of my socks that I'd just put on my feet before I tied my shoes. I stared to the ceiling where the fan twirled in a circle, and I blinked with the tap-tap of the movement, stuck for a second in-between living and wishing for invisible.

My satchel slipped from my shoulder, and the latch popped open, my extra overalls cascading to the wooden floor. A photograph floated from inside like a feather, landing beside me. "Willie. Sweet little brother. I don't know. I'm a broken mess and scattered pieces. I've tried so hard and thought I could do this on my own, by coming here. But …"

I kissed the photograph. "You are my own blood. Even if we only have the same daddy. I need you. And you need me." I found my strength rising, my hope stirring, and my feet itched to escape.

Tossing my things into the satchel, I ran to the four windows, pushing aside the panels of red, and peered out the window. "What's that? *A Schwab.* And *Dyer's Burgers.* Over there is a café and a theatre."

I pressed my nose on the window, pushing the two levers in the middle of the long window, and lifting the pane upward, sticking my head out, catching a glimpse of a tall white church to my left. Cars chugged along. A few trucks inched to the A. Schwab store. A lady in blue danced on the sidewalk across from me. Two Negro men in suits strummed guitars, singing by an open spot between what looked like entrances to bars. "Goodness, I can't get out of here. This is the highest second story ever."

Shaking my head, I jumped onto the mattress. The headboard with knobs pointed me to the window with a white blind. Pushing it out of my way, I cracked open the window that was no bigger than a crate. The opening was large enough for me to get through, and I hung over the ledge and spit. "A side alley. I can get away through there."

The fire escape hung below me, off to the side a bit, so I grabbed the sheets, tied them together, and made a fat rope. Wrapping the one end around the post on the headboard, I hung the rest of the sheet from the window.

Running my fingers along the soft sheets, I remembered the Bible story Toby told the Crush Boys and me by the tracks in Jefferson when the fireflies danced. "I'm glad he told me about that Rahab lady. She escaped from her attackers just like me. And she lived. So maybe I will."

I sighed, unsure what to do or where to go, but if I found the railroad tracks, I could find my way to the hobo camp by the cemetery, that is, if I follow the rail east from the river. Then I can find Peg Leg and White Beard, if they're still staying in the woods. Whining, I prayed for Archie to find me. "God, give me Archie. I need him, too."

I climbed out the window, dangling on the red-sheet rope, my satchel bouncing in the air, and I wrapped my legs around the fabric, sliding downward and dropping the extra few feet down, landing on the fire escape. I hurried down the ladder and stood in the alley, not sure which way the river ran or how to get my bearings.

I rushed to the street, where a sign hung like a flat ball in front of 'Jolene's Crystal Palace.' "Well, at least she told the truth about having an oyster restaurant, but why—why did she lock me in the room? I need Archie to tell me, but right now I need to get out of sight before she gets back."

Running, I dashed in the direction of the church, slowing when I found myself in front of three arched and oversized doors. A dozen steps led up to each entrance, and I prayed one more time with my eyes open, while staring at the three red doors. "God, call my name. Say it. Come on. Just say it. I need to hear someone call me, so I can find my way."

My prayer made no sense. My undone heart and lost puzzle pieces were stuck at the base of the river at the end of the Harahan Bridge. I moved to touch the giant clasp on the door. "It's locked. Who shuts you out of a church? I need to see God, and these people are locking me out. I knew it. I knew it. I'm not good enough to be in a real church. Even God is shutting me out of His house."

One minute I talked to God like a girl who liked Him, but the next, when my pieces were shattered and breaking into a million slivers of sadness, I'd scream at Him.

"Sorry, God. This is not the way this is supposed to go."

*Choo-choo. Choo-choo.*

From behind the church, a familiar call to my heart, the sound of a train roaring into town broke the silence of my glaring at the red doors. I raced toward the sound of the chugging train, charging to the side of the church, counting the stained-glass windows. "Twelve arched windows. Three stories. A giant church for a huge God. So, this means, God could be big enough to fix me, if He would. Maybe my life is a painted rainbow of glued glass. Maybe …"

I powered myself with all the will I had inside me, thankful for the strength from the biscuits and eggs. Now I could keep searching and hiding, and looking for my brother. The rumble of the train grew louder, and the hum of the clacking of the wheels knocked on the rail, and I stood beside the boxcar rolling by me like lightning.

I hurried alongside of the tracks to my left, because the sun hung low and the shadows told me it was early morning. That meant the river and the hobo camp were back to my right, where Tin Can Mahlee forced me to read. She wanted me to be smarter than those kids in school on the other side of the tracks.

The train disappeared down the tracks, and I walked on the ties, breathing hard, tired of running. Wrestling with my questions, I stopped in the middle and spun around, noticing the pebbles. Picking one up, I tossed it as far as my arm allowed the rock to fly. "This is the spot. This where I played the alphabet game with Skip. Where he gave me his engineer's cap."

Falling to my knees, I turned back to face the way toward the river, and noticed the dirt road that crossed the tracks. "Daddy got out of a car there, with his gun, with our Thanksgiving fruit. He was ready to run and escape Memphis that night. Which we've done plenty in the past few years.

I remembered his smile, his holding me, and his carrying me. I remembered his anxious glances as he watched the trails, his nervous jitters. Something worried him, something he never got a chance to tell, or most likely never planned to let me in on, since I was his girl—and he protected me.

Shaking my head, I yelled, "Daddy, you never took care of me. Tin Can Mahlee did that, she's the one who watched me.

You just disappeared with your women and your card games. Daddy, why didn't you love me?"

I let out the anger of not having a daddy who could love like he should, and yet, no matter how mad I got, I loved him. I sobbed, my tears falling like pebbles to the ties of the tracks.

*Rumble. Rumble. Rumble.*

Glancing up, a black shiny car rolled up to the track in the same spot where my daddy had caught a ride with someone that horrible day—when he died that night.

A window in the back rolled down, a face I'd never see before offered me a grin. The man with white hair, bushy like Santa Claus without a beard, but wearing glasses and a brown Fedora hat waved to me. "Come here, little girl. You can help me."

I took a couple of steps toward the car. "Help you? I don't even know you." My heart raced, and the eggs backed up in my throat, my mouth slobbering with fear. "I have to go."

The door opened on the other side, and a man taller than a small giraffe held onto the arm of another person, dragging the wobbly man with him.

I blinked, trying to focus. "Archie? What's wrong?"

Archie stumbled. "Run, Shoelace. Run! This is Boss Crump, and he's out to get the money I owe him. You need to hide and never show yourself."

Storming the other way, I stampeded across the tracks, cut to the left, zigzagged back to the right, and rushed up a hill. I stopped behind a tree, waiting to see if I was being followed.

"Little girl, we'll find you a good home. You can make a family happy. And it will pay Archie's debt. Come on now. Come out."

The giraffe called to me, his stomping on leaves let me know he was near, and then a *whalap* from somewhere in the shadows gave way to shrieks, "Leave her be. She's mine. You best be on your way." A boom and *whalap* sent squirrels to their hiding places, and I realized I was hiding behind a tombstone and not a tree.

I shook, not sure who else was with me in the wooded cemetery. The quiver of my feet and the tingling in my arms told me I was weaker than a bird without wings. I hugged the marker, and spotted the face of a towering person—someone with saggy wrinkles and no teeth.

*Pam Kumpe*

### The Elmwood Cemetery Blues

"Take me over? I'm yours?" I spouted at the smacking savior. "And ... and how did you survive? You were shot by Buster." I rose to my feet, backing up with each word and with each breath.

The woman reached for me. "Quiet. They may send another one of Crump's cronies. He's not one to let a person owe him. I'm not sure what they think you'll bring. Too scrawny. Too old. No one wants to adopt a girl your age."

"What are you saying? Adopt me? I have a family. They're coming for me. Or they will, when they know where I am." Choking on the misty fog rolling into the cemetery from the steam of sadness following us, the afternoon brought a chill worse than fear. Worse than a train barreling down the tracks at me. "How did you live? You were supposed to be dead."

The woman rubbed her hands together and wiggled them in front of her face. "I'm not dead. Thankfully, Buster never could shoot straight. The doctor stitched my head up though. It seems I hit my head on a rock when I fell. Poor Buster, I hate he lost his steps and took the path of the river's death, but his world capsized around him."

"What? You knew Buster?"

"Sure. Everyone around these parts knew him. He's Archie's brother."

Backing up a few more feet as the woman shuffled herself toward me, I put a tombstone between us, using an angel to guard us from each other. "So, you know Archie, too?"

"I's know everyone. Well, everyone who is someone worth knowing."

"You talk like the rail has taken your mind. My Tin Can Mahlee used to sound like you. She made no sense most of the time."

"I make sense when I want, and I have reason to cry. Reason to fly. Reason to ride the tracks and find the tears from all of my whys."

I shook my hand with a fist. "Stop it. You're acting crazy. You speak in riddles. You just want to catch me, to take my satchel."

"I not need your satchel. But I do need to know why you bring trouble to Memphis. We have enough without the likes of you."

"I came for someone. I came for …" A flitter to my left caused me to stumble. "Did you see that? We're not alone. That man might have gotten up. He could be coming for us."

"He's not going anywhere. He's out cold."
*Swoosh. Swoosh.*

A blur swooshed by at the top of the hill, and I twirled, darting behind a patch of tombstones, six in a row. "You can leave now. I don't need you. Did you see that? There's someone up there."

Afraid of the woman who appeared less wrinkled the closer she got to me, I blinked to clear my sight. Her face sagged less too, her hair a brownish red. Her teeth mostly rotted out, not entirely gone.

In the shadows of the trees a few days ago, she reminded me of an ugly grandma. But today, a shower, a brush, maybe clean clothes instead of nasty ones; she would look as young as Ms. Susan. My heart cracked into pebbles of a longing, one for Ms. Susan's touch, for Mr. Boyd's punishment for my bad attitude, and for Lizzy Beth's words. "You're my big sister. I love you."

The crazy woman from the rail yelled at me. "Stand still. Stop moving away from me, and tell me why Crump would trade my Archie for you?" She coughed and wiped her mouth with the back of her hand.

"Trade your Archie? He's my Archie."

The woman shook her head. "Not true. He gives handkerchiefs to many, but he has plenty. He's mine. Not yours."

"What's with you? Not everyone is your possession."

"He's my friend. Mine since we were little. My friend. Not yours."

"Well, he's my friend too, whether you like it or not."

"I've known him all my life, mostly. He doesn't need another friend." While she lost herself in a memory, I took the chance to charge across the winding cemetery road, hurrying up the hill, hiding behind a large tombstone.

I halted face-to-face with the *blur-swoosh*, and gazed into the eyes of a small boy who rocked side-to-side next to a tombstone. A tombstone holding praying hands, little boys' figure.

I put my hand out, but my fingers went right through him. "Oh my!" I shook as if the earthquake of my heart would crumble with the next wave of fear. "What's going on?"

The boy wearing knicker boxer pants and a sweater, smiled as if he was glad someone could see him. He faded faster than my next reach for him, and my hand went to my throbbing head. "The knot. I still have a whopper on my head. I'm seeing things."

A squeeze on my shoulder from behind me caused me to fall forward with a leap. "Stop that! You keep scaring me."

90

The woman hollered, "I saved you back there on the tracks. Don't forget how I could have rescued you." She wiped her nose on her sleeve. "So, who were you looking at? Were you swatting at flies??"

"A little boy. I saw this child. He grinned at me."

"It's probably one of Georgia Tann's babies, one of those she killed." The shriek in her voice brought her to her knees, and we sat together on the grass where she rocked like Mahlee when she went to her dark place.

Trying to decide if I should run off for help from the police or someone who isn't trapped by a lost life on the rail, I rocked a little myself.

She touched my hand. "This is Joseph Norman McDonald's grave. He was three when he died. He's not one of Georgia's though. But right there over by the elm tree," she pointed to a marker with a curvy top, "that's the tombstone for the children who never lived to leave the orphanage. It's also for the lost babies no one can find."

Her language took on a clarity, her words concise, her slurring not causing me to miss what she said, and I could tell her heart joined mine in pieces on the ground. I shook my head. "Who is this Georgia Tann? I've heard her name before."

Not wanting to reveal too much about my reason for coming to Memphis, I didn't know if I should trust the woman with things about me and my brother. I wasn't sure she would let me leave to continue my search. And now I'm so confused about why Archie is in trouble, too. If she's really Archie's friend, she might become mine, too.

A low mournful sound of music drifted into the cemetery as the woman moved to the marker, where she petted and traced her fingers over the curves. Her sways came with the notes dancing through the air.

I joined her, stepping in front of the tombstone where a carved image of a small child prayed in the middle of the marker. We glanced in the direction of the music as the next low sound dug low with a sorrowful blend of gospel and blues.

Deep within the guitars, a tune, heavy with blended hums sent her to the ground like a broken china doll, sobbing. "Baby Charley, where are you? I wish I had a clue. Stolen from me. You'd be thirteen. Shoes for you each year. I'll never forget. You were stolen from me. I'll never be free from the pain of losing you. It's your birthday next week. I've come home to see you."

I backed up, leaning on the tree, and got lost in her words, those that could be mine. Words that sounded much like Tin Can Mahlee's ramblings, whenever she spoke of her giving up Lizzy Beth in 1943, in Memphis, in this town.

Lost in the low, mournful music, I trotted toward the singing and came upon four Negroes sitting on the ground by a freshly dug grave. The one man's rich tenor voice sang slightly behind the beat, and another man used a knife to slide up and down the strings of his guitar. All of their voices had a drawl, and they sang, "There's nothing like the Handy Band that played the Memphis Blues so grand. Oh, play them Blues."

I stood there caught in the hypnotic music as if a sorrowful song might transport me to feeling invincible. But then the woman joined me, whispering, "These boys lost one of their own. He was in their band on Beale Street. They spend their days singing WC Handy's songs, and you can hear the Blues at their stage on the corner down from A. Schwab's General Store."

She sounded like a commercial for this group, and yet I cringed, realizing my lost steps were causing lost time. I had no one to look up to, and no one to help me. I've gotten caught in something and it lives by the tracks, in the alley, and in the secret of tombstones of little children. And in that person Georgia Tann. "What should I do? I need Ms. Susan and Mr. Boyd."

I looked up and into her face, the one streaked with salty tears. "Can you help me? Or are you going to kill me? What will we do about Archie? We have to help him, too!" My questions crawled from me as if I wrote my own Blues song.

The men turned their heads in one fast swoop, singing, "Folks, I've just been down, down to Memphis town, that's where the people smile, smile on you all the time."

The woman gazed into my eyes. "I suppose I should tell you my name. If we's going to be friends on this bumpy ride, I need to tell you who I is."

Sighing, I agreed, not sure why, except my options for getting help were not great. I was in a cemetery after all. "Fine. I'll go first. My name's Shoelace. My daddy gave me my hobo name when we rode over the Mississippi River almost two years ago. But he fell from the coal car, and died."

"Well, sweetie. My name's Kissabelle."

"Kissabelle?"

"Yes, that's me. And I know where we can go. We're going to need more than me and you to figure this out. Crump's boys are bigger than Memphis, and his power to control things and take things and kill things, mean we could come up missing. So, let's go find ourselves before we lose ourselves in this place."

We spun around together, running back toward the tracks. I shouted, "Are you sure we should go back to town?"

"Yes, they'll come looking for their man and for us. But we'll go up the wrong alley, up the right street, and double back to the right alley, to find our wrong way home."

I galloped with Kissabelle as if I knew I should, but scared of where she'd take me. "Are you sure this is the right way?"

"I'm sure. We're almost there. Keep up. Watch for Crump's car. Or any other dark, creeping car with its windows up. He's bound to show, and we must get off this street before he returns."

We rushed into the next alley, and zigzagged back, rushed down another short alley, and cut between two buildings. We then hurried with now-loud pants from our chests to the next alley, with me tagging behind Kissabelle.

A red flag waved above our heads, which brought me to an abrupt halt. I wrinkled my brow. "No way! What in the world?" The red sheet dangled from the second story window of Jolene's apartment like a flag. "I can't go this way. I'll get in bigger trouble. I can't go with you." I stopped at the end of the alley, the brick wall to my right, the brick of the next building to my left.

Kissabelle pulled my arm. "We're here. Come on."

She yanked me to the street where the sign above my head told me the truth of my worrying. I screamed, "No, this can't be. I'm back at Jolene's Crystal Palace?"

"Yes, we're here. It's my sister's restaurant. Her connections in Memphis will save Archie. And get you to a safe place."

"No, she's going to kill me. She locked me inside of her bedroom."

"So, you know my sister?"

"Yes, she's horrible. Well, her eggs are good. And her biscuits. But she lied to me. She said she didn't have any children and there are kids shoes in her closet."

"Oh, the shoes. I buy those. Every year I ride in to Memphis and have a birthday party for Charley, my son." She sniffled. "I leave the shoes at his gravesite, and Sister keeps them here for me after I go down the rail."

"You? Those shoes belong to your boy?"

"Yes, he was taken by the nurse at the hospital. I lost him to Ms. Tann, and I have no idea where he lives."

"Then why have a party at a gravesite? He's not buried there."

"I'll never see him again, so he's dead to me because of her." Shaking her head, she barked, "Enough about that. Let's get inside."

I pulled back from her grasp. "Maybe you should go inside without me."

## Lies, Lies, Lies

"Stop yanking on my ear. I'm not your daughter." My screams bounced to the bottles of whiskey and swirled around the vodka. The only reason the hollering got trapped was because of the bar and stools where my words wrapped in circles falling to the floor.

Ms. Jolene let go of my ear. "Get up the stairs. I'm right behind you. We need to talk. Archie left me with you, and I'm trying to do him a favor. Then you destroy my bedroom, escape like a wild animal and tear up my curtains." She stomped behind me as I crawled up the stairs.

At the bend in the steps, I swirled around to defend myself. "But you caused me to run. You locked me inside your bedroom."

Jolene reached behind her, and her fingers grabbed Kissabelle's ear. "Tell her the truth. Tell her what happened."

Kissabelle hopped next to me. The two of us faced Jolene and silence fell like empty vapor. "I don't know what you mean."

"Tell her. Tell her that you were in the house, hiding behind the sofa. That you jumped up and locked her in the room when you heard the arguing. That you were scared to let her see you since you had a run-in on the tracks. Tell her!" Jolene shook her fist, her cotton dress waving with wiggles of anger from all the shaking.

Kissabelle shook her head, moving up five steps, then more, turning back to stare at us like a tall tree. "Jolene, I told you she's mine. I found her. I need her."

I clapped my hands as if to wake everyone up from the dream. "Hey, I do not belong to either one of you. I belong to myself. I came here, got caught in all the crazy shenanigans with Buster. I'm fine now. I just need to find my brother!"

A hush fell from the sky like heaven opened and let the angels fly out, as if they surrounded the building. A small voice with a high pitch sang out, "Swing low, sweet chariot. Coming for to carry me home."

The three of us gazed upward like we could see through the third-floor ceiling at the top of the stairs. Nudging Jolene, I asked, "So does the cook have any boys, or not?"

"Yes, two. One young. One who thinks he's grown. The cook came from New Orleans with the oysters some years ago. He's raising them boys alone." Her hand went to her mouth, covering up the slippery answer. "I mean, well … he believes God is guiding his parenting."

Kissabelle bumped her way back to the bottom of that set of stairs. "What she means is, she lied to you about the shoes in her closet. She didn't want you to know I leave them at Charley's grave. She puts them up. If you look in her closet, way in the back, there's shoes for each year. Baby shoes. Loafers. Even PF Flyers."

I marched past her, noticing the singing had ended, and climbed to the top of the second-floor stairs, holding the rail as if I might slap someone if my hand let go. Spinning around, I argued, "So, you both lie. That's it. You have a life filled with pretend. I'm real. I don't lie. I have nothing but the truth to tell."

Jolene grabbed my arm. "Then why would a little girl with a home, with new adoptive parents, with a little sister and with folks who care about her—tell me why she was riding in a boxcar?"

Stuttering, I fished for words. "I am looking for someone. I have to find him." I slapped my hands to my hips. "And I can do that without the likes of you two. And how in the heck would you know I had a family or a sister?"

Jolene barked, "I've told you, Archie left you in my care. You were easy to watch for three days while you slept. But goodness, no wonder he dumped you on me. You're a handful."

"Dumped?" My bravery escaped with the next breath. "He dumped me?"

Kissabelle tapped my shoulder. "He was caught between a spot in Arkansas and the spot he left behind in Memphis. Seems he owed Boss Crump some money. Now they want to sell you to the next highest bidder."

"What? Highest bidder? I'm not for sale!"

"Well, in their world you are for sale. Little girls go for a pretty penny. You can make a good hand for someone at a ranch."

Jolene butted in, "Stop it. She doesn't need to know all about that right now. We just need to keep her safe. I've sold Archie's car to pay his debt with Crump. I just came back from doing that, when you two disrupted my afternoon nap. Now I'll need to get ready to open the restaurant for tonight. Friday nights bring the best tippers."

I began my descent on the stairs. "I'm leaving. I can take care of myself. I don't need either one of you." I sucked in my stomach, the growls of hunger trying to burst from my insides. "And that truck! Well, it's not Archie's to sell. That truck belongs to Marion Kane in Jefferson, Texas."

With the final yell, Jolene and Kissabelle each moved at me like tarantulas, and they each grabbed me at the elbow, lifting my feet from the ground. Jolene giggled, "Well, Archie will be here soon. He's going to be tired and hungry. He's going to be flat out mad, too. Especially when I tell him about the trouble you caused."

I mouthed, "It's not like he didn't see me at the tracks."

Kissabelle nodded. "And it's a good thing I followed you. You sounded like a rat trying to chew through the apartment wall. I knew you were leaving, so I hurried down the stairs and followed you. It's a good thing, too. Crump's man would have taken you up the river for good."

Mouthing, my feet in the air, I swallowed hard. "Up the river? Don't you mean down the river?"

Jolene popped my backside. "You're not too big to take a switch to, and I have good mind to do so."

The sound of a small child singing rose again, as they put me down by the apartment door. My ears heard the words, "I looked over Jordan, and what did I see? Coming for to carry me home. I saw a band of angels coming after me. Coming for to carry me home."

"Who is singing? Who lives up there? I mean, who really lives up there?"

Unlocking her door with a key, Jolene shrugged. "I have two apartments on the third floor. One is for Lottie and her boy. The other is for our cook." She made eye contact with me. "Really. That's who lives there."

Kissabelle grinned, bumping into me as we both tried to go through the door. "I could take her boy. This girl's too much to deal with, brings lots of questions and is so mouthy."

Offering her another piece of my mouth, I confirmed her remarks. "I can leave any time. I don't need you."

Jolene popped me again, a little firmer. "Sit down on the sofa. I'll let Archie deal with you when he gets here."

Plopping down, I smarted off, "And I'll let him deal with the both of you."

Jolene moved closer to me, a firm and confident and determined walk. She sucked in a deep breath. Your little sister and your little brother don't deserve you. They need someone to look up to, and that wouldn't be you."

She stormed to the table where our breakfast dishes sat, and stacked the china faster than a bee flying from its nest. "A little girl with no manners. That's something a good switch could fix."

Kissabelle tiptoed up to me, sitting on the other end of the sofa. "You've done it. You've gone and made her mad. She's bound to hurt the both of us now."

## Things That Go Bump in the Night

Sitting on the sofa, leaning on my elbow, I cringed at how the trip to Memphis had trapped me inside this building. Pursing my lips, I sighed, talking to no one, but mouthed, "I'm a girl too old to be a child. And I'm too young to be a woman. I'm too sad to cry. And too weak to run away again. I'm too confused to know what to do next—and worried I'll not get the chance to find Willie."

Waiting for Archie to return came with Jolene changing into a night dress, a sparkly red long gown with the same slit, like the one in the painting in her bedroom. She bounced in high heels down the stairs to open her restaurant for the night, telling me how Friday nights bring the best customers.

The bedroom's back in order, after Kissabelle and me made the bed, swept up the broken glass, and hung the curtains on the rods. Now it's me and Kissabelle in the apartment together, and she's singing like Tin Can Mahlee did around Lizzy Beth's birthday on Halloween. Only thing, Mahlee cried and mourned but Kissabelle's celebrating her son's birthday. They have the same heartache, but one weeps, while the other parties and bakes a cake.

Kissabelle rattled the room with her high-pitched voice. "My sister's serving oysters tonight, and she's taking care of her own oysters, too. She'll be in late."

"What does that mean? Her own oysters?"

"She entertains the men who don't want to go home, and she makes some extra cash for rent that way. She's just lonely, but ya can't fill up empty with emptier."

Kissabelle spun back to the counter swinging the spatula around the bowl.

Whispering to myself, "Empty with emptier? My pa tried emptier, on too many nights. He came home hung over and worn out, and hungry. Then we were usually running from his late-night secrets. Some daddy he was, some daddy ..." I shrugged, the ugly latching itself to my memory of my daddy. "He loved me. He did. I know he did."

Turning to watch Kissabelle, who was baking a cake for the party, a celebration for a dead boy, I couldn't remember one birthday my daddy celebrated with me.

Wiping a tear, I glanced at the thirteen pairs of shoes on the floor, those along the space heater near the wall. Kissabelle had brought them from the closet like a monument to her son. She has baby shoes, to big shoes. And every size in-between.

I stepped to look at them, shaking my head. "Kissabelle, what happened to your Charley?"

"My Charley?" She stopped stirring, and put the spatula down, splattering chocolate cake batter around the bowl.

She hovered near the shoes. "My Charley was taken from me. Not being married and pregnant and alone, I was a target. The nurse said he was sickly, but I didn't believe her. I had to see my boy. But they wouldn't let me, and kept me away."

She marched back to the bowl, swooping the spatula in a whirlwind of circles in the batter. I moved next to her. "So, he died at the hospital?"

Sighing and sucking the joy from the room, she blurted, "No! I snuck down the hallway in the hospital to see him in the nursery. Something felt wrong. I knew he wasn't dead. He was born perfect. His brown hair. Pudgy nose. Matching ears."

I smiled. "So, you saw him?"

"No! Well, yes!"

"What are you saying? You saw your dead boy?"

"No, another person had him. A lady with glasses, and she had a wide part in her hair on the right side of her head. Wavy, short hair. Light colored. A smirk on her face told me she held my boy."

"No way. She was stealing him?"

"Yes! Her name's Georgia Tann. I told you about her. She's a baby stealer, and she sells our children to not only rich folks, but to people who wants farm hands. She's the baby thief of Memphis!"

"Why didn't you chase her down?" My quizzing was spoiling the birthday party.

"Chase her? They held me back. They let me scream so loud, I thought the walls would crumble. But no one came to save Charley from being snatched away. No one!"

I put my hand on her arm. "I'm sorry. My Tin Can Mahlee had Lizzy Beth here in Memphis, too. That's my half sister. Mahlee was talked into giving up her baby, too."

"I wasn't asked or talked into anything. Charley was taken from me."

Gulping, I added, "I wonder if that Georgia Tann took my Lizzy Beth, too. She was a twin. And now he's missing. I don't know what to think."

"I bet it was Georgia Tann. She's everywhere. She pays off people, so we can't find our children. All the records get lost. And the judge here is dirty, too. Judge Camille Kelley handles Georgia Tann's fake adoptions. She's as evil as they come."

"I'm sorry. I only came here to get my brother. And this has collapsed in on me like sadness from a grave. My adoptive parents hired an attorney to find Willie, but I figured my friends White Beard and Peg Leg would help me."

"White Beard? Peg Leg?" Kissabelle twisted to look down at me. "I know them. They's long gone. Last I saw of them, they were up around Nashville."

I inched back to the sofa, unsure what to make of having nobody I could trust. But right now, having somebody I didn't trust was better than being out there alone. "When's Archie coming? Jolene said she paid his debt, I figured he'd be here by now."

"Crump's men probably gave him one last walloping before tossing him in a ditch somewhere. When he comes to himself, he'll come. You'll see."

*Clump-ca-clump. Clump-ca-clump.*

We jumped together, glancing at the apartment door. I choked on spit. "Is that Archie? Do you think?" I ran to the door, twisting the knob, and peeked outside. "Hello. Archie?" I called to the silence, thick on the stairs.

Hollering to me from the kitchen, a mere spot off to the side of the room, Kissabelle asked, "Well, is it him? Let Archie come inside."

I closed the door. "It's nothing. It's not him."

Kissabelle glanced to the ceiling. "Hush, did you hear that?"

I looked up, peering at the yellow plaster. "What are we listening for?"

"I heard some bumping upstairs. Might be the noise we heard a second ago." She stirred the batter, mumbling, "Might just be nothing."

"So, who lives up there?" I knew I'd asked the question more than once already, but I wanted to see if the same answer rolled from Kissabelle's lips this time.

"What's with you, girl? We have a cook upstairs. And Lottie. Lottie lives there."

"And her boy?"

"Yes, a boy. Jolene said it's a cousin of ours. I haven't met him yet."

*Clump-ca-clump. Thud!*

Kissabelle poured the batter into two round pans. "What is going on up there? We might need to check on Lottie."

"So, who is Lottie?"

"Lottie is …" Kissabelle opened the oven and pushed the two pans inside. "Lottie is our pa's daughter."

I swiped some cake batter with my finger from the edge of the empty bowl. "What? She's your other sister?"

"She's my half sister. See, our pa had this restaurant, and our grandpa did, too. Our pa strayed with our house maid and she had a little girl when Jolene was five, and I was three. She's our baby sister."

"You have a little sister, too. Just like me."

"But it's not that easy. When pa died, he left everything to Jolene and me. But in his will, he wanted Lottie to be taken care of too."

"And … she lives upstairs? And you don't know who the boy might be?" My quizzing and confusion grew into a puzzle of puzzles, with breaking pieces and lost answers. "I don't understand."

"Our ma loved Lottie like she was hers, but her heart was never strong after the rumors and ugly words cut our families apart. Lottie moved with her ma to the slave quarters. Not that they were slave quarters, but it was the old house behind our main home. She grew up our sister, but not our sister."

"So, who is the boy?" My curiosity about the boy was greater than the half sister part, and it felt like Kissabelle was not telling me all she knew. Maybe the boy was her son, and she's not normal enough to raise him. Maybe she's crazy like Tin Can Mahlee, and she's trapped with voices inside her head and maybe they're mixed up like cake batter. A cake-batter ma doesn't need to raise her boy.

"Happy birthday to you. Happy birthday to you." She peeked into the oven, singing a song to a boy who might live right above us, in the apartment on the third floor.

*Clump-ca-clump! Thud! Thud!*

Kissabelle stopped, shut the oven, and tossed the bowl into the sink, marching to the door. "We need to check on Lottie. Too much noise going on. You stay here. I'll go."

Not listening or obeying, I followed her out the door, and up the stairs. At the top of the next flight, she paused, glancing at the door to her right, then to the left.

"Don't you know which room is hers?" I squinted, tugging on her sleeve. "It's your sister. You should know which apartment is hers."

"I know which one is hers. I'm not sure she wants to see me. We're not too fond of each other. She thinks I'm ..."

I finished the sentence. "... crazy."

Spinning around, Kissabelle pursed her lips. "Girl, you have no idea what you're saying. I'm not crazy. Losing my son sent me to a deep well where the waters is so far down, you'll never quench your thirst. It's awful."

"I'm sorry. I think out loud too much." I pointed to the brown door to the left. "Does she stay there?"

"Yes, that's her room."

I knocked once, but I didn't get to knock twice. The door swung open with a squeak of death, and a woman lay on the floor. Kissabelle pushed me aside. "Lottie? Oh, my goodness what happened?"

I froze, unable to move, and I couldn't take my eyes off the Negro woman crumpled in half, whose eyes were stuck wide open.

My throat stuck together and I couldn't breathe, and my heart caved in with heaving. My skin crawled, and I shouted, "I'll get Jolene. I'll get her now."

Stomping down the stairs, I cried, "Jolene. Jolene," only to crash right into Archie. "Get Jolene. There's a dead lady upstairs."

Archie shook me. "What? What are you saying? Jolene's not here. I was asking for her myself. Seems she left a while ago. Seems she left with our Willie!"

## When Truth Hurts Worse

A gurgle of lies rolled over the tracks of the Mississippi River into Memphis way before I came to town. These people bubble up with lies and part truths. They mix like cake batter in a bowl until I'm not so sure they know when to tell the truth or lie.

Now the apartment smells like smoke too, the birthday cake ruined from the chaos of a dead woman, from the return of Archie, and especially from the fact that no one has seen Jolene for hours.

The cops questioned me along with all the people inside the oyster bar, from ladies in gowns to men in suits, to Archie and Kissabelle. But why me? I didn't even know this woman, and I had never been to the third floor until tonight.

Rocking with my knees pulled up to my chest, I hid inside Jolene's bedroom closet, with the door cracked. The windows were opened to the night's party taking place on the street and the sound of cheering and laughter bounced on the walls around me. Guitar strings squealed. Drums pounded. Gospel music mixed with the soulful swoons while the voices hung like harmonica notes held too long. The cadence of letting go of the day danced in the air. But I couldn't get over the past few days!

Inside the apartment silence fell like cracked plaster from old walls, as if wounds were leaving marks on lives that crisscrossed with my life. No birthday party would take place for Charley. And no one could console Kissabelle. I'm not sure if she was more upset about the cake or about her sister dying from a blow to her head.

I had yelled and screamed at all of them. First at Kissabelle for sobbing and blocking the doorway. Then at Archie for blurting out the fact that my brother … my brother may have stayed with Lottie. But why? Why would she have my brother? And how did he come to live there?

I touched the wall near the shelves, wishing for the closet of my new bedroom, the one I shared with Lizzy Beth in Jefferson. The one with crayon-colored dream catchers. The one with dolls and toys and laughter and hugs. "Lizzy Beth, I'm sorry I left you. I need to come home. I need to be somewhere safe. And this isn't safe. And these people aren't my friends!"

Sighing, my chest rose and collapsed with leftover sobs from not understanding, from not knowing what to do, from being trapped, and feeling lost. "Daddy, why am I without you? Come for me. Daddy, please come."

My tears dripped like a faucet of tainted water. "That's it! I'm leaving. I'm going far from here." I stormed from the closet, jumping and jolting, rising and standing with my hands on my hips. "It's over, Daddy! You never really came for me. You only returned for me whenever you finished those card games, and only after chasing the bottle. You stayed out with women and other people. But not me! You hunted for empty, when you had plenty. You had me!"

I choked on the next words. "Why did you kidnap me from my grandma? I was only five. Who does that? Who makes a little girl live in boxcars? Or in missions? Or under bridges?"

My yelling and stomping and shouting brought Archie to the bedroom, and his face searched me up and down, with a glare of sadness. He reached for me. "Come sit with me. Here's a handkerchief."

"What? A handkerchief? You think that's the answer for this? Don't you see? Don't you even care that I'm here to find my brother—and you knew? You knew Willie was here all the time!"

"Sit. Sit and let me talk to you."

"Talk to me? How will I know if you're telling me the truth?" I plopped on the bed, folding my arms. "I snuck off to find Willie. And, I was that close! What is wrong with you? What is wrong with all of these people?"

"Let me explain. This is more complicated than you see or know." Archie slipped to the edge of the bed, clutching his own handkerchief, the one I refused to accept.

Biting my top lip, I shook my head. "Where are they? Why would Jolene leave with Willie? And how did she get my brother?" What felt like boiling water pouring over my head scorched me with wounds that bled with sorrow, and the anger gushed out from my mouth. "And who would kill this Lottie?"

"Lottie?" He choked, wiping tears from his face. "One question at a time. With my brother dying, and then Boss Crump found out from some of the officers that I was back in town …"

"What? So the cops told him where you were?"

"There's plenty of folks inside the Crump Camp of crime. And I'm on the list of threats to their ongoing deceit."

"Crump? Who is that man?"

"He's power. He's politics. He's money. And he's deadly."

"What? You've been riding the rails with me!"

"Well, not before I met you … in Millerton, Oklahoma. I lived right here in Memphis."

"What? Who are you? I've known you for almost two years. You were on the train when my grandma died, when I rode to Jefferson, Texas, and then you showed up in Washington, Arkansas. Just when were you going to tell me I had a brother?!"

"It's complicated. I had to wait until we knew Willie was out of Memphis and safe. But then Buster got involved and sent me back here. Too quick. And too soon. In Memphis, I'm a man who owed a debt I couldn't pay, and they wanted to capture you and sell you to shut me up."

"Sell me? What for? I'm not for sale!" I unfolded my arms, slapping them crossways like directing traffic. "I want my brother! He needs me! I don't like the trouble you bring."

Archie wiped his head like rubbing away his painful thoughts. "Crump's men found me down by the river. My brother was gone and I wanted to find his body. Well, they worked me over pretty good, even showed me to you in hopes of making an exchange. But you got away, thankfully."

"I only got away because Kissabelle knocked out that man."

"But we both have Jolene to thank. She brought them the money." He sighed. "I hate she sold Marion Kane's truck though. I'll need to pay that debt, too."

I spouted off, "Which you can't pay!"

"I'll work it off. I'll make good."

"Or maybe you can sell a kid."

"Stop it. I don't sell children."

"But you hide one. You hid Willie from me."

"No, I didn't hide anyone. I had no idea Jolene took the boy. Last I'd heard when I came looking for Lizzy Beth at Wheelock Academy." Archie coughed. "Last I heard, he was staying at the orphanage where my precious Ms. Lottie worked. He took a liking to her, and she took a liking to him."

"Precious Ms. Lottie?"

"Yes, she was precious to me. Little Willie loved her."

"But now he's gone. Probably for good."

Archie sniffled, "Maybe not. We have God on our side. A miracle might fold up like a fresh clean handkerchief."

"Really? Tell that to Lottie."

\*\*

Archie paced the floor in his disheveled suit, and he used six handkerchiefs to catch his tears. He sobbed, dropping the white cloths to the wood floor, muttering to himself, and he kept stomping in his loafers with a force like he was the wind behind a fierce storm.

His torn sleeve flopped, and the bruises on his face held the dry blood behind his ear and on his neck from his attackers, reminding me of the hurt Archie felt, too. But his wounded heart bled from the invisible knife I'd forced at him with my words. I hated that I'd talked ugly about God. Archie loves God. I love God, too. It's just hard to be loving when all the ugly rides in like a thief, stealing everything from you.

The lightning strike of regret pierced my entire being, and watching Archie fume—and not shout at me left me with only one thing to do. I had to tell him how sorry I was for his brother's death and for losing Lottie. I'm not the only one hurting tonight. I whispered to the ceiling, "God, I know You can see through stuff. So, I know You know what's going on in Memphis. Please, let me say something so Archie won't hate me. Amen."

I paced with Archie and reached for his hand, wrapping my fingers inside his sweaty palm. "Archie, you've been nothing but good to me. I'm sorry I was so mean. My grandma would wash my mouth out for saying such ugly things to a grownup."

Archie sighed, bumped me a little with his side, and squeezed my hand. "This here life we get, well, it comes with rushing waters of life and death. I choose to cherish life. I cherish having Lottie in my world even for a season. She's a gem of hope when life dealt her nothing but blows. She's a hero to me."

"A hero?" I coughed.

"Yes, she kept your little brother safe for more than a year. Without her, Willie might have died at the hands of Georgia Tann."

"Gulping, I apologized. "I'm sorry. I don't mean to be so horrible to you. It just slips out. My gut leaks from a deep well of ugly. One my daddy put me in when I was five. I didn't know it was going to drown me. And others who got too close."

"Your daddy got much wrong, but giving birth to you was the syrup of richness to this world. You're like Marion Kane's sorghum. A little sticky. Tasty. And you can stick to the roof of a mouth and latch onto a heart faster than a boxcar barreling down a mountain. You are special to Mr. Boyd and Ms. Susan. You just don't see it yet."

When Archie compared me to syrup, my tummy growled and my hope slipped from hiding. "Thank you. That was almost nice of you to say."

Archie squeezed my hand again, and sat down on the end of the bed. "See those china dolls on Ms. Jolene's dresser. They are each priceless. Each is designed with a unique imprint from the artist who molded them. You are like a china doll. God mastered you for this time. For this season."

My eyes glued to the spot where I'd knocked off one of Ms. Jolene's dolls. "But when I break for good, will I end up in the trash?"

"Trash? You're fearfully and wonderfully created. You are a masterpiece. You're just a little unfinished right now."

I sat close to Archie, wondering what to do, where to go, and if I should leave for Jefferson tonight.

He interrupted my daydreaming. "You know, Lottie only snatched up Willie once Georgia Tann pulled the twins apart. She sent Lizzy Beth with a group of girls to the Choctaw orphanage. Seems your little sister looked too Indian for Ms. Tann."

"What? So, Lizzy Beth was taken by Georgia Tann?"

"Yes, Tin Can Mahlee lost her to the baby snatcher. But, Mahlee didn't know she had twins. She thought she'd given birth to one baby, a girl. So, when I heard about them separating the two of them, I knew this might send Lizzy Beth to losing herself more. She wouldn't talk to anyone but him. As for Willie, with his ailment, he needed his twin sister."

I jumped to my feet. "Ailment? What's wrong with him?" I stomped, my ankle itching from the wound on my leg. "And why would you know all of this, unless you worked there, too?"

Stuttering, Archie sighed. "I did work for Ms. Tann. I was her chauffeur until last year. I couldn't stand working for such an awful woman. She paraded around Memphis like she saves babies, but I discovered she sells them to the highest bidder. I had to get out."

"Get out? By following Lizzy Beth?"

"Yes, to let … to let the love of my life, Ms. Lottie, know we could have both of them, and give them a proper family. I was going to marry her." His words cracked into splintered wrinkles of pain. He held his face, weeping like a girl, sobbing like a man, and shaking like I do when all is about to break apart.

I found my hand reaching for him, and I pulled his hands from his face, taking his handkerchief and blotting his eyes. "So, you and the Ms. Lottie were … in love?"

"Yes, we were. She was the kindest and prettiest thing this side of Beale Street."

"Beale Street?" I puckered my lips.

"Yes, that's where the Blues light up the night with songs. Like you're hearing out them windows."

I scooted to the opened window, my face damp from the moisture of the night, but the heat from the June day landed like a warm sock on my face. "I like the way it makes me want to sway." I called to the night. "Willie, where are you?"

"He's out there alive. I'm sure of it. The music sings tonight, and Ms. Jolene can disappear like a ghost in plain sight."

Shaking my head and turning back to Archie, I brought my angry voice to our chat. "But … but why did Jolene take Willie? And, where are they? Do you think Georgia Tann killed Lottie?"

"Ms. Tann? She doesn't do her own dirty work. But I'd say someone is on to Jolene and Lottie."

"On to her? About what?"

"You're not going to like this part." Archie now stood next to me, the flickering light from the restaurant sign lighting up his streaked face with red and blue colors.

"Why? How much worse can it get?"

"Jolene has her own investigation going on. Lottie brings home records and takes notes about the baby stealing and how they change the records. She is wanting to help Gordon Browning expose this horrible crime. He's running for governor and she's fed him some details."

"What? She's like a spy?"

"A spy for a good cause. She wants to save the children. Especially since losing her own nephew, little Charley."

The doubt of what Archie told me rang like truth inside my head, the information too much. Too confusing. Too scary.

A nervous twitch in my neck made me scratch. "I can't stay. I must go. This is more than I came to see. I want to go back to Jefferson."

"In time, my little one. You need to stay in hiding. We can't afford to lose you, too."

"No! I'm leaving. I need to see Ms. Susan and Mr. Boyd. I need a hug from Lizzy Beth. I saw how much they want Willie, especially when they saw his photograph. It's the way they look at me … it's the way they look at me when they tuck me into bed. When they kiss my head. When they say prayers over me."

Archie nodded. "They do love you. And they love Lizzy Beth. But we've got to find Jolene and find Willie before it's too late."

I shrugged my shoulders. "I can't do this. I must leave. You've seen Kissabelle. She's put all those shoes in a circle around her on the floor in the parlor. She's sitting in the middle, crying and rocking. And cradling different little boy shoes."

"She's mourning. She's endured so much. She and Lottie never talked much. A life of regret can consume you."

"If I stay, I'll turn into her. I have to go. I'm catching the next train out of here." Fear circled me and swallowed me whole. "I can't stay here. I'm leaving!"

Charging past Archie, grabbing my satchel on the way by the door, I clutched the strap.

*Ring-a-ling. Ring-a-ling.*

I slung the bag over my shoulder, pausing long enough to see Archie pick up the receiver. I shouted, "I have to leave!"

Darting from the apartment, my chest pounding, I leapt down the stairs. I charged into the leftover, smoke-filled restaurant where the haze of a party that never happened hung like death. The cook swatted flies by the window as he held a small glass in his hand by the bar.

Pushing the restaurant door open, flying to the sidewalk, and landing in the road, I tumbled to the brick cobblestone. I felt hope rising in me and leading me from this place. But a tinge of worry for Willie clouded my view, and it's as if I carried my own cloud above my head.

Inside a bar across the street, a Negro woman sang, "I hate to see that evening sun go down. I hate to see that evening sun go down."

I barreled between rows and rows of Negroes, men who smiled and women who wooed. Not one person noticed my blonde pigtails, overalls, or my red PF Flyers. In the shadow of a night, we're all one with God. We match because He made us.

Charging between elbows and wobbly people who were drinking their supper while walking down the sidewalk, I wondered if my daddy used to come to these bars. To this street where guitars strummed and bands played. Where laughter drifted from alleys. Where women giggled and clung to sloppy men who could barely stand up.

The swirl of activity sent me running and screaming, not at Archie, but at my daddy again. "Daddy, I hate to see the evening sun go down, too. I know now you didn't love me like a daddy should, you loved me like a lost daddy, who didn't know how to raise a girl. I wanted you to love me. And now it's too late. I'm leaving you behind. I'm leaving Memphis for good!"

*Pam Kumpe*

## A Fountain of Courage

Running from corner to corner, I bumped into the profane and the proper. "Ouch!" I collided into the back of a horse carriage. "What in the world?" Counting five horses and five carriages, all standing in a row, I twisted my head sideways in front of the tallest building I'd come across so far. Gazing into the starlit sky, I added up the floors as they rose toward the heavens. "Thirteen, maybe. Whoa!"

A man marched up to me with a tall woman attached to his arm. Her poufy hair took up more room than four faces. The man brushed me aside. "Kid, get out of our way. Tommy Dorsey and Glenn Miller are up in the Skyway Ballroom. And we're late. Tick-tock. Move along." The man and woman rushed inside after giving me a gentle, but firm shove on my shoulder.

Mouthing at him, I added my mocking, "Tick-tock. I am a rock. I follow no clock." Spinning around, I peered inside the double glass doors. "Wow! Lights. Chandeliers. Fancy stuff." I shrugged my shoulders. "A world inside of a world. Look at those ladies. All dressed up. And the men. Shiny shoes. Furs. Everyone has been to the beauty shop. And the men. Their hair is slick like an oil spot."

I pushed my nose on the glass, my hand cracking the door open, letting the musical notes escape from inside the lobby even though the other set of doors were still closed. Stepping inside, I swung the other glass door wide, my brain soaking up sights with my eyes to replay later in a dream. My ears hearing piano keys notes from a song I'd never heard.

118

"Look at those dangling chandeliers hanging from the second-floor ceiling. There's a balcony around the edge, and there's the music lady." She beat the white and black keys with dinging and banging of her fingers, her body swaying on the bench. Her gray hair and wrinkles moved with their own rhythm, too.

I slipped my feet across the floor, coming to a glass-windowed store. "*Lanskys Brothers*. Fine clothes. Too fine for me." I ran my fingers over my overalls, wondering if my street clothes clashed with the polished and ironed suits and dresses surrounding me. But no one noticed me, or cared. Each couple. Each person. Each man or woman lost in their nighttime fun, of playing in this hotel that was fancier than fancy.

The flashing neon sign had announced its presence blocks away. A sign the size of grandma's manor. Huge! Big! The Peabody Hotel held people captive with its bar, arm chairs, small round tables, sofas and hypnotic jazz with the Blues sounds.

Running to the trickling waterfall fountain that held a centerpiece of pink and yellow flowers on top, the statue beneath the base pushed the blooms taller than four of me. I ran my hand along the edge by the pool of water. "Look at this marble circling the fountain."

Across from me two boys danced like they never went barefoot, and like they never slept in a tree. Giggling and pointing at the fountain, the boy with ears that hung low clapped. "Tomorrow we'll see the duck march when they come from the rooftop and ride the elevator and walk on the red carpet to the fountain."

The smaller boy nodded. "The Duck Master will roll out the red carpet for them."

Squinting, I interrupted them. "Ducks? Why would there be ducks in this beautiful hotel?"

The ugly-eared boy shook his head. "It's tradition. Twice a day the ducks come in for the march. They stay in the fountain for a while and swim."

I turned my back to him, cackling, "Sure they do."

A flash of a toddler ran in front of me. "We saw them today. They have ducks. They even have their own house on the roof."

I patted the boy wearing church clothes on a Friday night. "Isn't it past your bedtime?"

"We get to stay up late. We're on vacation."

I weaved between a sofa with cream and red stitching, and circled a set of green arm chairs with a small table in front of them. Two ladies sat at the table. The first lady wore a pink dress and a giant pink flower in the center of her chest, right above her stomach, but below her neck. She shook like cherry pudding whenever she sipped her drink, all of her body wiggled with a jiggle.

The other woman looked tired, and she wore a brown fur and a sideways hat with a broach on it, and a pin with a peacock. She crossed her legs and her floor-length dress flowed with grace, even though she almost seemed out of place with her sour-faced features. Ugly glasses. Pointed nose. Heavier than regular, but not as big as the wiggly lady.

A potted-faced man sipped from a small glass, and the golden colored liquid reminded me of my daddy's whiskey. Seems there are other men who drink when the sun goes down. Only thing is, my daddy liked to drink in the sun, too. "I'm sure that's whiskey. My daddy drank straight from the bottle. He didn't dress up to drink away his problems. These people have more stuff to hide, I guess."

The lobby was bigger than a basketball court, and the chairs and sofas filled the room with families, as people poured into the first floor like ice tea. Not all drank from whiskey glasses. Some clanked ice in their glass and sipped from crystal goblets.

A little girl wearing a hot pink sundress reminded me of pink cotton candy. She tiptoed over to me. "Hi." She held an orange. "We're attending a wedding here tomorrow. Would you like a slice of my orange?"

For a second, I felt like I was back in Texarkana with Clara, the snotty girl who made me so mad that I spit orange on her dress. I had to bite my tongue to keep my words from causing an ugly reaction.

A tap on my shoulder made me spin on the marble with my shoe, making a squeaking noise. The girl held the orange slice under my nose. "Hey, little farm girl. Would you like a bite of my orange?"

Swiping her hand from my face, I scowled, "Leave me alone. I'm not a farm girl. I'm me. Just me."

"Sorry. No need to be rude. Manners matter. You may be poor, but you can be kind."

"What makes you think I'm poor?"

"Well, look at what you're wearing. You don't fit in here. Did you wander into the wrong hotel?" The curly haired girl flittered away from me, as if she was tired of talking to the lower class.

Sliding to the fountain, I sat down on the marble edge. "I don't fit in on Beale Street. I don't fit in at the Peabody. I don't fit in on boxcars anymore. Where do I fit in?"

I lost myself in the chatter, the music dancing off the glass of the chandeliers and realized being lost in downtown Memphis in this hotel felt lonelier than being in a cemetery by a tree. "Where is the river from here? I don't know where or how to find the Harahan Bridge so I could hop a train out of town.

The two plump ladies and the man burst into laughter as if they were making fun of me, but they weren't looking at me. They were singing a Blues song and cackling like a pack of hyenas. The flower lady folded her hands in her lap, clasping her own whiskey drink. "I'm so worn out. The courtroom has been so full this week. Placing all the children came with quite the pocketbook of pennies. But we found all of them good homes."

The lady who rocked next to her in a chair that didn't rock, smiled. "I sent three girls on the train to California. And we have four new babies from the hospital. Selling babies has made us rich. We're set for life." She turned to the flower lady. "Camille, you make it happen in the courtroom. You are vital to our work."

The man sitting between them listened, sipping another drink just handed to him by a waiter. He stretched his legs, and leaned back, closing his eyes. "Yes, I'm the attorney who can make your dreams come true. If you need help. Just call me. Abe is your man." He tapped his shoes on the carpet, his smile reaching from ear to ear as if he said something that made him important.

Watching the circus of people loading up in the elevators, I wandered to the shiny doors. Party dresses scooted by me. Suits on men made them appear clean and proper. And couples out on the town laughed and made goo-goo eyes at each other. I hung out by the elevators for minutes, upon minutes pushing the button whenever I could, just to see the duck imprint on the elevator floor. "Look, it's a mallard." I shouted this a hundred times, before a man wearing working clothes from the hotel, put his white-gloved hand on mine on the wall. "Enough, little one." He glanced around. "Where is your family?"

"Umm. Over there." I pointed and moved away from the man, but stayed close enough to enjoy watching a new bunch of shiny shoes fill up the elevator again. They disappeared when the door shut, and I felt like disappearing, too. Maybe I could ride up to the rooftop where heaven might be within my reach. Then I could talk with God, and see what He thinks I should do next.

The dinging on the piano brought me to the fountain again, and I twirled twenty times, dizzy from staring at the chandelier lights. I got lost in the music, stuck in a world where I'll never belong. Not that I wanted to, but belonging somewhere would be better than running. I'm tired of not being someone to someone.

A familiar man's voice sent to me the floor, to my knees, to hiding behind a sofa. Whispering to the back of the arm on the sofa, I announced to the fabric. "That's Archie. He's followed me."

I glued my eyes to the back side of raggedy suit, and he shook hands with the flower lady. "Ms. Camille Kelley, a woman like you taking time to enjoy the weekend. Good for you. You must be exhausted from signing off on all those adoption papers." Archie used a rude tone, a harsh emphasis on the word adoption.

Camille yanked her hand from his grasp. "I heard you came back to Memphis. Are you hoping to get your old job back driving for Ms. Tann?"

"Driving for Ms. Tann?" He scowled at the lady in the other seat. "I think not. I'm ready to expose her to our next governor. You'll see."

The woman with glasses frowned. "Archie. You're not welcome at our little party. I'm meeting with my attorney

tonight. Maybe you know Abe Waldauer. He's taking care of
my finances and that of Judge Kelley. We are planning our
retirement."

Archie snapped, "Well, Ms. Georgia Tann. I'm sure you
are. Maybe you should plan it in jail. Your men can't think for
themselves. But I can. I have a plan. And it's to take you
down."

She grew four inches in her chair as did the Camille lady
and the attorney. "Archie. I suggest you watch your words.
They may be used in a court of law or in an alley with a gun."

The man whose eyes were bugged now, calmed the
conversation. "Let's have another drink. Archie, stay and join
us. The ladies are a little testy. But a couple more drinks and
we can solve everything."

Backing up, Archie shook his head. "No, thank you." He
started to turn and leave, but glanced back at the man. "So,
your name is Abe Waldauer?"

"The one and only. I win every case I take. And every case
I take comes with a price."

"I see. Sorry to bother the three of you. You best enjoy
tonight. Your days of lies and stealing and killing are coming
to an end."

The attorney called, "Threats? Coming from you?"

"Yes! I mean to take you down myself!" Archie waved a
fist at him.

Pursing my lips, I crouched lower when the attorney
peeled himself from the chair. He screamed, "Mr. Archie.
Threatening me comes as a serious infraction. I suggest you
leave while you can."

Archie tipped his head. "Serious infraction? Stealing and
selling babies! Now that is a serious infraction." He moved
toward a hallway, and I darted behind lamps and tables and

caught up with him. He had collapsed by the wall, breathing with a panting sound. And he wiped sweat from his forehead.

"Archie, I've never heard you talk like that to anyone."

Startled, he sucked hard on his lips, coughing. "Shoelace, where were you? And where have you been? I've searched up and down Main and Union, and Beale Street."

"I've been here for a good bit, and I heard you talking to those people. That's the horrible Georgia Tann, huh?"

"It is. And her judge who helps her in court. But I wasn't expecting to see … to see the very attorney who, under the pretense of helping Ms. Susan and Mr. Boyd, sitting with them. He's playing them. He's not going to find Willie. He's just making money on the poor boy."

I touched his torn sleeve. "But you were brave and bold. You showed courage. Do you have a plan on how to stop them?"

Shaking his head, he sighed. "No, I was about to pass out. I'm sure she's got some of her men close by. After the way I talked to her, I'm not likely to live through the weekend."

"What? But you said you were going to expose her."

Archie stepped to the black phones lining the wall, each on little wooden shelves. "I need Jolene. I need all her notes, and they are missing. Even her typewriter is gone from Lottie's apartment. I noticed it earlier when the officers were here. The proof we had and need is no longer ours. Whoever killed Lottie must have taken the research. Almost 18 months of gathering information to take them down."

"But Archie … we can get more proof. It's not too late. We can find Jolene. We can save her. We can find Willie, too. We can do this."

Archie huffed, moving to a bench. "I don't know where to start. I don't know what we should do. I'm at a loss."

Marching around him, I challenged him with the bravest words I could think of. "So, when I get scared you talk to me about how God will help me. I think we need to find God. And the way we can do that is to … to go to church."

"Shoelace, this is no game. We're in real trouble here."

"I know. Isn't God up to the challenge? He's been testing me for two years. Let's go find Him."

"Find Him?"

"Yes, He has three red doors at the church by Jolene's place. Let's go find the door that He's behind."

"You're acting silly now, my child." Archie pulled me along the hallway toward the stairs, going past them, and we darted into yet another hallway.

"Where are we going?"

"We are keeping out of sight. We need to keep moving. I know their men are near. I just don't know how close." He jerked on my arm. "Come on."

"I'm coming. But where is God? He is Who we need!"

Bolting to a stop, Archie faced me. "Wait! You're on to something. I know what to do. I know where to go. Let's go to church."

"That's what I said."

Archie smiled, "It's time to watch the sun go down on Georgia Tann! And the Tennessee Children's Home Society!"

## A Good Door with Bad Men

Archie swirled around like a top on the floor, whispering, "Come on. Those three men are watching us. Two of them are from my ride through town today. I may have gotten Georgia Tann too riled up."

Peering back over my shoulder, my pigtails flopped from the bouncing. I tried to keep up with Archie. "Where are we headed? I hope you know these halls."

"I'm not sure where they lead, but getting away from those guys will be our only hope."

We charged to the left, stomping up a flight of stairs that took us to the balcony with the view of the flowers on the fountain. Archie yanked me from the rail. "To the elevators. We're taking these boys for a ride."

Pushing the button, the doors slid open, and we jumped inside. I placed my shoes right on top of the emblem. "A duck. They have ducks in all of the elevators."

Archie wiped his brow, pushing floor number six, and we crept upward like a bullet in slow motion. Our chamber opened to a hallway, and we tumbled out, only to run to the next elevator where we joined a woman and man dressed for a party. But they must have started early as she was sloppy and wobbly, and falling all over the man. She clutched two empty glasses, and laughed at nothing.

The man pushed the button to the top floor, the last light, while Archie pushed floor number ten. In seconds, we were waiting for yet another elevator. "Archie, they're going to catch us. Or we'll run into them."

"They have no idea where we are by now. We're taking the next elevator down and we're getting out of this hotel."

"I hope you're right." I glanced down the long carpeted hall, and back the other way.

Archie assured me. "We're going to the church. It's time to move ourselves to somewhere where we can get help."

*Ding.*

The door to the elevator on the left, one of the three, opened and we jumped inside. My huffing and wheezing sounded like a worn-out dog from chasing a cat. "I can't breathe. I need to rest."

"Rest? We have no time for such. Time to lean on God. But we must run to Him first."

At the first floor, we faced the flowered marble fountain again. "They're gone. And so are those men in black suits."

"This way. Back the way we came."

I followed Archie since no other choices made sense. I had no other friends, and no other ideas. We pushed our way through the crowded lobby, slipping along the polished floor to the glass doors. We barreled out to the street, and Archie pulled me to a horse carriage. "Sir, we need a night ride to Beale Street."

The man in suspenders and long hair, not much older than a high school boy smiled. "Sure thing, sir."

I climbed into the seat of the white carriage, and Archie planted himself on the other side of me, leaving me with a dog licking my face. "Stop, I don't need your tongue up my nose."

The driver corrected his dog. "Shadow, stop now. Sorry, little girl." He turned to his yellow dog. "Shadow! Manners! We don't lick girls until we know their name." He glanced back at me from the driver's seat of the carriage. "And your name is?"

"I'm Annie Grace Kree. My friends call me Shoelace."

He grinned, looking down at my PF Flyers. "Is that because you forget to tie your shoes?"

I nodded, and saw my shoe was untied. Bending down, I made a double knot with a bow, and Archie whispered, "Stay down. Just keep low."

The horse trotted down the street making clip-clop noises, and Shadow yapped at something. I couldn't see what it might be, since I was bent in half.

Finally, Archie pulled me up by a strap on my overalls. "Phew. That was close. Tann's men or I should say, Boss Crump's men ran right by us as we pulled from the Peabody Hotel."

Turning, I got on my knees. "So they're gone. Will they leave us be?"

"Not likely. But we're going into hiding. We'll be safe. Only two more blocks." Archie tapped the driver on the shoulder, the boy who held the reigns to the horse. "Will you drop us off at the corner by Beale Street Baptist Church?"

"That's not on my regular route. I'm to turn on the street before that one."

"But, my little girl loves the Blues, and that will put us right in the spot to hear the bands and music."

"Well," he glanced at me. "Sure thing. It's only another block."

Shadow licked my face as if to agree. "This dog reminds me of the one in Jefferson that belonged to the whole town."

Archie petted the dog's head and my head, with a rub for the pup and a rub on my ear.

I grinned. "Archie, you are the strangest man ever. You know more scripture than most preachers. And you didn't use any on me tonight."

"Fear got in my way. It happens. But I know plenty. But not enough. I do want to save a life somehow. Even if I couldn't save my brother, Buster."

"I'm sorry about him. He got lost on the wrong side of the tracks, huh?"

"He was born troubled and stayed in trouble. He never understood our hard life and never considered following God. He followed himself, which led to horrible and terrible and lonely places."

"My daddy was lonely, too. He let trouble get into his soul. He didn't tell me much, but his secrets were scribbled in his face and in his choices."

Archie hugged me. "You're a smart girl, Shoelace. You see things. You see what's important."

"I see things?"

"Sure, you see beyond the sin, to the possible life of forgiveness and living strong."

"You think I see all of that…?" I wrinkled my nose, unsure who or why Archie thinks deeper than my little brain understood.

The driver whipped the reigns, pulling them tight. "We're here. This is where I turn around. Enjoy Memphis. I hope you come to see us again."

I played the part of a tourist. "We will. We had a great time riding in your carriage." I used my high-pitch voice, the pretend one that frilly girls use to impress others.

Archie handed the boy some extra coins. "Thank you, we're off to find us a band listen to, to learn some catchy songs."

I hovered near Archie, the music of long tones and squeals from guitars strumming made my shoes tap on the brick road. "There's the church over there to our left."

130

"Yes, hurry. We need to get inside and off this street."

I paused, looking down the street with bustling activity. "There Jolene's Crystal Palace. It's only a couple blocks from here."

Archie laughed. "It used to be called Jolene & Crystal Belle's Palace, but there wasn't room for the Belle part on the sign. Right now, the 'and-sign' is not blinking so it looks like it's just Jolene's place."

"What? So Kissabelle is Crystal Belle?"

"Yes, she slurs her name. And it's stuck with her." Archie grabbed me. "Hurry. There's a black car. It's moving too slow." Archie tugged on me with a firm grip. "Run. Run to the church."

"But the doors are locked. I tried them earlier."

"No, they stick. That's all."

At the base of the steps leading to the three red doors, I heard the plop-plop of shoes stepping. Twirling, I spun in the shadow of the night, catching the glimpse of two faces, two long-lost and familiar ones. "No way! Mr. Boyd? And Mr. Marion?" I started to run but my feet froze in place, the car inching closer.

Marion Kane waved from a short distance away, calling to us. "Archie. Shoelace. We've searched everywhere for you two."

Mr. Boyd ran to me like a father, like someone who loved me. "My sweet girl. What have you gotten yourself into now?"

He wrapped me inside of his arms, tightly, and held me close to his beating chest, and he wept like a baby.

"Mr. Boyd, you do like me!" I got swallowed up in the hug and realized my daddy's embrace never felt this good or tender.

"I love you, Shoelace. You need to stop running away from life."

"But I was running here to get Willie for you, and for Ms. Susan, and for Lizzy Beth."

"I know. But you need to leave these matters to the grownups. We have an attorney who is on this."

Archie was shaking his head. "No, sir. It appears the Mr. Abe you hired is also connected to the crooked baby stealer here in Memphis. He was never going to get your Willie."

"What? I paid him good money."

Marion reached for me, taking my hand as Mr. Boyd put me down. "Shoelace, aren't you tired. Aren't you tired of trying to fix everyone? Maybe you should let others take care of you for a change."

"I'm sorry. I just wanted to find Willie. I'm good at riding the rail." I sighed. "Well, I used to be good at it. I'm sort of rusty now."

The car we'd forgotten about idled up the block, and the headlights flashed. Then the engine roared, and the car raced at us.

We darted, dodged, and jumped, all four of us, running to the curb, getting nearer to the church. Then as fast as the black four-door, mobster-type car charged, it slowed and the passenger window opened as did the back window on that same side.

Archie hollered, "Get down! Guns! They have guns!"

*Pop. Pop. Pop. Pop. Pop. Zing. Zing. Pop.*

A forest of bodies toppled like trees being cut down in the street. Yelling, I screamed through the gun fire, "Mr. Boyd! Marion!"

Archie shoved me to the steps, shouting at someone unseen. "Get her inside. Keep her safe. Don't let anyone have her. Don't let her die."

As the middle red door cracked, the face of the person receiving those instructions grabbed my arm.

"Let go of me! That's my daddy on the ground! He's bleeding!" I struggled to get free, racing a foot, but the long arm of the shadow-person yanked me back.

I screamed again, as I watched Archie fall to his knees. I yelled, "No! Archie! They've shot you, too."

Within four seconds it seemed, I found my real daddy only to lose him in gunfire! I had waved at Mr. Marion only to watch him fall like a tree cut down! And then, Archie landed on the cobblestone, his head pounding to the bricks, and a spot of blood rushed from beneath his body.

In seconds the forest of love running for me toppled like three trees. Three lives. All knocked over in a blast of guns firing. With blood gushing. With lost breath. And I wanted to die!

"Get inside this church. And now!" The not-grown voice, the not-known person holding my arm dragged me through the door of the church, as we both seemed to crawl. He forced me along like I was a potato sack, and once inside the darkness, the person turned the knob making sure the door was secure. He put a hand over my mouth. "Quiet! They'll be back. Don't move."

Kicking, I bit his fingers.

"Ouch! Stop that."

"Then leave me alone. I don't need rescuing."

The shadow bent my arm behind my back. "Stop fighting me. I'm not the enemy. I'm not your friend. But I am the one God sent."

*Pam Kumpe*

## Because It's Real

*Ahhh! Ahhh!* "Not again. Not now. Not three people at once. I just got me a real daddy. And now he's gone. Mr. Boyd! Mr. Boyd came for me! And he wasn't drunk like my old daddy, and he never drank whiskey. He came for me!"

"Rest your head my weary friend. Rest your head and shed a tear." The arms of someone stronger than me, but with a half-boy, half-man voice kept me in a bear hug as if I might run.

Fidgeting my hands toward the face in the shadows, I felt swallowed up by the eerie darkness, like a blanket of death hovered over me. Being inside the church left me confused. I'm alive but stuck in a pit of shadows. I couldn't figure out who pulled me to safety and yet, I was afraid of the rescuer.

"Stop wiggling. You're being saved."

I argued, "Let go of me. I'm not yours. I belong to no one. I keep losing the ones I love, and the ones who love me keep saying goodbye. Everyone I love keeps dying."

"Show you? What about your showing someone you love them?" The voice challenged me, and pushed me to a corner, holding me against the wall, or maybe it was stairs.

"No one loves me like I need. No one shows me until I bleed."

The shadow whispered, "The love you speak of comes from God. The love you need is here for thee."

"You talk in circles, part preacher talk, part Bible talk, and part nonsense talk." Wiggling, I kicked at the person who held onto me.

134

"Hush! Quiet! They're outside, they're near, and they'll blast through these doors with gunshot, unless we go now." The hand guided me to my feet, yanking on me, and I was dragged to a staircase where my legs bumped and climbed. "I can't see. I have no idea where we're going. I need to go and see if Marion Kane is alive. And check on Mr. Boyd. And what about Archie? He needs a handkerchief."

In a low, but stern voice, while breathing in my face, the voice warned, "If you want to live, you must do what I say. I am your answer. I am the way."

"You may know the way in this church at night, but I'm not following you anywhere!"

*Pop! Pop! Pop! Pop!*

The crack of wood snapping stopped my wiggling, and the gunshots rang out below, somewhere. The bweep-bweep of sirens blaring grew louder, too.

*Bweep. Bweep. Bweep.*

"Sit still. Don't move." The voice shook my guts with its firmness. "I'll go see what's taking place. If you come outside, they'll take you to jail to question you. But they won't take me. I'm the janitor. I'm the one who cleans up the messes here at the church. Seems I'll clean this one up for you."

I froze with fear, not wanting to spend one second in jail. But I shook my head wondering how and when does a janitor have the say over me. "I'm not staying here. I'm going with you."

*Kaboom.*

The shove sent me backwards, my head bouncing off the wall. "Stay put. Or you'll die."

Quivering with a shake of doom, I pulled my knees to my chest. The stomping of the shadow lessened, a creak of a door opening and closing sent chills up my neck, and muffled talking slipped from the basement of what seemed like death.

The eerie place where church and death, where life and hope crisscross. Where I could stop breathing any second.

I whimpered, falling to my side and felt the warm hand on my face, a soft touch, and I popped up. "Grandma? Is that you? Are you here?" Shaking, I wiped my face with my hand, the dampness real, the wishing for my grandma real, the absence of her too real. The hurt like a bullet to my wounded heart!

I rocked, and rocked, and rocked, and rocked, and then rocked again, whining, worrying, and suffocating from what I saw, of seeing bodies tumble to the bricked road. "No! No! I don't know what to do without Archie, or Marion, and even Mr. Boyd."

I waited, and waited, and rocked some more. The talking and noises outside went away, and I stood to my feet, testing the floor with my shoe, and finding the stairs that went down, taking it with a tiptoe, and then another step. Until I was standing in an open vault of charcoal darkness where musty carpet reeked. Where the scent of a thousand shoes left their dusty prints, and caused the smell of moldy cheese in my nose. "What is that smell?"

*Creak!*

A light slipped through the cracked door, and my copper-armed shadow, a mere teenage boy, held the red door with his hand, his body half inside, half outside. "Good night, sir. I'll lock up after I dust the pews. Cleaning is my game. I wish I could help you with your case. I only know that a car drove by as I was coming to work to get the church ready for Sunday services. I hid in the nook at the end of the stairs. It's a miracle I'm alive."

A deep voice echoed through the foggy air. "If you remember anything, call the police station. Three men gunned down in front of a church. This will make headlines and stir fear."

"Yes, sir. I'll call my pa to walk me home tonight. It might not be safe." The boy closed the door, locking it with a click of a key. He switched on a light from somewhere, facing me, staring at me, sighing, and wiping his hands together.

I stood there frozen, caught in the not moving, not breathing, not having one person to turn to for help. "Who are you? Let me go."

The Negro boy moved toward me. "Come with me. Let's go up the side stairs. Either way will take you to the sanctuary. We can pray there."

"Pray? Will praying bring Archie back to life, or Marion, or Boyd? Or my daddy? Or my grandma? Or my mama? Or Pastor Cody? Or Tin Can Mahlee? Or … or Lottie?"

The boy shook his hand with a fist. "Prayer will connect your heart with God's heart. Prayer will change you from thinking everything's about you. Because little girl, it's not."

"Don't talk to me like that. I'm no one to you. And you aren't sent by God."

"Really, and how would you know? When do you listen to God? When do you obey Him? When do you follow His ways?"

Backing up, stepping sideways, I inched my way toward the zigzagging carpeted stairs to the side of me. If I charged up the stairs, I could fly away, far away, and run to a pew. I could fall to the floor, hide and not show myself. I could disappear, and not breathe, and not cry. Or think. Or live. I could die, if it weren't for the sobbing pouring from my soul. "Stop bothering me. I need to find Kissabelle. I need her. She's the only person I know here, who's alive. She's someone who can help me."

"Are you serious? She's not in her right thoughts, and she's stuck. She buys shoes for a dead boy. Is that who you want to help you?"

"How do you know her?" I cringed at his knowing glances, and his words that stung with power over me.

"She lives along the tracks in towns where sadness rides, where life breaks and where she can hide until she's found. She's the lonely part of a broken mother's heart. She's my neighbor."

"Your neighbor?" Shaking my head so hard the tears flung from my face, I cried out. "I can't do this! I can't!"

"Then let me help you. I live ... live next door to Lottie. My pa is the cook. My little brother is in the hospital. He's sick. He's only six. Our ma lost her life giving him his, and he's never gotten strong." The boy wearing brown pants, and a white cotton shirt, who had wet marks under his arms from sweating, wobbled, talking of his family. Just like I wobbled thinking of mine.

"You knew Lottie?" I coughed. "So did you know Archie?"

"Know Archie? He taught me to drive. He taught me to play pool. He taught me how to iron my shirts, so I'd look crisp and clean. He taught me how to love the Bible, and to listen to God."

Smiling, I whimpered, "You knew him better than me. I didn't know he played pool."

"He's the best. He wins. I lose. He's ..." The boy's voice cracked. "He was so good to Lottie, too."

"So, you were coming to work tonight?" My feet itched, my toes wiggled, and readied to run.

"Naw! God sent me!"

"Stop it! Why would He send you if He wasn't going to stop the shooting?"

"He sent me to get you. To save you."

"Whatever!" I took his last words and charged up the stairs, running like a deer caught in a maze. I bounded up and to the right and through a set of glass doors, tumbling like the carpet had trapped my foot with a deep hole, like I was sinking deeper into the pit of no return.

The stomping thud from behind me stopped, and I knew even in the hazy darkness of the sanctuary, I was dead. "Fine! You've caught me." I rolled onto my back, and the light slipped in through the rainbow glass of arched panes running up and down the oversized room. The rainbow of color sent me weeping, blue for losing my pa. Yellow for lost sunsets. Purple for the luck of the draw for people who could eat and drink at the Peabody Hotel. And the color of red for blood. For death. For how it happened whenever I came into someone's life.

Sobbing, I knew my mama died because of me. My pa, too. My Tin Can Mahlee. My pastor. My three friends tonight. Screaming at God, I kicked and wallowed, and stammered, "It's not fair! I don't get to pick anything! I get nothing."

The boy touched my shoulder. "Hey, my name's Que, short for Quedellous, the pool shark."

Sniffling, I moved from his reach. "Stop it. Don't bother me."

He lifted his fingers, the ease of his touch gone, like a candle snuffed out. "I'll switch the light on the chandeliers. You need to see this place."

"Sure. So, I can yell at God in the light?"

"If you must. But tonight, we stay here, until you heal."

"Sure. And who's gonna make me?"

The brightness of the lights breaking into the shadows made my eyes burn. I blinked, and rubbed my eyes, taking in the dark wood of the pews. The red carpet. The white walls. The rainbow stained glass that reached to yet another story, to the third floor. The side balcony circled us on the top floor, like a horseshoe. And the giant painting on the wall behind the choir loft showed someone beating Jesus, and another part showed Him carrying His own cross on His shoulders.

Charging down the center aisle, seeing the words on the wall beside it, I spoke out loud as if Tin Can Mahlee wanted me to practice my reading. "If My people, who are called by My name, will humble themselves and pray and seek My face and turn from their wicked ways, then I will hear from heaven, and I will forgive their sin, and heal their land."

Weeping like those words were for me, I glanced to the face of Jesus on the wall. "God, I have nothing and am nothing. I cause pain. I even kill things."

With my knees on the carpet, the smell of sweet perfume drifted by my nose, a fragrance I'd not noticed. "Do you smell that?" I asked the boy with chocolate eyes, who appeared like an angel in the light. "Do you smell that?"

"Yes, it's the fragrance of hope in Christ. He's wanting to heal you heart and give you strength. He's calling to you like never before, because now you'll need every bit of life left in you. Every step you've taken has led you here. All the other steps of your life have mattered."

I sobbed, and let out the rest of the volcano of pain. "I don't understand."

"God brought you to Memphis to do this. This is your purpose and it will give God glory and cause others to draw hope from your pursuit."

140

I felt the tears and snot mixing on my face. "I can't do it. I can't go on. I'll end up shot like everyone else."

Que knelt beside me, his head two feet higher than mine, and he spoke in a gentle voice. "Together me and you—we're going to get your brother back, so he can go home with you. Remember, God sent me, which means I know where Willie is, and I can get you to him."

## Of Willie, Other Babies, and Me

Rocking and sitting, crying, I placed my legs under me and became a statue like stone. One that had fallen over. Like a tombstone on its side. Like a rock. I curled up beneath a pew, quivering and shuddering, afraid and worried. Weak and worn. Tired beyond tired. And sadder than a tombstone without a name on it.

"Shoelace, you need to come with me. We've got to leave now, they'll be back. It's not likely those men didn't see you. You were after all at the Peabody Hotel with Archie. So, they know you exist."

"I wasn't beside him when he talked to that judge and the witch-lady. Rolling to my side, I whined, "And what? So you were at the hotel?"

"Yes, I've been assigned to you. I'm to keep up with your wanderings. Your Jefferson folks were coming for you. Jolene and Kissabelle were afraid you'd come up missing before they got here. Kissabelle figured you for a runner as did Jolene. And we all have prayed for God to send someone to change the river's tide. And then you rode into Memphis!"

Sniffling, I scowled, "So, you're a spy for God? And for two sisters? That's a nice job for you. Spying on me!" I wiped my bangs from my eyes. "I guess you're not even a janitor, are you?"

Que sat cross-legged, bending sideways to get a closer look at me. "I do clean the church, and sweep the basement and the stairs out front. I'm a janitor for God, too. I help clean up things."

"Sure, you do. You were just on your way to work, that's what you told the cop. But you … you were following me?"

"I have been with you since you left through the window of the apartment. When you met up with Kissabelle at Elmwood Cemetery. When you came down the alley with her. When you snuck out the front door tonight, I became a shadow of protection."

I rolled from beneath the pew, popping to my feet like a soldier ready to fight. "Protection? Are you kidding me? Three men died tonight. Three! And they were … were my friends. One was my daddy! My first real daddy!"

He stood like a tombstone towering over me with anger. "I control nothing. I'm here to watch you. To keep you. I have my task. And I'm good at what I do."

"Good at what you do?" I shook my fist. "You say that we're going to find Willie, but I don't think you have a clue about what you're doing. Besides, Jolene took him somewhere."

"Stop yelling. It makes your face red."

Shaking both fists. "I like red!" I shivered and wept. "You know, maybe those men got Jolene and my brother. I'm leaving. I'm going back to the apartment to find Kissabelle. To see if she'll ride out of town with me. Or I could call Ms. Susan …"

Before the words dried from my mouth, I caught myself sobbing, and worrying how Ms. Susan was going to react when she heard of Mr. Boyd's death, and how it was because of me.

Stepping backwards, I searched the pews. "Where's my satchel? I need my satchel. I had it on my shoulder. I need it."

Que glanced around. "I haven't seen a satchel. You didn't have one when I pulled you from the street."

Charging through the side glass doors at the back of the church, I pounded down the carpeted stairs. The zigzag took me to the three red doors. Shaking, I hollered for Que. "Get me a key, so I can get out of here."

Que's voice trickled down the stairs like a ghost. "I'm coming. But you don't need to go into the night."

I wobbled in the darkness, my feet aching, my head throbbing. The light from upstairs in the sanctuary lit the staircase, but the dimness was eerie as if this Friday night would become the worst memory of my life. "Que! Bring me the key!"

"It's not locked. It's just stuck. The key is for looks. Anyone who knocks on the door will find God invites them inside—always."

I moved back to the bottom of the stairs. "Where are you? I saw you lock the door. You did it to keep those men from getting us."

"I pretended. It's not locked. I promise." Que's voice turned lower, a strangling and gurgling sound came from his next sentence. "Shoelace, run! Run! And hide! Go now!"

Yanking on the door, I felt the weight of the giant door move, and I slipped between the crack, falling down the concrete steps. Landing on the sidewalk, I scanned the cobblestone. The activity on Beale Street told me the night was alive with parties, drunks, and plenty of music for the soul.

"There's my satchel." I fumbled for it by the shrubs, next to the church steps. Slapping it onto my shoulder, I darted around the side of the building into the darkness, and slammed into something hard. "What? Ouch!" Falling backwards I gazed upon the bumper of a black car. "No way! This is the car from earlier. I'm sure of it." I peered around the bumper.

"The side door's open to the church. I've got to get Kissabelle. We need help!"

Charging to the alley, I barreled across the street toward the brick buildings, running by the bars. Hurrying, I crossed one alley and then another, I stormed between the long stretch of guitar playing sounds and bands making music.

I slipped onto the street, glancing up at the neon signs, wading between wobbly and wiggly bodies. I'd gone too far, and missed the alley to Jolene's place. "There's her sign. It's flashing like a beacon calling to me. It's back a block!"

Stepping into the shadows, I rushed down the alley out of view. I became the invisible hobo girl, creeping and running, hiding and darting. At the next cut-through, I rushed to the fire escape below Jolene's apartment. "I can't reach the bar to pull the steps down." Looking around the alley, I found a crate holding trash and scooted it below the spot. "There, I can do it now."

Swinging my feet, I yanked and clawed and caught my foot onto a rung, climbing up toward the window leading into the bedroom. Peeking inside, I couldn't get a glimpse if anyone was there, until the flashing lights from the street flickered with a glow. "There's Kissabelle asleep in the bed."

Pushing on the window, the unlocked glass moved open, and I tumbled through the opened window, landing like a rock on top of Kissabelle.

"What? Who's here?" She came up swinging and kicking. "Oh no! Who's with me? Don't hurt me! Don't kill me!"

"Stop it! It's me, Shoelace! I came in through the window."

Shaking me, she yelled, "What are you doing? Where's Archie? And where's Q…?"

"Where's Que?" I filled in her question.

"You know about Que?"

"Yes, we met tonight but it was after … after …" I fell into her arms. "It's a nightmare. They've killed Archie. And Mr. Boyd. And Marion Kane."

"What? Archie's dead?"

"Yes, he smarted off to Georgia Tann and a judge and an attorney at the Peabody Hotel. Then we were chased and a car rolled down its windows and shot them in front of the church."

"That explains the cars that keep trolling and watching the apartment. It's probably the same ones who shot Lottie, and now Archie."

"And Mr. Boyd. He's my adoptive daddy. And Mr. Marion Kane is my … my … he was like a grandpa." Sobbing, I shook and my heart throbbed in my head. The dampness of the late night felt sticky and wet, like my eyes.

Kissabelle gathered herself. "We've got to leave here. They'll be coming inside to get me or you. To see if we're here." Kissabelle sighed. "Where's Que?"

"He told me to run. And there was a car at the church on the side. I think they've got him. He saved me from … being shot. He said God sent him."

"Well, he does listen to God more than some." Kissabelle shut the window. "Let me show you something. But hurry. Then we're leaving this place."

"What? Can't it wait?" I plopped to my bottom on the bed, and let my feet dangle. "We need help. I don't know what we're going to do."

"Let me show you this first." Kissabelle moved the torn curtains, peeking from behind them. "We don't have much time."

"Then let's go. I need to go. I can't stay. I need to be somewhere else."

"Follow me." Kissabelle shuffled in her long pants, in her boots, and her wrinkled shirt.

"Why are you dressed?"

"I've been figuring on when to leave and how to leave. And where I should stay."

"Don't you mean, we?"

"Yes, we. I knew you would come. You are light. Light comes back."

"I'm not light. I'm not. I bring bad things."

"No! You bring hope. Unwavering hope to all of us."

"I think you have me confused with someone else."

"No! We need to do this for Charley."

"Do what? And why am I following you to the front door of the apartment?"

"Because I'm showing you something. Something you need to know. Something to help you know why Que is listening to God, and why he is sent by God, and why Lottie was helping God."

"What? Lottie was helping God?"

"Yes, Que's pa caught me up on what Jolene and Lottie and Archie and Que have been doing this past year." She reached for the knob on the door. "We're headed to Lottie's apartment before we leave."

"I'm staying here. If those men come inside, they'll come right up these stairs." I inched back a couple of feet.

"No! You come! And see! You need to know this, in case we don't come back here."

"I don't want to know anything."

"You need to see. So you will know."

"Stop talking in circles. I can't do this. I'm just twelve. Twelve! I'm a little girl! I just want to be little and go home." I clutched my satchel like it was a doll, wishing for Lizzy Beth and a pillow, wishing to sleep with her and forget tonight.

"Take my hand." She reached back for me. "Take my hand."

"All right." I clasped my hand in hers and we stepped to the outside of the door, and headed up the stairs, standing once again at the third-floor apartment door, leading into Lottie's apartment. I yanked on her hand. "I don't want to go inside there."

"You need to see." Kissabelle pulled a flashlight from her pants pocket, switching it on, shooting a beam into the room. "Look at those photographs. Little boys. Little girls. Babies. Newborns. Some older. All white babies. All perfect for the right price."

The sitting room was littered with faces and faces of children. "What are these?"

"These are the children Georgia Tann sells. Some are still at her orphanage. Que cleans the orphanage, and Lottie worked there. They were gathering information about the stealing of Memphis children."

Bending down, I stared into the eyes of a little boy, a grinning toddler with a wispy piece of hair. I wondered where he lived. Was he somewhere—maybe sold, maybe not. Maybe sad. Maybe lonely. What about his ma and pa? I dropped the photograph and my tears landed on the slick paper like they were the baby's tears.

Walking on the lake of photos, I felt like I was falling from the Harahan Bridge into the pit of sadness. Babies lost in a world they never asked to be a part of, and little toddlers stolen and living with the wrong parents. I wanted to save them all. To hold them. To rescue them.

Reaching for as many photographs as I could hold, I put them to my heart, crying, "I'm so sorry. I'm not the saddest kid, you babies are sadder. You just don't know it, maybe."

Kissabelle called to me. "Come over here. Look, this is what you must see." She shined the light to a spot by the wall, a place with one photograph and it was surrounded by baby, toddler, and little boy's shoes.

"Those are Charley's shoes."

"Yes, I'm letting him go. He's got my heart. That won't change." The flashlight shook, and she coughed. "And maybe I'll see him again one day."

"Do you think that's his photograph?" I bent over gazing at the face, as she shined the light onto the photo. "Is that? Is that your Charley?"

"Yes, I'm sure of it." She wept, the flashlight wobbling with her shaking.

"But, how do you know? How do you know it's him?"

"A mother knows her baby. He had a triangle mole on his neck. It's him! And someone has my baby boy! He'd be so grown up by now. Thirteen nearly!" She sobbed, with cries louder than some of the voices singing on Beale Street.

"Kissabelle, we need to go. This isn't safe. This is scary."

She picked up the photograph, slipping it into her pocket. I released the photos from my hands and they floated like butterflies to the hardwood floor.

Kissabelle moved to the door. "Yes, we must go. We must now."

*Kaboom. Kaboom.*

A rattle from below the floor caused me to jump. I turned to Kissabelle. "Someone's coming."

She put her finger to her lips, and turned off the flashlight, gently closing the door to Lottie's apartment.

We slipped to the floor like mice, holding our breath, and tears from deep within my eyes burst like a waterfall. I hugged Kissabelle. "Are we going to die?"

She whispered, "No, there's no way. You've been sent to us. You can't die."

## Where Steps Matter

*Clump. CLU...mp. CLUM...p. CLUMP!*

Kissabelle placed her calloused hand over my mouth. "Be quiet. Whoever that is, he didn't stop at Jolene's apartment. He's right outside the door. He's at our door. Here." She shook and scooted on her backside with me next to her, and got us next to the solid spot on the wall. "If the door opens we'll be behind it."

Mouthing to myself and to her hand. "Great, then we'll be stuck here and shot for sure."

"Be quiet. Hush."

*Creeeeeaaaak!*

Before I could pass out from fear, a voice echoed like someone was inside of a tunnel, the fierceness of the yell made Kissabelle and me tremble like a double-earthquake.

"So you're late again? We've talked about this. I know you clean the church on Friday nights. But it's after midnight. Midnight! That's too late for a boy who gets lost in the pool hall. Who gambles away his nickels faster than dissolving salt."

Another voice joined in, "That's not what happened tonight. It's worse than playing pool. Or staying out too late. Or gambling!"

"Boy! I don't need your lip tonight. We've not heard from Jolene since they've found Lottie dead. I'm not sure what's happening, but the heaviness in my chest won't let up. And then you stay out on the street." The growl in the man's voice reminded me of those nights when Mr. Boyd yelled at me, which was most of last year.

I pushed Kissabelle's hand down. "Who's out there? Is that … could that be Que?"

"It might be. But he could have someone with him. Someone who's hiding downstairs. We can't let ourselves be seen. We must stay here, until I'm sure."

The stomping on the other side of the wall came with more hard and heavy and sad words. "Pop, you have no idea what's happening."

*Caplunk. Caplunk. Caplunk.*

Kissabelle whispered, "More steps. Another pair of shoes."

Shaking, I put her hand back over my mouth, so I wouldn't scream while we sat in the dark like ducks on a pond. A pond where no one flies away. Where life gets snuffed out.

"Son, it's late. And who is that?" A pause in the man's question allowed the boy to interrupt.

"Pop, Archie's dead. And a man name Boyd and another man, Marion-something. Georgia Tann and Boss Crump have killed them. Or their men did."

Removing Kissabelle's hand, I mouthed. "Marion Kane is not just a something. And neither is Mr. Boyd."

"What? Dead? When? Where? You sure, boy?"

"Yes, it happened in front of the church before I got there. I was going inside when Archie and that Shoelace girl got off of a carriage. I had lost her for a minute, that little baby brat of a bother you had me watching is trouble. I tried to follow her like Jolene and Kissabelle asked me too, but she kept getting away from me. Then she was tossed at me as the three others were shot down."

Kissabelle pushed me aside. "That's Que. I'm sure now. But I heard other footsteps." Crawling, she moved to the door, trying to peek through the keyhole.

"You can't see through there. It's Que, and you heard how he talked about me. I'm not a brat. I need to let him have a piece of me. Then we'll see if he calls me names."

Kissabelle pushed me backwards. "Everything isn't about you, girl. You act like we should stop what we're doing for you."

Sighing, "But you said I was sent to you all."

"I did say that. I had to hush you up. Now hush again. I can't hear them. Someone else is talking. It's a man."

"Leroy, we need to put you and Que at the parsonage. It's gotten too dangerous here. Que told me about the gunfire, the deaths, and saving the girl."

Mouthing, I talked to the wall in a low voice. "He didn't save me. It's not like he even knows where I am."

Kissabelle kicked me. "Hush!"

The talking on the other side of the wall went fast, and the third person picked up the pace of his breathing. "Let's get you a change of clothes. I've got my car. I brought Que home. Seems that cleaning a church will have to wait. We can't afford to lose you, Leroy. Or Que, for that matter. Losing Lottie after all she's done for this case. It's too much."

Kissabelle knocked me away and stepped on my hand. "Ouch!"

"Girl, we're going with them. It's Reverend Roberts. Nothing to be afraid of here. We can go with him." She turned the knob, and the light from the staircase stung my eyes. "Come on Shoelace. Let's go."

Before I could focus, Kissabelle barreled from the apartment. "Hey, can we go, too? I was just listening in on your conversation."

Mr. Reverend answered, "I see that. And what were you doing in Lottie's apartment?"

Que drilled her, upon seeing me sneak behind her. "And who do we have here?"

Peeking from behind the door, I answered. "She was showing me the photographs of the babies."

No one responded. They stared at me instead with questions not said, with worry not spoken. Que stood in the middle with Leroy, his dad on the left. And the reverend towered to my right while Kissabelle pushed me forward. "Seems our little helper here, she's gotten things stirred up. We best keep her safe."

Smiling a pretend grin, I reached to shake hands with anyone.

The cook grabbed my hand. "Well, I've seen you around, but we've not actually met. I'm Leroy Quedellous Crigle."

"Hi. I'm Shoelace. If you will send me to Jefferson, I can leave all of you alone." Shaking my foot, I glanced down to see a photograph stuck to the bottom of my PF Flyer. Reaching down, I pulled the paper from my shoe, and found myself staring at a small boy, whose Indian features glared at me like my brother's photo, like the one I'd seen back home.

Crumbling like a withered leaf, I fell to the floor in sobs that wouldn't stop. The reverend knelt with me. "My poor girl. This old world's toppled in on your heart. I see those scars. I see your wounds. You are crying for love and love is escaping you at every turn. It's like the handkerchiefs won't stop the bleeding. Let me hold you."

For what seemed like days and days and days, I rested in the fold of the suit of a Negro man whose giant arms wrapped around me. It felt like I was resting in a cloud of safety where nothing could get to me, or hurt me, or cause me any more pain.

Leroy broke through my sobs. "Que, let's get our clothes packed. Kissabelle, if you have any other clothes, go get them."

I watched as she moved down the stairs, and I watched as Leroy and Que went into their apartment. The reverend brushed my bangs from my eyes. "I'm taking all of you to my house. My twins will love to have the company. They're ten. Both are pianists. Quite skilled in music."

He led me down the stairs like we were in a parade, and Mr. Leroy and Que came behind us, and Kissabelle charged up holding a china doll, and a burlap sack packed with bulging items. I turned to her at the bottom of the stairs on the first floor. "And that's what you bring? A supersized china doll from Jolene's dresser?"

"Yes, it's full of hundred dollar bills. It's money she puts back for emergency. And this is an emergency."

In seconds, we piled into the black car parked on Beale Street where late-night partying was louder now than earlier. I sat in the four-door mobster type vehicle that acted like a reverend's car. Sitting in the back seat between Que and Kissabelle, I shook and lost my will to speak. My eyelids fell with each blink like they might not open. I became worried, got lost in the wondering, and I wished for a new day where nightmares like tonight end up not being real. I wiggled. "No! Wait! I don't have my satchel!"

Mr. Leroy held something up. "Here it is. I picked it up for you. I've noticed how you carry it with you wherever you go." He passed it to me over the seat.

"Thank you. It belonged to my real daddy."

Que whispered, "I thought Mr. Boyd was your real daddy."

"He was. They both were. One just did a better job than the other."

The Reverend broke into our exchange of words. "We all can learn from the mistakes of others. We can change the course for our family. We can make a difference and be the hope for the ones who will look up to us." He drove the car around the bend, heading along the road next to the Mississippi River.

Glancing out the window, I shook my head. "We've been this close to the water the whole time?"

Kissabelle nudged me. "Memphis is on the water, girl."

"I know. I got turned around." Sitting back, I remembered the times riding the rail with my daddy, how I never got mixed up on the way to go. I knew how to find my way around. But tonight, being a regular girl instead of a hobo girl almost felt normal, except for the part about losing Archie, Mr. Boyd, and Marion Kane. Death never feels normal.

Sighing, I leaned against Kissabelle, and my eyes closed as I drifted to a place in my past. To the place by the ocean where I first met Tin Can Mahlee. To the place where I met Skip on the rail in Memphis. To the place where I met Taddy, my first best friend back in Texarkana. To the place by Swampoodle Creek where I met Pastor Cody Howard in Texarkana.

To the place where I met an angel named Chula, who looked like a Choctaw girl, and who smoked a pipe. To Wheelock Academy, to the place where I first met Lizzy Beth, my half sister, along with the other Choctaw orphans.

To the place where I met Crush and his boys in Jefferson, Texas, by the bayou. To the place where I met Uncle Silas and Molasses Jones in Washington, Arkansas.

To the place where every step I've taken has mattered. And now, I'm in a car going someplace down a dirt road where the light of the headlights cuts the layers of darkness into slices like pie. "Where are we going?" I leaned on the seat peeking between the reverend and Mr. Leroy, tapping the seat with my fingers.

The reverend pointed. "Up ahead. That's the parsonage. It's our old farmstead. Two floors. Big porch. And lots of rooms. A place to think and pray and meet and decide."

My heart skipped with the bumpy ride from the holes in the road. "How will I ever find Willie out here? Or get home?"

Que nudged me. "You'll see. I know where to find your brother. You'll see."

"Really? It's not like you were able to keep up with me, remember?"

## Fastest Shoes in Town

Stretching, I rolled over to my side, bumping into a warm something. *Yawn!* "I'm sleepy. I need more sleep." Rolling the other way, I collided with another something. "Where am I?"

My hand hugged a pillow, and from behind me, a teeny voice with a squeaky sound answered me, "You're in our bed. I'm Siri. I'm five minutes older than my sister. You're facing Iris. She's a bed wetter."

Popping straight up, I yelled at the room, "Where am I?"

Like lightning Kissabelle fell into the room. "Shoelace, there are other people in this house. Some are still sleeping. You're in the twins' bedroom. I'm downstairs with the reverend and Leroy, and Que's still asleep across the hall. It's early Saturday morning. Get some sleep. We're planning how to stay alive and how to stop Georgia Tann."

In the bed, the girls with curly black hair and green eyes yanked on each other's hair, squealing and laughing. I pointed at them. "Kissabelle, tell them to be quiet. They're making more noise than me." I stared at the identical twins, and they giggled the same as if using one voice.

*Haha! Haha!*

Iris touched my hair. "It's so yellow. Like straw, but soft."

Siri hugged me. "You're like a big sister. I get tired of having just a twin. She copies me, and wants to be me. And she bothers me."

Iris reached across me in the bed, slugging her sister. "I'm ten like you. And I don't want to be you. I am me, already."

I slipped to the bottom of the bed, thankful I was wearing my overalls and even more grateful to not have slept in a wet spot in the bed. "Where are my shoes?"

Together the twins spoke, "Over there, by the window."

Tying my shoes, Kissabelle warned me to stay upstairs, which I nodded that I would, but I didn't mean it. Out the window the meadow of fields went to the edge as far as I could see, then a forest of trees stretched their arms to the sky. "Where are we? How far are we from Memphis?"

One of the twins stepped next to me at the window. "We're about three hundred miles from everywhere."

"Perfect. I'm missing. And I don't know where I am."

Kissabelle moved to the door. "Be quiet if you must stay up. But let the grownups have our time to talk." She shut the door, and the other twin glued herself to my other side.

Glancing at the mirror of sisters, I asked, "So who is who?"

Together they answered, "I'm Iris. I'm Siri."

I pointed to the twin on my right. "So you're Siri?"

"Yes, and she's Iris."

"Goodness, I'll get you two mixed up for sure."

They replied in unison, "We're used to it."

The sisters returned to the bed leaping in their gowns to the mattress, jumping and roughhousing like tomboys. They tossed pillows at each other like a battle might erupt, so I crept from the room, and climbed down the stairs to listen to the grownups planning our next move.

Sitting on the base of the steps, I put my face between the rail, wishing for food when the smell of sizzling bacon caught my nose by surprise. Whispering, I begged, "Will somebody feed me? That smells like my grandma's cooking."

In the front room, Kissabelle argued with Mr. Leroy, her hands waving as if directing traffic. "We can't just stay here.

We need to be doing something." She went on, debating and bossing, shaking her head and raising her voice. "We've got to think this through, and be ready."

Her meltdown sent me to staring out the front window of the parlor toward the morning sun's beam of newness, and the opened drapes let the day shift the shadows into places behind furniture and into cracks in the hardwood floor.

Leroy danced with a nervous twitch, moving out of Kissabelle's way, but she followed him. I hadn't noticed his bulging arms with muscles like someone planted baseballs beneath his bronze skin.

Leroy barked at her, "Kissabelle, we've gathered so much information and to think it's gone now. Well, I don't know what we can do for Jolene. It's likely they've … they've hurt her, or worse."

"This can't be. You said you saw her. I remember. And there's something you're not saying. I know it. I can see it in your eyes." She held up both fists like a boxer who had held her own, on too many boxcar rides.

Leroy backed up and sat down on the sofa. "I may have been confused. There was a lot of customers at the restaurant." He picked up his coffee from the table, sipping the warm drink. "Losing Lottie from our team has added to our sorrow. Since Christmas, the random shootings have gotten horrible and more frequent. This is real. We could all die."

Not able to shut my mouth any longer, I charged down the stairs and into the room. Standing in front of Leroy, I noticed the reverend stopped rocking in his chair and he blew a puff of smoke from his mouth, holding his pipe. He interreupted my interruption. "Shoelace? That's your name, right?"

"Yes, sir."

"Maybe you could join my wife in the kitchen and have you some biscuits and bacon and her famous over-easy eggs with cheese."

"No thank you. I want to be in here."

"I think you'll do better in the kitchen." He rose like a tower of righteousness and gave me a stern glare. "Why don't you go into the kitchen and think on things that are not so pressing. Think on the lovely things in life."

Ignoring him, I blasted my words at Leroy. "Mr. Leroy. What are you not telling us? This is worse than real. We're talking about my little brother. I need to find him. I need to go home. I need to get out of Memphis and never come back here. I need to take my brother with me." My words tangled, and my heart longed for home, but I knew Willie belonged with me, too.

Leroy reacted with quietness in his voice. "I know this is real. You're just a little girl. You have no idea what we've been doing all last year. I've already lost my wife because of this investigation. Why do you think my younger son is in the hospital? He's in a coma. Do you hear me? A coma! He's been that way since before Christmas when his mother was shot at the park. When he caught a bullet in his head!"

"Oh my! Too many people are dying!" My hand went to my throat, and I spun around to run, crashing right into Que. He wiped the tears from his eyes. "I've told you. This isn't all about you."

I gulped. "I'm sorry, Que. I didn't mean to …" Running from the room, I crashed into the kitchen table, knocking a glass of milk over, spilling the drink to the floor.

A hand touched my shoulder. "Sweet girl. Sit down. I'll mop that up. Are you hungry?"

I plopped into the chair sobbing, and she placed a plate of eggs and two biscuits in front of me. She pushed the platter of bacon toward me. "Help yourself. If Siri and Iris get here, you'll not get seconds."

"Thank you, Ms. Reverend. I need to go home."

She rustled my hair. "You're welcome. We'll get you home. We'll pray for God to make a way. You'll see. He does answer our prayers." She turned a burner off on the stove. "I'm gonna call my girls in a minute, but first let's have a talk."

"A talk? I don't need to talk. I need to go home." I bit into the bacon, my tummy growling with each swallow.

"Yes, we need to talk. Just you and me. I need to look you in the eye and get to know the real you. And how did you come by the name Shoelace? Seems a girl in overalls and red tennis shoes might need a real name."

I interrupted her. "I don't wear any ole tennis shoes. I wear PF Flyers. And my real name is Annie Grace Kree."

"I met a Kree in Texarkana. A plump woman who ran a manor." She rubbed her chin. "It was on the Arkansas side close to the Catholic Church. I made her some quilts for her beds when we met downtown. I was selling them from the back of my wagon outside of Hart Drug Store. It was about five or six years ago. She bought three from me that day. Nice woman, had manners, too."

I choked on the biscuit, spitting the bread onto my plate. "What? You met my grandma? No!"

"What, did your granny have a manor?"

"Yes! Yes!" I jumped from the table, and ran to Ms. Reverend, wrapping my arms around the round woman who reminded me how loved I was by my own grandma.

She held me close to her stained apron, and my fears dropped like crumbs. "Oh, my goodness. I miss my grandma."

"She sick? Or gone?"

"She died January last year. She loved me."

"I can see why she would. You're the prettiest little girl with the whole world at her hands. I think you're changing lives for God and for good. She would be so proud of you."

I sniffled. "Do you think she would?"

"Oh, me! You're made in God's image and He never makes ruined little girls. He makes hungry ones. But not bad ones." She guided me to the chair, and I gobbled the food down like I'd not eaten in forever.

She peeked under the table. "I do love your PF Flyers. Iris and Siri love PF Flyers, too. They each have a pair. One wears the dark blue. The other wears white."

"For real?"

Ms. Reverend lifted her long cotton dress and pointed to her feet, revealing a brown pair of fuzzy slippers. "Someday, I might get me a pair myself. If I find them on sale at the surplus store."

Laughing, I wiped the egg from my face. "You remind me of my grandma. Except … for …"

"Except for my skin?"

"Yeah! But you have good skin. God made it."

We chuckled together, and for a few minutes I felt like me again. Like hope was inside me. Like laughter might return.

*Knock. Knock. Knock.*

The door creaked in the front room, and Mr. Reverend invited someone inside. "Officer, come inside. We hope you have good news."

## Learning to Pray Learning to Act

Scooting the chair away from the table, I smacked on one last bite of eggs after chomping down five pieces of bacon. All the gobbling left me drooling for more bacon and for more eggs. I was starving. Peering into the front room, I tore off a piece of bacon from the strip in my hand. "Why is that officer here?"

Ms. Reverend shuffled in her slippers to the doorway, blocking me from leaving the kitchen, acting like a gate. "Time for the twins to join us. Their chores are waiting for them."

As I squeezed between Ms. Reverend and the doorjamb, her hand seized my shoulder, snatching me to her side. She squeezed hard but with the grandma and ma touch. "And maybe if you did a few chores with the girls, your mind will ease up, and then you can let my husband and Leroy talk without interference."

"Interference? I don't interfere. I have a lot to say."

"I expect you do. Which gets in the way of your listening."

"You just met me. What do you know about me? I can listen. I just prefer talking."

"I know your will is strong. And God is chiseling away the *you* so He can shine through in your life."

"Huh? I just want to get my brother and go home."

"I know you do, but when you listen, you hear what matters. When you listen, words form inside your ears and sweep down to your heart. Then you can make sense of the ugly in this world. When you listen, you discover how much you don't know. And how much God does know."

"I know a lot. I can make a chocolate cake like my grandma. I can wash my own clothes. I can climb a tree higher than any ole boy. And I can jump onto a boxcar when it's moving down the tracks."

"But, sister. What do you love to do? Why do you think God's brought you here to the farm?"

Smarting off a little, but not too much, I squinted my eyes since it helped me to think. "We came here because it's not safe in Memphis. People are after Leroy and the others for trying to stop the baby stealing." I pursed my lips, proud of my answer.

"And do you think that's why you're here?"

"I'm here to get my brother."

"Are you?"

*Kaplunk-plop. Kaplunk-plop.*

My answer lingered in my throat as Siri and Iris bounded down the stairs to my left. They jumped on the staircase that zoomed straight up and straight down, but made a zigzag at the top to the rest of the bedrooms.

 The twins with their curly black hair smiled with grins of joy. "We're hungry."

One twin yelled, "I smell bacon."

They chattered like ducks clucking, jumping in their blue shirts and matching overalls.

I couldn't tell them apart. "Hey, which one is which?" I quizzed them as they sailed into the kitchen around their ma.

The one wearing white PF Flyers picked up two pieces of bacon. "I'm Iris."

And the twin swallowing her milk gurgled, "And I'm Siri. I wear the blue PF Flyers. Unless we trade."

Laughing, "You two must be pranksters."

Iris swished her fork in her plate, sitting in her chair. "I'm really Siri."

Ms. Reverend corrected the twins. "Iris has a little blue in her green eyes. That isn't something they can trade."

I glanced at the circle of blue in Iris's eyes, smiling that I would know how to tell them apart if they swapped shoes on me. Siri grinned using a piece of bacon for teeth. "I have bacon. I love bacon. I will eat all of it."

Ms. Reverend responded, "And then you need to gather the eggs. Give the cow some fresh hay. And sweep the porches."

They nodded while smacking and chattering in low twin voices with a weird language of their own. And they disappeared into the enjoyment of a breakfast made by their ma.

She tapped the table with a spoon. "And who forgot to say their blessing? We thank the good Lord for every meal and every day and every breath."

Together they answered, "Sorry. We forgot." The twins folded their hands. "Thank you God for our food. We praise you for loving us. Amen."

I tugged on Ms. Reverend's arm. "Why didn't you make me say a blessing over my meal? You let me dive in without a word."

"Do you normally pray and thank God for each new day? And for your meals?"

Shaking my head. "No. I haven't in a long time. Ms. Susan blesses our meals. Or Mr. Boyd. But I just wait for them to finish. I haven't thanked God too much for stuff."

"Well, I prayed over your food for you, silently."

"For me?"

166

"Yes, sometimes praying for another person helps me remember that God provides and guides and gives new life. He knew you were hungry. And I love to pray."

Iris nodded. "Mama does pray. She walks in the fields praying to God. And on the front porch. And the back. And in the barn."

Ms. Reverend kissed Iris on the top of her head. "I pray for my two muffins, Iris and Siri, and for their pa. He's carrying a responsibility to lead his church. I pray for wisdom for him. And I pray I support him like I should." She kissed the top of Siri's head, too.

I took their table-talking time to head from the kitchen to catch up on the officer's reason for coming to the house. A farm you had to drive to on purpose.

Ms. Reverend blocked my way. "Sister, you might learn more in the kitchen."

I stepped around her and into the parlor to get closer to the whispering by the big window. Putting my hands on my hips, I twirled around to glance back at Ms. Reverend at my successful escape, when I bumped into the end table. Knocking the lamp to the floor, I dove to catch it before the porcelain smashed, and caught the lamp shade, instead.

*Splat-a-crack!*

With my back on the floor and my pigtails tangled in splintered glass, Mr. Reverend reached for me, standing me to my feet. "Don't move. The glass is stuck in your hair. You'll get cut."

Leroy hovered like a pa who worried I might be bleeding, and Que picked up the big pieces of glass. The twins peered at me with big stares, their lips puckered like punishment was close. Like a paddling might come in the minutes to follow.

My heart beat in my chest. "I'm sorry. I just wanted to know what was happening. I wanted to know if we were going to find my brother. I didn't mean to break the lamp. I didn't mean not to pray over my food. I didn't mean to come to town and get trapped inside this terrible-awful spot."

Ms. Reverend handed a broom to Que. "Sonny, sweep up the mess. We can fix this. We can open more curtains until I get a new lamp. But getting a new Shoelace, well, the good Lord made only one. And she's pretty special."

"So, you're not going to punish me?"

Mr. Reverend Roberts picked glass from my hair, answering, "Why would we punish the first glimpse of hope that came our way? We've been stuck in the collecting of papers to save the children under Georgia Tann. You have reminded us that we need to act. Every day we make another note, another baby crashes like broken glass into the lost world of illegal adoptions."

Leroy dropped the glass into the trash can by the wall just inside the kitchen, turning back to peek at us. "You're our messenger of hope. You're the catalyst of change we needed. You reminded us how valuable all life is, and how we need to save the children. And our waiting has cost us dearly."

The uniformed officer hovered, holding his wide-brimmed hat in his hand. "So, this is our little girl causing havoc in the city? Seems she's one mighty warrior."

"Me? A warrior?"

"Yes, you've escaped Buster's grip. You've hidden from Boss Crump's men. You've escaped from windows. And hidden in cemeteries. Your walk is known and we need to protect you."

"How would you know what or where I've been?"

Que sighed. "I've gotten him caught up. He needed to know the whole picture. He needed to know who he came to see."

I moved from the clean spot by the sofa, and backed up, sitting down. "You're here to see me?"

The officer sat next to me. "Yes, I come with a message for you. It's from a survivor who got shot in front of the church. He wanted you to know he's alive."

"Who? Who's alive?" I caught a glimpse of Kissabelle staring out the big glass window, like she was lost somewhere and not in the house. She hadn't come to me when I fell. She hadn't yelled at me for making a mess. She wasn't moving. She seemed like a lamp stand, like porcelain. Like life escaped her with each breath.

A tapping on my knee brought me back to the conversation. "Oh ... tell me who's alive!"

"Archie. It's Archie. And he sent you this." He handed me a handkerchief.

I sniffed it, weeping like a waterfall of tears might soak the cloth. "Oh my! He's alive!"

"Yes, he is very much alive. He took a bullet to the shoulder. He'll be in the hospital a couple of days."

Embracing the officer with my long arms, I screamed, "My Archie? He's alive?"

"Yes ... and I have even better news."

I sat back. "What?"

"Mr. Boyd and Mr. Marion Kane will make it, too."

"What? You mean all three of them are alive?"

"Yes, very much alive! And they'll be on the mend, but they'll live to see you and to be with you. They sent me. They wanted you to know."

"How did you know where I was?"

"Well, Archie had me call his friends. Seems his list is short. And we found out you were here from the reverend."

Hugging everyone, I jumped from person to person like a rabbit, hopping all around the room. "Oh, my goodness! They're alive. They're alive!"

I danced in a circle with the twins, who were laughing and smiling, too. I kept repeating, "They're alive! They're alive!"

Iris nodded. "We heard. We heard."

Screaming, I grabbed for Kissabelle who pushed me aside. "I'm happy for you, girl. I am. I just have trouble getting past my own hurts sometime."

"Then hug me. Let me share this with you. We'll find Willie and he'll have you to thank!"

Kissabelle fell to her knees. "If only I could see my own boy! Is that too much to pray for?"

Ms. Reverend wrapped me up in her arms, holding me like a baby. "Precious girl, what great news the Lord has brought to you. He has blessed you with answered prayer."

I looked her in the eyes, my voice tapering off to a whisper. "But I didn't pray. I yelled at God."

Ms. Reverend put me on the floor. "Sometimes yelling sounds like prayer to God. He knows our heart."

I spoke words inside my head, *Thank you God. This is a miracle.*

Kissabelle rose to her feet, wiping the tears. Her long hair was wrapped into a bobby-pin bun and the strands of brown hair fell like spider webs around her ears. Her old pants and wrinkled shirt showed me she was standing in the same clothes from the night before, and she looked too tired, beyond one night's lack of sleep.

I held her hand. "I can't believe they're alive."

She turned to me. "So, do you think God could ever return my son?"

170

Leroy inched toward Kissabelle, holding her like a father, even though he wasn't much older, and I moved back to hug the twins.

Leroy spoke the saddest words ever. "I'm sorry, Crystal Belle. I'm so sorry. Today is ... today is Charley's birthday. I can't believe we didn't remember."

I moved to her side. "We can bake a cake for him. Let's bake a cake. The other one burned. But I can do it. Let me do it."

Ms. Reverend hugged my neck from behind me, and whispered. "You heard her cry. You heard her need. You listened and God is using you to heal her heart."

I spun around. "This is almost the best day of my life."

The officer interrupted me, "I have one bit of bad news. It's seems that the Jolene's & Crystal Palace burned to the ground last night. And we've got the police watching the church to make sure it's not torched."

*Spakunk. Spakunk.*

I turned to glance at the stairs, as did everyone because of the noise on the creaking stairs. Silence fell in the room as a woman appeared in a cotton dress, holding hands with a little boy. A child with a bandage over his eyes. My mouth fell open. My eyes were wide. And questions jumped from inside my head.

Ms. Reverend cut the silence with her greeting. "Well good morning! Look who's finally up!"

## Oh Brother! Oh Brother!

"Jolene? Have you been here all along?" My first question led to another. "Is that ... is that my Willie?" I slipped toward the small boy with black hair. It was shiny, slick and wild. Around his head a white bandage covered his eyes, and Ms. Jolene held his hand, guiding him into the room.

Kneeling, I reached for his face to touch him, but moved my hand back when he spoke. "Who's here, Mama Jolene?"

Ms. Jolene patted his shoulder. "We have company. Precious company. We're at the reverend's house, remember?"

"I know where we are, Mama. But who is that other kid?"

"It's someone who came to meet you."

"Me? Someone knows me?"

"Yes, she's a girl from Texas who has a message for you. We'll talk about this later. Right now, you need breakfast."

Ms. Reverend took the cue. "Good morning, Willie. The day is perfect now. Now that you're up and with us." She ushered Willie in his dark pants and a white shirt. The part of his face I could see reminded me of Lizzy Beth. Same hair, just shorter. Same size body as his twin, except for the bandages.

The little voice of my brother sparked hope inside me. He fumbled to his seat at the table. "Can I have some oatmeal? I likes me some oatmeal."

Ms. Reverend placed a bowl at his spot, turning to the already-made oatmeal on the stove. "Sure, anything for Willie, our guest. We must keep you strong. The choir is singing tomorrow, and you'll sing your first solo for all of us."

"I'm scared. What if the other kids laugh?"

"If they laugh, I'll sick Iris on them. She's good at fighting. Not that she should be fighting." Ms. Reverend chuckled under her breath.

Siri nodded. "Iris hits me when I take the covers. She's ready to punch any kid who makes fun of our Willie."

We scooted toward the kitchen while Ms. Jolene joined the grownups in the parlor, and I glanced back, wondering why they marched to the front porch with the officer.

Following Willie like a puppy, I bumped into a twin. "Sorry, I can't keep from staring at him."

Iris scolded me in a low voice. "We've been told to treat him like any other boy. He may be blind. But he has feelings."

Defending myself, I apologized, "I didn't mean it like that, I have never seen him before today."

"Why did you call him your Willie? He's our Willie and he belonged to Ms. Lottie. Or he did until yesterday." Choking, Iris sighed. "The bad men got her. But they don't know where we live. We are safe. Mama said so."

Whispering, I filled in the blanks for her and Siri leaned in to listen, too. "Willie is my half-brother. He's a twin, too. His sister's name is Lizzy Beth. She's at home in Texas. I can't wait for her to see him." The joy rushed inside my veins and popped like trumpets playing in my ears. I shouted. "I have my brother! Oh, I do!"

Ms. Reverend shushed me, "Shoelace, some surprises need time to unwrap. Let's move a little slower with your news."

Willie sat at the table in the very chair where I'd eaten, dishing up his oatmeal, using one hand to guide, the other to hold the spoon. He smacked, "Who has a brother?"

Ms. Reverend assured him, "You, my dear one, are a brother to everyone. You're like family to all of us. We love our Willie."

Willie smacked on his food, and I plopped down in the chair next to him, gazing at him, drooling with love. A love found hidden but ready to escape from my soul. "I'm Annie Grace Kree. My friends call me Shoelace."

Willie laughed. "I've never known …" He reached with his left hand, fumbling for my face, running his fingers over my eyes, touching my hair and holding a pigtail. "You are a girl. I had to see. You sounded like a boy."

Giggling, "I sound like a boy?"

"A little. I not know a Shoelace before."

"I'm a one-of-a kind. I'm twelve. I used to come to Memphis with my daddy." I nearly told him *with his daddy*.

Nodding, Willie lost himself in his oatmeal, and the girls helped Ms. Reverend with the dishes. Iris argued, "It's my turn to wash. And your turn to dry."

Siri shouted, "It's not your turn to wash. It's mine."

Ms. Reverend moved between the girls. "It's time for extra chores, if you two can't work this out."

Together they answered, "Yes, ma'am."

Willie laughed, "They fight like boys."

Again, the twins answered, "We're not boys."

Ms. Reverend held her apron, wiping her hands, laughing. "Silly girls. Silly Willie." She smiled, nodding at me like she knew my whole story. "I see that the Lord is making family come together. It's precious to behold."

I swung my feet under the table, keeping my eyes glued on the boy my daddy never knew. Still though, peace rose up in my heart from lost places and lost steps. It was invisible joy, like a mist of love rolling around the kitchen to all our hearts,

174

and tears dropped from my eyes. "Willie, you're about the best thing I've seen in my whole life. Nearly!"

Giggling, he touched his bandage. "I have bad eyes. But my ears like you. You is nice."

I touched his arm, and a tingle shot up my arm. "I can't wait to know you like a ..."

Ms. Reverend cleared her throat. "Let's see. The girls are done with the dishes except for Willie's bowl. I'm headed to the yard, got a basket of wet clothes to hang on the line before they sour. The sun is shining. The breeze cool. And there's nothing like towels with baked-in freshness."

I stopped talking, since knowing and telling Willie how we were related would come later. But I could barely keep the excitement inside, and my feet danced inside my shoes. "Hey, I thought we were having a party for Charley. Can I make the cake?"

Kissabelle stepped into the kitchen. "I'll help you. Charley gets a cake every year. Always has, so this year is no different."

I smiled at Kissabelle. "I want to help you. Will you let me?"

Ms. Reverend picked up the clothes basket. "Girls, you can help Crystal Belle with the cake too, and little missy."

Screaming in their duet of joy, the twins shouted, "This will be fun. Our chores will wait."

Ms. Reverend stood at the screen door. "Yes, they'll be waiting for you after the baking."

The collecting of the flour, the sugar, and the bowl landed on the table in front of Willie while he finished his breakfast. And Kissabelle opened the ice box. "Eggs. We need eggs."

Willie asked, "Can I lick the bowl?"

I kissed his cheek. "Yes! Always!"

"Yuck, no kissing. Ucky!"

"Sorry, it just happened."

*Ha-ha! Ha-ha!*

The twins burst into giggles and stirred together, each with a large spoon in the bowl. Kissabelle dropped the egg yolks into the mix, added cocoa and grabbed another bowl. "Frosting! We need us some rich chocolate frosting!"

I pulled the bowl from the girls, taking their spoons. "Let me help. I want to do this, too."

The tug-of war over the bowl began, and the batter lapped over the edge and splatted to the floor. "Oops!" Slipping, I tumbled to the floor, and the green eyes of the twins peered at me. Iris pointed at me with a chocolate covered spoon. "You are making a mess."

Siri laughed. "A big one!"

"I have you two to blame. It doesn't take four people to bake a cake." I pulled myself to my feet and my hand plowed into a puff of flour from where the package had tumbled over. My fingers wrapped into the flour and without thinking I tossed a flour-cloud at Iris. "See if you like that. Messy is fun."

Iris screamed, "What? Look at me!" Her eyes jumped from her face with a sparkle, her brown skin covered in white.

Siri giggled and stomped her feet. "You look like a ghost."

Iris reacted with a flour-cloud of her own, tossing it at Siri. "Well, so do you."

*Ha-ha! Ha-ha!*

The laugher and chaos and disaster became one of cake batter flying and flour sifting, along with a chocolate coating on most everything in the room. A mist of dusty four floated above our heads, and Kissabelle moved to corral us. "Girls! Girls! Stop this." Her foot slipped on the floor and she nearly did the splits.

*Ha-ha! Ha-ha!*

We all roared at the near dislocation of Kissabelle's hips, and she acted like nothing happened out of her normal stance. She gathered herself, slipping and sliding and muttering.

I blurted, "Are you hurt?"

Kissabelle barked, "Why would I be hurt? I'm as limber as a rubber band."

*Ha-ha! Ha-ha!*

Willie joined in with the laughter, his small hands holding his chest with each giggle. I exploded with more laughter at the twin white ghosts, who giggled like they'd not had this much fun since forever.

I pointed at the twins. "Oh, my goodness. Your mama is gonna get you both."

Siri spoke up, "Not just us. You made this mess, too."

I put my hands on my hips. "Willie, who made this mess? Was it you?"

Laughing, he spouted off, "Not me. It was you! You did this!"

I pointed at the twin in spotted white PF Flyers. "No! Iris did it! She's the one! Her shoes have cake batter on them now. It's her fault!"

With that Iris reached for the goo in the frosting bowl using her hand, slinging it at my face. "There!" *Ska...plat!* Iris laughed with a burst, hollering, "Oh my! Look, you is one of us now. You are brown!"

I wiped the chocolate from my eyes, and the tossing and splattering and swooshing and flour mixed with all the gooey batter, and I stood in a mess. Even Willie had cake batter on top of his head.

*Creak! Creak!*

Silence fell. We froze when the plump and firm Ms. Reverend moved into our chaos. Iris held a spoon. I held a bowl. Kissabelle stood with a handful of flour. And Willie licked batter from his arms. Siri whimpered as she gazed into the face of her mama. "We … we are sorry."

With that Kissabelle's feet left her and she slipped beneath the other end of the table, but not before the soaring of the flour-puff mixed with frosting soared like a bullet across the table. The goo flew between the twins and Willie, flying past my head and *poof-platted* into the face of Ms. Reverend.

The hollering of laughter seeped into my throat, but I was afraid of the wrath of Ms. Reverend. Her hands went to her face, and she wiped the goo off, leaving streaks of cake batter on her cheeks. "Now, who is next?" She tossed the batter like a baseball and the chaos and laughter erupted until we spent all of our giggles. Until every single drop of cake batter landed on us, the floor and the table, and even the walls.

Ms. Reverend wiggled on the floor, holding an empty cake pan and put it on her head like a hat, giggling like a child. Mr. Reverend interrupted our birthday party. "My word. What is happening in here? I had no idea baking a cake was this hard."

Ms. Reverend took a piece of batter from the table leg, and slung the blob at her husband. "Here's your piece."

We roared with a final burst of laughter. *Ha-ha! Ha-ha!*

Ms. Jolene showed herself, her glare frozen, and her mouth open. "I can't believe this! I just can't!"

Ms. Reverend called from the floor. "What do you mean?"

Ms. Jolene pointed. "This is the first time I've ever heard Willie laugh."

That's when I lost it, and ran to him. "I love you, my little Willie. I love you." I kissed his ear with at least ten smacks.

Willie pushed me off. "No kissing. No hugging."

"Sorry, it just happened."

178

Willie laughed. "It's not so bad. You smell like chocolate. And I like chocolate."

Mr. Reverend ordered us to cease. "We need to meet and talk and discuss the things we have to do. Children, help your mother with this mess. We have much to do. And not much time to do it."

Leroy stood behind Mr. Reverend. "My kitchen never looked like this."

And we all burst into another round of laughter, but then the officer who I thought had left, came rushing inside the kitchen, sliding on batter. "We have company. We need to hide you all. Not the Roberts family. Just Jolene and Willie, and Shoelace. And Leroy And Que."

I glanced around. "Where is Que?"

## Hide the Truth No More

Mr. Reverend ushered the officer to the front room, their steps erratic and too fast. "Let me see you off. Act as if you're on your way and wave like the summer sun is warm and you're without a care."

"You know I'm not one of his cronies. There are good officers in Memphis. Not all are being bought out."

"I know this to be true, or you wouldn't have come this morning." The reverend patted the officer on the back. "Boss Crump is making his monthly visit to me. His curiosity is leading him to an early death. He already has his monument set at Elmwood Cemetery. His secrets and crimes are known by many, and with my speaking of his connection to Georgia Tann in the pulpit, he wants to check my pulse. To see if he can control me. I can handle him."

I peered at the reverend whose strength consumed the room, not because of his size. He was a regular man, but he was calm like a sleeping cat, but fierce like a lion. His hands were like claws ready to fight for good. His heart like Jesus. The inside of this man drew me in, his gentleness, his confidence, and his faith—an invitation to stand firm. He reminded me of Mr. Boyd and how he takes care of his family. Or will when he gets out of the hospital.

Mr. Reverend shut the door and hurried to the rest of us. "Everyone. Down the old cellar." He pointed to Ms. Reverend. "Not you, my dear. And girls, get to your chores. Go on now."

The twins rushed through the screen door, jumping without a word, obeying as if they knew serious grownup talk was not for them. Ms. Reverend pointed to a rug. "Shoelace, lift that up. Then open the cellar door. There's a switch on the side next to the first few steps leading below the house. Go on now."

"Cellar door?"

"Yes, it once hid slaves back in the day when they'd take the train out of Memphis. It's our cellar now." I reached for the latch after tossing the rug. The dust danced in the beam of light shooting through the window pane. "Are there snakes in there?" I went down a few steps and glared into the small room, a darkness of dark, fumbling for the light switch.

Ms. Reverend hushed me. "Snakes? Only snake I know is Boss Crump. And he's coming into my house to hiss and wiggle, to strike and blow. To leave his poison."

"Yes, ma'am." I moved to the side as Jolene helped Willie down the steps, to the damp room with walls full of jellies and burlap sacks. Leroy followed, glancing over his shoulder. "Que best be hiding. I'm sure he's fine. He's good at disappearing."

I filed in with the others and I sat on the steps, remaining high enough for my head to pop above the floor. Ms. Reverend waved her hand. "I have to shut this door and put the rug over the entrance. Crump doesn't need to know that any of you are here. He's bound to be bringing some rattlesnakes with him."

I slithered down a step, and the dust tickled my throat. "Can we breathe down here? I might suffocate."

She peeked at me around the lid. "You can get air through the vents. They lead right into the front room and there's a small window between the jars. You can crack it open if you feel like the walls are closing in on you."

Willie whined, "What are we doing? Am I gonna stop breathing?"

Ms. Jolene held Willie close. "We're playing hide and go seek again. You know that's my favorite game."

Willie's lip quivered, "So are we still looking for Lottie? We forgot to find her yesterday."

Trying to remember if I'd heard anyone say Lottie's name around Willie or that she'd died, I wrapped my arms around my brother. "I'll play with you. One, two, three, you're it."

Willie cackled, "You don't decide who's it. I do. I'm the one who can't see. So I'm in charge. Ms. Jolene always lets me pick."

Ms. Jolene slapped her knee. "I love it. Willie's found his laugh."

I nodded, stroking Willie's cheek. "Sorry. Go ahead." I sucked in the joy and courage found in a five-year-old, and knew my daddy's strong will was alive in my brother.

"I've decided. I'm it. Let me hide my eyes." Willie turned his back to me as though he could see, as though he really was letting me hide.

I darted behind a bin with a sack of potatoes on top, and ducked low, hiding my face, wondering if snakes were ready to strike my ankles. Wondering if spiders were crawling above my head. Wondering if Willie would ever love me like a sister.

*Boom! Boom!*

Leroy yanked on my arm, pulling me to my feet. "Quiet, everybody quiet. Boss Crump is in the parlor."

Staring at the vent where little specs of light cut the shadows, Leroy, Jolene and I kept our eyes upward, frozen. Willie held my hand after fumbling down my arm, grabbing my fingers. I squeezed his hand. "We're safe. We're safe. We're hiding from the bad man."

*Kaboom. Kaboom.*

The shuffling of shoes, and the slamming of the door echoed like someone shouted into a canyon, the noise so loud we all stepped back a foot. I turned to Jolene. "Is Mr. Reverend going to be hurt?"

Leroy pounded his fist. "Not if I can help it."

Jolene pulled on his sleeve. "Stay here. He'll shoot you. He's not scared of you."

Leroy squawked, "He don't shoot nobody. He has his spotters do his dirty work."

"True. And I'm sure he didn't come alone."

Up through the vent, Ms. Reverend's voice rose with offerings of tea. "I have sweet tea. It's my special sun tea, Mr. Crump. Can I get you a glass?"

"Yes, ma'am. With lemon, too."

"Yes, sir. Lemons to go with your sour face."

"What? What did you say?"

"I only said that the lemons this year will pucker your face. They're good though. Fresh and sour. They make your tea taste like brewed summer."

A deep voice cut through the fresh and sour words. "Boss Crump. Now what brings you out here on this Saturday? You should be counting your money."

"I'm here to bring you these season passes for the upcoming football games at my stadium. You might want them. Special seats at the fifty-yard line just for you and your deacons."

"Sir, no offense. But no coloreds can sit there. We have an end zone just for us. I'm not sure I'm ready to be the first colored to sit in the E H Crump Stadium just to cause a riot. It seems the risk might be too high."

"Reverend Roberts, the tide's a changing. We just hired nine Negroes on the police force. They are doing a great job, too."

"Thank you, sir. But, no thank you."

"It's in your best interest to consider my gift. We need to work on the same side. We both live in Memphis."

"You may not be the mayor now, but we both know you run Memphis, and that you appoint the incoming mayors. That you help Georgia Tann. That she has control of the Children's Home, and Judge Kelley has control of the courts."

"I support them because they love our little ones. They give babies good homes and save lives."

The growl of the men grew louder as each spoke, and Mr. Reverend shouted, "These are deadly women. Deadly! And I aim to put a stop to it."

"What are you talking about? Eleanor Roosevelt takes advice from Ms. Tann. Everyone respects her."

"Well, I have proof. Proof that will take her down. Do you hear me?"

"Now, it appears you're making statements you won't be able to back up. The Crystal Palace burned last night. I expect the documents you had disappeared in the ashes and flames. They went up in smoke."

"And it appears you don't know what you're talking about. We have all we need. More than a year's worth of forged birth certificates and paper work that Ms. Lottie gathered for us."

"Well, she won't be telling you anything now, will she?"

"Her voice lives. You'll see."

*Kaboom. Kaboom.*

"What's that you have there?" Boss Crump asked someone something but he wasn't talking to the reverend.

"I caught this one roaming through the field. He was carrying this typewriter."

"Que, what have you got there? And how's your job going at the orphanage? Are they treating you right, boy?" Crump's questions poured out like someone was striking the keys on the typewriter.

"My job's good. I'm helping the reverend this weekend."

"Que's a good worker. He was helping me give that typewriter away, to our neighbor. She is learning to type and that old thing could use some use. I was giving her ours." Ms. Reverend calmed the dust and the snake with her voice.

"I expect this isn't a typewriter that's been sitting around. I have a feeling it's the one missing from Ms. Lottie's apartment. And if so, you must have her documents. That's Ms. Lottie's typewriter, isn't it?" Crump's voice turned into a lion's roar. "Where are the papers? Get them and get them now."

"No … I'll never give them to you." Que yelled with a fierceness that sounded more like a lion cub.

"Fine! We'll take you with us, and we'll see what you have to say about riding down to the river for a swim." Crump announced, and the shuffling on the floor sounded like sand scooting across the floor.

"No! Wait! Don't take Que!" Ms. Reverend screamed, which sent me to quivering like it was cold, but the temperature was hot. And I screamed in my throat, shaking and crying.

Leroy barreled up the stairs, pushing the wooden entrance open, the lid booming to the floor. I followed like a jack rabbit, stomping into the kitchen. He shoved me back, and shot to the pantry as Ms. Reverend came into the kitchen. "Nothing wrong in here. My canister fell from the shelf. I'll get this cleaned up." She shouted over her shoulder, reached inside the pantry beside me and held two long guns.

Leroy backed up, guarding me with his arm, and we went down the cellar steps. I was afraid to breathe, afraid to move. Afraid that hide and go seek was not a game after all.

"Honey! Take this!" Ms. Reverend hollered in the front room.

*Click-clack. Click-clack.*

"Now! Now! No need for you both to point your shotguns at me and my man. I'll let the boy alone. We can talk about this without shedding innocent blood. I'll be off to mind my business. You best tend to yours. Are you sure you don't want the football tickets?" Crump offered his goodbye with a token of nothing.

"Get off my property. Get off. Ya hear!" Ms. Reverend shouted, "I can shoot with the best of them. And I don't miss."

"That's right. She's able to take out a snake from the front porch. A snake slithering in the corn field that gets his head snapped right off!" Mr. Reverend added his comforting words, "And I'm not bad with my gun, either!"

## When Prayers Go to Heaven

Swinging my feet from the end of the tailgate on the rusty brown and blue speckled truck, I smacked on the birthday cake Ms. Reverend baked for Charley. I announced, "This is the best cake ever."

Iris bumped me with her shoulder from my left, her feet swinging in rhythm with mine. "I have the most fun with you here. Can you stay?"

"No, I'm going home soon. Like tomorrow, maybe. I have my brother. I need to get back to Ms. Susan and my Lizzy Beth."

"How old is Lizzy Beth?"

"She's going to be five. Smart as any eight-year-old though. She can do big school math. And can do some words in cursive."

Siri rocked on my right, her bare feet dangling, touching the top of spindly weeds that popped up after we drove out to the pond behind the barn. "I'm smart, too. But I'd rather fish and eat. I do love frosting. We don't get cake much. We do eat good vegetables from Mama's garden though."

Across from the truck, to the side, Que and his pa were stretched out under a tree, napping. Mr. Reverend and Shotgun Mama were sitting on the quilt with Willie keeping watch over the fried chicken and the nasty ole livers. Jolene sat back on her arms like she might topple over from being so relaxed, and Willie gobbled up another liver when Ms. Reverend handed him one. He acted like he was eating cookies.

"Yum! I love me some wivers…"

Ms. Reverend responded, "They're livers. And I do have to say, I can't swallow one without gagging."

Willie chomped on the liver as if he was teasing her, his lips stuck in the air, his smacking wide open.

Jolene corrected him, "Willie, now I know you have some manners."

"Yes, ma'am." He grinned, pushing the bandage on his head into place after it slipped down over his ear.

I so enjoyed the picnic, and the surroundings were perfect. A pond. An old truck. New friends. Birds chirping. Tree branches swaying. A reverend who loved God at his home, not just at church. He loved like God on *off* days too. But the cloud of Boss Crump crept in like the lowering of the sun behind the trees. He was bound to come back or doing something bad to hurt someone.

However, Ms. Reverend figured a trip to the pond, to move away from worrying might help our spirits, and it did. She offered us the picnic in trade for cleaning up her kitchen too—and yet, worry hovered like a mist of poison.

My mood was better though, because for a few hours now, I've lingered and pretended I live with Mr. Reverend and Ms. Reverend. That they are my family until I go home to Jefferson. I've stopped running, and haven't cried once this afternoon. But I can't stop staring at Willie. I have my *real* brother. My very own brother and my very own sister and my very own family to go home to in Texas.

*Boom. Boom. Boom.*

I pounced to my feet in the bed of the truck, yelling at Kissabelle. "Stop hitting the fender with your hands. You just woke up Leroy and Que."

She smiled. "And scared the dickens out of you! Come on. Let's go swimming."

188

I scowled, "I can't swim. I don't even like to take a bath. Besides, snakes slither in ponds. And fish bite."

The twins bounced on their toes in their matching pink shorts and sleeveless tops, jumping next to me. They screamed, "We'll go. We can swim. We love to swim."

The three of them hurried to the pond, and the girls dove right into the green murky water in their good clothes. Kissabelle also waded into the shallow end, tripping, landing on her tummy, splashing like a kid. She didn't care that she was wearing a cotton dress. Until she got wet, she looked nice in a dress. The laughter and the splashing sent a flock of birds from the trees, and I moved toward Que who was leaning up on the trunk of a tree. Leroy now sat with the Roberts eating his third piece of cake.

Crouching down, I whispered to Que who reminded me of Crush. "I need to go see Archie. I haven't seen him since he tumbled to the bricks in front of the church. I can't believe Mr. Boyd's not dead. I've been horrible to him this past year. I've gotten away with things he never caught me doing, in trouble for some I did do, and lied about a few I thought about doing."

Chewing on a piece of grass, he muttered, "You're a bother to most folks, aren't you?"

I plopped down, crossing my legs. "I've gotten mixed up on how to treat people. I think too much, and speak all my thoughts out loud. That can get you in big trouble. Tin Can Mahlee taught me to read, but some of her bad habits became my habits. I'm working on stopping some of them. But they leak out just the same."

Que swiped at a fly. "Who is Tin Can Mahlee?"

"Hey, you're the one who said you were following me. You probably already know who she is."

"No, not really. Tell me."

"She's …" I glanced over to the chicken and cake eaters, to Willie who giggled at everything and nothing. "She was Willie's birth mama. And Lizzy Beth's birth mama. And my daddy was … was their daddy like he was mine. My real mama died when I was born."

"So, Georgia Tann stole them from Tin Can Mahlee, huh?"

"Yes, but Tin Can Mahlee died last year." Coughing, I choked on my sorrow. "… in an accident. And she only knew about Lizzy Beth, not Willie. She never really knew either one of them."

Que nodded. "Archie's the reason for the good we see happening."

"Good? It's scary here. I don't want to stay in Memphis. He'll die if he stays."

"Yes, we've been afraid. But we know what the right thing to do is—we must help the other babies and children caught in the lies behind those doors at the Children's Home."

"But you work there? So, you knew they stole babies?"

Standing to his feet, peering down at me, he kicked the grass with his shoe. "What? I cleaned the floors, and did windows, and trash. How was I to know? But when I did find out, it was because of Lottie. She was on to them in no time, once she went to work there. She saw beatings, and crying, and children in closets. She heard stories of babies dying, and babies being stolen from their mothers. She's the reason we know what we know."

"But she's gone."

Wiping tears falling from his eyes, Que bent down and got right in my face. "She's in heaven. And God must have said well done to her. I want Him to say that to me. I will do what I can for God. He's the reason for life and we can change the lives of some of the children, even if many are gone or worse, dead. Georgia Tann must be stopped."

"I'm sorry. I didn't mean to get you all mad. I don't like her, either. She did take my sister and brother. She stole them from Tin Can Mahlee. And she stole them from me."

Mouthing with a whip of words that snuck out, Que piped in with, "But I heard she didn't want *you*."

Popping to my feet, yanking on his arm. "What are you talking about? I wasn't born here! I was born in Texarkana, and lived with my grandma until I was five. Five! Do you hear me? My daddy rode the rail, and came for me then. That's how we came to Memphis and rode up north and down south. We stayed here some. But Georgia Tann never tried to sell me."

"Sorry, I got caught in another memory, mixed it up with another story. There's so many of them. So many kids." Que turned his back to me as if he might slip with something he was hiding from me, but I had no idea what he knew that he wasn't saying.

I tugged on his arm. "Will you help me go see Archie tonight? And Mr. Boyd and Mr. Marion?"

"Talk to my pa. We usually go see my little brother at the hospital and maybe he'll go tonight. Maybe he'll make a stop there, too."

Bouncing like a ball, I let my words fall. "Do you think so? Do you really think we can?" I stopped jumping. "But wait, those spotter men will be watching. What if they see us?"

"They won't see us. Pa knows the roads no one takes. He can do it. If we can talk him into going into town with all that's happened."

Running over to Leroy, I cupped my hands over his ears. "Are you going to see your boy tonight?"

He licked the crumbs from his plate. "This cake is your best, Ms. Roberts. You've outdone yourself."

Ms. Reverend smiled, hugging Jolene from the side. "It's a grand day to be alive. A grand day to do God's will. A grand day to see the beauty in the day."

I almost forgot that I'd asked Leroy about going to town, when he jerked with a hug and kiss on my cheek. "I'm headed to see Bubba in an hour. You and Que can come with me. I need to see the beauty of my boy tonight. I need to see the grandest part of what keeps me going besides my Que. I need to go and kiss him, no matter what life brings. I always go on Saturday night, and I won't let Boss Crump keep me away."

Hugging Leroy, I thanked him. "If I could have asked for a pa, you would be the type of daddy I would have asked God for, and yet, God gave me Mr. Boyd and he's a lot like you. Strong. Has faith. And he loves his family."

Mr. Reverend added his thoughts. "We have this race to run for God. We don't want to get to the end and not be finished. How we run now, will determine how we stand before God." He rose to his feet and came over to me, holding both my hands. "May you stand tall and win your race. And if you fall, fall into God's hands."

I wept at his words, the hope I needed seemed to fall in his prayer over me at a picnic I didn't plan, at a farm I don't know how to get to, at a pond with my brother.

Ms. Reverend joined her husband, and touched my shoulder. "I don't know what tomorrow holds, but remember you can change the world by praying to God, by sending your words to heaven."

That moment etched itself into my heart, until ... Jolene screamed. "Snakes! We have snakes!"

"Girls! Out of the water! Now!" Ms. Reverend charged to the pickup, snatching open the passenger door, and swooped to the pond carrying her shotgun. "Where? Where are they?" She aimed the gun at the water. "I don't see no snakes. Where'd they go?"

Jolene hurried to her side, along with the rest of us while the twins screamed, running to the bed of the truck.

Mr. Reverend took the gun from Shotgun Mama. "All of you get away from the edge. Too many weeds here."

I hollered, "Look! It's Kissabelle, she's floating on her back out there in the middle. She doesn't know about the snakes."

Jolene pushed me aside. "No! No! The snakes I'm talking about are those two men at the tree line. They're watching us. Crump must have sent them."

Mr. Reverend pointed the barrel at the trees, glanced to the sky whispering as if talking to someone. Then he called to the man-snakes. "If you want to live, I suggest you leave my property. And get on your way."

With that Kissabelle's feet went to kicking, and she glanced our way, arms waving. "No need for a gun. I'm just swimming and singing. Can't a person sing when she wants?"

I listened to her babbling, and the snakes hovering by the trees disappeared without answering. Mr. Reverend, without a word, without a song, without shooting, without responding in violence; he must have prayed them away—for now.

*Pam Kumpe*

## Emergency Room Prayers

Scrunched between Leroy and Que, I wiggled like my feelings might explode on the windshield like a million mosquitoes. "I can't believe we're going back into Memphis. And I'll see my daddy, Boyd, and Archie, and Marion Kane."

Que pushed me against the seat, as the pickup bounced down the road, turning toward the tracks. "Be still, you're like a wiggle worm."

Leroy corrected Que, "Leave her be. If Bubba were awake, we'd be the same way." He clasped the steering wheel of Mr. Reverend's truck. "We'll be there in about thirty minutes. The way I need to cut through will take us up some back roads."

I sat up tall. The haze of sunlight cut through the trees, leaving streaks of a perfect day dancing in my mind and in the road. And there's even more good stuff to come. Kicking my feet, I shouted, "I can't believe I have a brother, and a sister, and a ma and pa who want me. If my daddy hadn't kidnapped me, I wouldn't be right here, right now, right in this truck. I wouldn't have ever met Archie at Wheelock Academy."

Leroy smiled at me. "God has a way of making good from bad, of using the wrong step to bring Him glory.

Que nodded, "I can't say I understand how God does what He does, but I know your being here is something I'll never forget. You have caused action to happen, not just wishing for action."

"Action?" I wrinkled my nose.

Leroy patted my knee. "Sure. You roll in like a steam engine. You go for what you want. You're the fire behind the

194

warm hope we now have for the other children. Willie will go
home with you. He'll be safe. And if we can save some of the
others ..." He sighed. "I only pray for my boy to wake up.
He's needing some special care. Some doctors who can help
him. If he could get that, I know there's a doctor who could
save him."

I wept as his words tumbled from the broken place inside
his heart, a spot I too hold for those sad times when nothing
makes sense. "I'm sorry about ... what's his name? I've just
heard you call him Bubba."

Que answered, "My brother's name is ..." His hands went
to his face, clearing streaks of tears from his cheeks. "I try not
to think of how sad I am, how sad it must have been for my
brother to see our mama get gunned down. Those spotters
weren't after them. Mama was watching one of the Planters
Peanut kids. His pa owns the peanut shop in town. And Ms.
Darnell was off to the store when ... when they took their little
baby boy right from the baby carriage."

"What? Did you say Darnell?"

"Yes, Mr. Daniel Darnell is the pa, and Ms. Rebecca is his
new wife. They had just had a baby girl."

Shocked, my mouth got stuck with letters collecting in the
spit inside my cheeks. "I know Mr. Daniel. He sold peanuts at
the circus in Texarkana for our county fair. My friend Taddy
is allergic to peanuts and nearly died on them. But Mr. Daniel
stayed at my grandma's manor. He is the nicest peanut man." I
coughed, "And he's married? He lives here?"

Leroy took over, "Yes, his shop is downtown on Main.
He's working there every day, but his wife hasn't returned.
She's at home mourning the goodbye of their first child."

I kicked the dashboard. "That's horrible! That Ms. Georgia
Tann needs to stop!" I glanced to the roof in the cab of the
truck, choking on the dust coming inside from the opened

windows. "God, help us! Help us do something that will change the entire world!"

Que shook and his chest heaved out a cry. "I pray that all the time! I pray to change the world for good and for God. I want to make something of my life. I want to see ... my brother become all God wants him to become."

I sobbed, and Que wrapped his arm around my shoulder. I looked up and into his face, seeing the freckles on his brown skin. "You didn't tell me your brother's name."

Que whispered between tears. "His name is Riley. Pa named him after Riley King who plays on Beale Street. Says Mr. King's going to go down in history for his Blues."

As Leroy tapped the steering wheel to the sound of his humming, the tone of the ride in the pickup changed from sorrowful to hopeful. "You should hear that young man's vibrato. He can stroke that guitar, too. I met him when he used to practice on Beale Street with the teens who wanted to follow in the steps of those before them. He's got a natural talent. You'll see. Everyone will know him."

I rocked with his cadence. "What song were you humming?"

"It's called *Three O'clock Blues*. He's been writing the lyrics for it, and comes by the restaurant to bounce the words off me. Who knows, maybe it'll become a hit."

I sat back, listening to the hum ripple from Leroy's lips, and Que put his hand out the window. "It's cooler tonight. We'll be at the hospital in a few."

For the next few minutes we rumbled along the pebble road, and made twists to the right, dashes through the alleys, and even backtracked to go another way. Leroy announced, "We're here. We'll see your folks first. Then we'll go see Riley at ... at the colored hospital."

I scooted toward Que. "Hurry up. Get out. Come on. Let's go."

"Let my pa stop the truck first, he's still rolling."

Leroy turned the engine off. "I've gotten the room numbers from Mr. Reverend. He called earlier to find out which floor they're on, too. Que, you go with Shoelace, and keep her close to ya. I'm going to stay outside and keep watch for anything … like snakes and such."

Que and me headed to the double doors of the hospital when sirens blasted. *Bweeooo. Bweeooo.*

"Look, there's an ambulance. We better hurry or they'll get in our way with that stretcher." The doors to back of the ambulance flew open, and the legs to the stretcher were let down, and the two men rolled the person right past us like we were invisible, like we didn't matter.

I mouthed, "Excuse me for getting in your way." I stormed up to the man pushing the stretcher. "You could have let me get out of the way. You didn't have to bump me."

I choked on my words, and the man never looked at me or spoke—and I found myself looking at the face of the old lady from the Peabody Hotel. Not the lady who does court stuff, but Ms. Georgia Tann. And she was not awake! Her skin was gray and her lips blue! I yelled, hovering beside the stretcher. "Could the baby stealer really be dead?"

## Snakes in the Hospital

"Stop pulling on my overalls," I yelled at Que, who yanked on me in return, who sent me sliding across the tile floor of the hospital hallway.

He shoved me against the wall and leaned in close to my ear. "You can't act like this in here. I'm with you. That brings enough attention already, and now you're screaming about a baby stealer? You need to learn some self-control."

I pursed my lips. "I didn't mean to, but I exploded like fireworks when I saw Georgia Tann." I peered over his shoulder. "Do you think she's dead?"

Que let me sneak around him, but he kept near, and I inched along the long hallway. He quizzed me, "Where are you going?"

"I want to see what's wrong with her. They took her to those rooms through those doors, somewhere."

Stepping in front of me, blocking my way, Que put his arm out. "Stop. We're here to see your three friends."

"My friends? They're more than friends. One is my new daddy. The other is like my grandpa. And Archie, he's like an angel with handkerchiefs."

"Then let's go the other way. Their rooms are upstairs. On the second floor. Come on." He motioned for me to follow him, and a nurse slipped into the hallway from a room.

She tapped her way along the tile, twirling back toward us. "Are you two lost?"

Que nodded. "I'm not. But she was turned around. I was helping the girl," he stuttered. "I'm helping her find her way to the stairs."

The nurse scowled, "Good, we don't need any trouble."

Mouthing to the backside of her all-white uniform, since she spun off down the hall, I let her have it. "Who does she think she is? Trouble? We're just visiting. Visiting isn't a crime."

Que tapped me on the shoulder. "It's me. She figured a colored boy meant trouble. I'll go wait with my pa outside. You go see your all your folks, and then we'll be on our way to see my brother."

I danced in a circle around Que. "Trouble? You bring trouble? I'm usually the one who gets blamed for trouble."

"Go get your visiting done. I'll be out front."

"Sure. I'll go find them."

I rushed around the corner to the next hallway, peering back around the corner until Que disappeared from my sight. "Good, I'm glad he's gone. I'm gonna find that Georgia Tann before I go upstairs." Moving to the front area, where chairs sat back to back and people gathered, crying, I realized the emergency room area was beyond the waiting room spot.

"Excuse me. Excuse me." A call from a nurse coming right at me sent me to a chair where I plopped down. She raced to the sobbing woman whose head was buried in her face. "Ma'am, come with me. Your husband is awake. They say he'll pull through."

"Are you sure? I saw him crushed under that tree. It fell over him."

"The doctor said he'll be sore and bruised, but no broken bones."

The lady collapsed, embracing the nurse. "Thank you! I thought I'd lost him."

"He's calling for you. Come now. Let's go see him."

They slipped down the hallway through two swinging doors, and I shadowed them like I belonged, like a visitor who searched for her sick relative.

The nurse and the woman darted into the room on the right, while I hopped into the room to my left. A man with no hair snored as if his mustache tickled his nose, and his leg extended upward with a cast, held in place by ropes. I whispered, "Sorry, wrong room."

Back in the hallway, I wiggled to the next room, pushing the door. "Nope, she's not in here. That bed's empty."

I barreled to the next three rooms, two were empty, and one held a woman who cried as she called to someone. "I need more pain medicine. My head is killing me. I hate migraines."

I boogied it from that room, and tore down the hallway, running from room to room, until I came to the last door. Pushing it forward, I ran inside, and found myself standing next to the woman who could have been a grandma, who looked not so mean, who had no idea I was staring at her.

But there she was … there was Georgia Tann, covered in a sheet, her head on a pillow, and her face shone with regular pink color.

Quivering in my PF Flyers, I marched closer to the bed. "Are you sick? What happened to you?" My whispering questions went unanswered, but I asked more. "What made you mean? Why hurt the babies? Why do you steal them? Just to make money?"

She took a deep breath, and a whizzing sound from her nostrils sent an eerie whistle to my heart. I put my hand on her arm, her skin soft, normal, like a real person. "You feel alive. How can you be as horrible as they say?"

Then a touch on my shoulder caused me to whimper, "What? Who's there?"

From the shadow at the end of the bed, the two men in suits stepped into the light, not smiling, not frowning, just watching me. The man closest to me, placed both of his hands on my shoulders, twisting me toward him. "What are you doing in here? How in the world did you get here from…?"

I interrupted him, lying, "I just … just want to pray for her."

The suit spoke, letting go of me. "You want to pray for Ms. Tann?"

"Sure, she can use a prayer." I folded my hands as if to begin. "I could pray for you, too."

The man with the wisp of curls over his ears shook his head. "It's not likely you'll change her heart. She's a tough cookie. Well respected, but firm. Strong willed, and determined. She may be fighting cancer, but now she's refused treatment. She'll go home to suffer with her disease. And her sins."

I argued, "I'm not the one to change anybody's heart. Jesus does heart stuff." I found myself thinking how this bad woman did need prayer. "I need to pray for her." I discovered the teachings for Pastor Cody rising in me, and that of Toby, the wanna-be kid preacher back in Jefferson. "No, really. I need to pray for her. It may be the only thing I can do, which might change everything."

"You can pray, but you'll need to leave her alone. If she wakes up, and you're here, it won't be the answer to your prayer." The suit on the other side, went on to explain. "She's set her mind on going home with her sickness. Tonight, she passed out, and that's the only reason she came into emergency. She didn't know she came. And now they've given her something to sleep. But she'll leave in the morning."

I placed both my hands on her heart. "Dear God, her heart beats with meanness, and she breathes out hate. I pray you do something to stop her from hurting the rest of the kids. And if you see fit, can you help us find Charley for Kissabelle, too?" I kept my eyes open to watch the two suits, but it's not like I ever close my eyes when I pray anyway.

The man to my right tapped my arm. "Are you finished?"

"Not yet. I have a little more to say." I moved my hands to fold them. "And God, if you have time, will You save this woman so she will go to heaven? Someone may have hurt her and then it got mixed up in her head. I know how that can happen. I also know You can fix her, if anyone can. Maybe she can still do something good with her life. Amen."

The curly haired man pointed to the door. "It's time for you to go. Scram."

I shuffled backwards, unsure why the two suits allowed me stay, or allowed me to pretend to be someone who might visit Georgia Tann, let alone pray for her, and then I saw a flash of something earlier in the day at the pond. The faces in the trees who watched us at our picnic flickered like a broken light giving way to a memory. "It's you. You were the men at the reverend's house today."

I backed into the wall, making eye contact with them, shaking, unable to even consider praying. I simply needed to run! I reached for the door, and the suit to my right blocked the door. "So, you recognize us, don't you?"

"Recognize you? I … I don't think I know you. I got you mixed up with someone at … at the restaurant."

"You saw us at Reverend Roberts' farm today, didn't you?"

"I can't remember. I think I'm in the wrong room. I think you might have me mixed up with another kid. I haven't been at Siri and Iris' house. I don't know anything about Boss Crump coming to the house and trying to steal Que. I don't know anything!" I charged from the room, racing down the hallway, screaming, "There's snakes in the hospital! We have snakes!"

The people in the end of the hall outside the swinging doors glared at me, standing and eyes searching. A woman yelled, "Snakes? Inside the hospital?"

A man called, "Someone lost a snake!"

Two ladies stood on a chair holding each other. "Snakes! There's snakes in the hospital."

Barreling through the chaos of dancing and running, and shouting and arms waving, I hollered, "The snakes are in that part of the hallway down there! Help them!"

I charged through the crowd of people running from the hospital to the front lawn, and I climbed the first flight of stairs to the second floor, sitting down at the top of the steps, breathing hard, wondering what to do, worrying who these men might bother.

The trash can to my left seemed like a good spot to toss my own trashy thoughts. "What do they want? I just want to go home to Texas. It's horrible here. They'll get to Archie, and Mr. Boyd and Marion Kane, if I don't tell someone."

I twirled around, spun the other way and fell, losing my balance, tumbling to the floor. I couldn't lead them to their rooms, I'll have to see them later. I had nowhere to go, except back down the way I'd come, so I jumped down the staircase and landed in front of ... the two suits. The one with curly hair pointed at me. "Go back up. To the top of the stairs. Go to the first room we see on the right."

His orders came at me like hissing, and I moved without a word, pushing the door open to the room by the water fountain.

Inside the room, I froze and the two men came closer, one of them switching the light on, and the one without curls held guard at the door. He kept his back to it, his hands inside his pockets, and the other suit marched up to me.

I backed up, hitting the empty bed with my legs. "I need to go. You don't want me. I can't hurt anyone."

"Stop and listen. Things are not as you think. I'm Blake. He's Blair. We're investigators. We're working undercover. You've got to stop interfering."

"What? Why would you tell me you're investigators? I'm a 'vestigator where I live. I know one when I see one, and you two are not investigators. You're snakes!"

"No listen! We were working with Lottie. Leroy and Que don't have any idea. We didn't know who to trust. She was helping us compile our evidence. She got too close, stirred up too much. Now Boss Crump's gone and had his men take care of her. We're working on the inside and we need you to control yourself. A little self-control will help us finish this, and I know you're just a little girl, but we're close to stopping the orphanage from these illegal adoptions. And you are causing too much noise."

Not sure I believed him, I shook my head and hopped on the bed, standing up in it. "How do I know you're telling me the truth. You're snakes. If you were at the reverend's house, then you're after us."

"No, we're watching you. To keep you safe."

"Safe? That's why my Archie, and my daddy, and Mr. Marion got shot, because you're watching out for us? You can't watch me or them any better than Que did."

"We didn't know they were after you Friday night. We can't be everywhere, and that hit came after Archie had words with Georgia and Judge Kelley at the hotel. He got them rattled."

"I don't believe you. You have me cornered. So, I'm not on your side, or you wouldn't have me locked inside." I shook my fist. "I'm not afraid of you."

The man by the door moved toward me. "You need to be afraid for your family. Georgia Tann's ruthless. The people believe her lies. She's conned many of our leaders. You'll come up missing."

"Missing? I can't come up missing." My words dropped with fear, and my big-girl talk switched to blubbering. "I need my daddy. I need Ms. Susan. I need to go home."

The curly headed man reached for me as I crumpled to the mattress, and he patted my head. "We're leaving. We're going back to the first floor to be with Ms. Tann. To keep our cover intact. Now stay clear of her. Do you hear? And go home. This fire's too big for you."

\*\*

Sobbing, I wiped tears from my face, and sat up. Seconds later, I wiggled from the hospital bed, and peeked into the hallway. The trash can and water fountain sat in the same place, nothing broken, nothing was moved or destroyed. I inched to the stairs leading to my escape, and slipped into the hallway, glancing both ways.

I mouthed, "I'm not sure where Mr. Boyd's room or Archie's room is, or even where Marion Kane might be, but I need to get help. Or leave. Or something. I looked to the ceiling, wishing to see heaven, and asked, "God, what should I do?"

A voice called to me, "You should get yourself to the pickup truck! And now!" Leroy's harsh growl came with orders, "It seems someone caused a ruckus downstairs and they have cleared the entire first floor, the emergency room area, and the waiting room because a little girl screamed she saw a snake."

I puckered, sighing. "I had to scream. The men from the pond were with Georgia Tann, and I had to run to get away. I had to hide and they came for me. I was going to die! They held me in that room." I pointed to the door behind me.

Leroy shook his head. "I think you got distracted, got caught and created a scene."

"No, they came for me." I declared my stance.

"I brought you here because I trusted you. Your behavior isn't helping matters one bit." Leroy held my hand like I was a toddler. "You will not leave my sight again."

At the base of the stairs, I whined as we stepped into the hallway on the first floor. "But I haven't seen …"

"You'll see them in a few days when you all go home."

Que came running up to us, rushing inside after shoving the glass doors wide. "Pa, the pickup is on fire! Someone threw a torch inside the cab."

## Sight to See

I'm wiggling and itching to catch the train home, but for now, I'm sitting in this church, the one with the three red doors on a Sunday morning. And I'm stuck between Que and his pa at Beale Street Baptist Church, the one where Que might have rescued me from those bullets Friday night.

From beside the pulpit, Reverend Roberts keeps smiling at Siri and Iris who are in the front pew with their ma. And some lady in a blue jacket and skirt is making announcements about feeding the homeless on Sunday morning which seems like a nice thing to do, but the other committee stuff she's rattling on about is putting me to sleep.

Whispering to Leroy, I leaned over to him on my right. "We've been here forever and that lady is still telling everyone about the prayer walk coming up. When does church get started?"

Leroy patted my leg. "Hush now. We are to act honorable in church. We stay for a while. No hurry for us. We worship and praise God and love to be here."

Folding my hands, I huffed. "They need to let my Willie sing!" My voice rose higher than it should have like a piano key stuck on a shrill note.

Que shoved me. "Hush it up. Now everyone's looking back at us and not listening. You are more trouble than a real snake."

Blowing in his face, I used my lower than a whisper voice. "I'm not good at being in church. And having to wear this dress Ms. Reverend borrowed from her neighbor feels scratchy. And I don't like yellow."

Leroy tugged on my ear. "Hush … or I'll swat you like my own child."

"Yes, sir." I flared my nostrils wide open, on purpose, and puckered my lips with my nose, and kicked the pew in front of me. Mr. Reverend grinned at his girls again, who were now moving to the front of the church. I leaned over to Leroy. "What are they doing?"

"They're singing *Amazing Grace* before Willie sings his song. You would have heard the announcement if you'd stop that chattering."

"Fine. I'll be quiet."

Que nudged me again. "I doubt it."

Biting my lip, I struggled to sit down, or stay put. I simply wanted to hear Willie sing and leave town. He looked funny, wearing a choir robe like the grownups, especially since Ms. Jolene pinned it up a dozen ways to keep him from tripping over the red shiny fabric. He's the only kid in the choir loft too, and the robed singers are right in front of that big Jesus painting on the wall.

The light streaming through the rainbow windows on each side of the sanctuary, along with the ones upstairs on the open balcony, are shooting beams of color across the room.

Ms. Jolene is sitting next, Ms. Reverend on the front row, and Kissabelle has slid herself to the end of the pew. She's mad at Ms. Jolene for making her come to church since she's headed out of town, too. She says she's catching the next boxcar that runs by the old cemetery. Says she won't stay for Lottie's funeral on Monday. Says she can't bury another person. Says this is not home for her anymore. I know I can be pouty, but she's worse than me.

Sighing, I'm still fuming mad too, and Que's my target. He lied to Leroy and me at the hospital yesterday about the

208

truck being on fire. Que saw the two men from the pond, whom I talked to, and they were headed toward him. He got scared like a baby and ran for his pa. He made the whole story up. Stupid boy. Stupid scaredy-cat.

I shot a whisper at Que. "So, you don't get in trouble for lying to your pa?" I snapped with another question before he could answer. "And you aren't so brave like your pa, are you?"

"I never said I was brave." He coughed. "You know why I had to get you out of there. Everyone had gone crazy, and all the people running from inside thinking there were snakes loose in the halls. And then, those men came too close, and one of them nodded at me and smiled like he knew something I didn't know, and the other man tipped his chin to the side and winked."

"So, you're scared of a nod and a wink?"

"Stop it! If they were watching us at the farm then they'll tell Boss Crump we were at the hospital. This isn't a game, you know. People get shot. Some are dead. We've talked about this. You just don't get it."

"I get it. You're a chicken." I giggled under my breath.

"My ma … my ma used to sit right where you are. Do you hear me? You've got her seat. And now she's gone and this isn't over yet." His words scolded me like an iron set on high, and the crease in my heart felt scorched with the heat of his words.

Unfolding my arms, I tapped his leg and felt uneasy in my spot on the pew, the place where his ma used to sing and pray. "I'm sorry. I don't mean to be like I am, but I am like this a lot. Mr. Boyd says I'm a stack or two short on the kindness in my soul. And that I'm filled with lots of selfish layers. And that I speak my mind more than I should."

"I think I'd like Mr. Boyd."

*Pam Kumpe*

Nodding, my eyes went to the front where Siri and Iris, dressed in matching green and blue striped cotton dresses chimed in. "I once was blind, but now I see …"

I got lost in the lyrics and in the bloom and hollow sounds coming from the organ. The swaying of the suits and the dresses swishing, along with the clapping of the white gloves on the women's hands kept pace with the organ tune. The gloves made a silent clapping puff, but the men made up for the pops with their calloused hands and stomping feet.

Most of the grownups gave out long drawn out notes as everyone joined in with the twins. The echo of the choir singing along on the chorus, and the rest of the folks singing along too sent the music bouncing from the chandeliers to the pews and back to the choir loft.

The chorus ended and Ms. Jolene ushered Willie to the side of the podium where she handed him a microphone. His creased black slacks and white shirt had been pressed by Ms. Reverend before I got out of bed this morning. She prepared breakfast for everyone before sunrise, and ironed her girls' dresses and the ugly yellow dress I have on. She wanted Willie to look like a polished penny for church. I guess she wanted me to look like a yellow squash.

*Tada-tu-so. Tad-tu-so.*

The woman with wide shoulders struck the piano keys and Willie's voice poured through the speakers like melted butter on a hot biscuit, like honey dripping on the side of the plate ready to be sopped up. He sang, "Swing low, sweet chariot, coming for to carry me home." He pushed his bandage into place over his eyes with a nervous twitch and his one loafer tapped the floor. "But sometimes still my soul feels heavenly bound …"

210

Leaning over to Que, I bragged, "He's smart. He can remember all those verses."

"He's smarter than you know. He can memorize anything in a flat second. His ears capture so much. Lottie worked with him daily once she saw how quick he learned. She took to his sad spirit. Said he was a lost boy who never fit in. She said he had that Indian blood in him, which made him darker and that black hair wasn't something Georgia Tann could sell. She made more money with blonde-haired kids who had blue eyes. Or green. Only white kids, too. But ... she didn't like you so much ..." He covered his mouth with his hand.

\*\*

I glared at him as if time stopped, as if the world fell from the atmosphere, as if the black hole of lost memories might find their way out. "What? What do you mean she didn't like me? She doesn't even know me!"

"Nothing, I got mixed up."

"No, you didn't. You didn't get mixed up. How does Georgia Tann know me? What are you not saying?"

The clapping from the men and the swaying and standing of the people in the pews let our voices mix with theirs, and no one picked up on our arguing. Most everyone sang with Willie now—so my screaming at Que went unnoticed, and Leroy moved to the aisle to clap with some other men and Willie sang, "Swing low, sweet chariot."

Que turned to me. "Stop yelling at me. I didn't mean to tell you."

"Tell me what? What are you saying?"

"I'm trying to say the truth will set you free. You need to know this, so you can live whole. I didn't mean to tell you like this, but you make me so mad."

"Tell me what? Please, I need to know what you aren't saying."

"It happened back a few years ago, when your pa kidnapped you and brought you to Memphis. He was going to pay a debt with you."

"What? Pay a debt? He wouldn't do that!"

"You're right, not if he loved you."

"He did love me. He did." I slapped his shoulder.

"Well then … why would he bring you to Georgia Tann to get money for you?"

He stared at me with a glare of wanting me to answer, but I had nothing. "He didn't do that."

Que went on, "He did. He brought you to her, to pay off his debt to Boss Crump from a card game gone bad. He lost more than he had on him, and had nothing to sell. And he knew Ms. Tann sold the babies and kids, and he hoped you'd bring him some fast cash, so he could bail himself out."

"No way! My daddy stole me from my grandma when I was five. Five, do you hear me? He came for me in Texarkana to save me. He wanted me. He wanted a daughter. You're lying again. You're making this up."

"I'm not. Your pa brought you to the curb that day at the orphanage and Archie was driving Ms. Tann's car. Remember, he used to work for her. And he drove up with her, and your daddy tried to sell you right there in the driveway. And Archie saw the whole thing."

Standing on the pew, I shook both my fists at Que. "Stop it! Stop it! My daddy loved me! He never would kidnap me to make money! Or to get rid of me! He had just gotten me!"

Que rose to his feet, meeting me eye-to-eye and he was standing firm on the hardwood floor. "You need to see how serious this is, and how it's not like you aren't a part of it. God has brought you through all of this, so you can help us crack this case wide open. And now you'll have your family, too. Maybe you won't have the one you first had, but you'll be loved and have a brother and sister. And parents."

"But why tell me about my pa? Why?" I shivered with doubt, but the flashing of faces and boxcars and jumping and falling and hiding and going with my daddy sent me to the front of a house in Memphis—years ago. To a house that held secrets. A house that I never went into, but the whispers I heard that day were like dandelions blowing across the yard. They flew into lost graves of places forgotten. But I remembered hearing this from the lady. "She's scrawny. Too little. Not enough. No one will want her."

My tears let loose like a boxcar broken from the rest of the train, and I felt dizzy, like I would fall to my death from such horrible memories. Whenever I tell others about my kidnapping, I make it sound fun, like an adventure. I make it sound like a beautiful waterfall of ripples of joy. There were many good parts on the rail, but there were shallow spots where I went hungry and wept like a lost child. Some days were ugly with cold and bleak or hot and sweaty.

I remembered the bump and roar of boxcars and how afraid I was at five. I remembered crying for my grandma, and getting sadder than a girl should feel at not seeing her. My pa was sloppy at night when he drank, and I knew about the cards. I knew about his women, and I longed for his love, but got leftovers on days after his partying.

I came back to the moment of now, and couldn't breathe, and those memories fell to the basement of my life, flashing horror and sorrow, like a pickup truck burning, like flames of sadness that left ashes in my heart.

I collapsed to the floor, with more thoughts popping into my head. And I remembered … remembered standing there on the curb at a three-story house and seeing that lady … the one I prayed for yesterday. I yelled in a not-so-sweet chariot way. "I met her! I met Georgia Tann seven years ago! She's the same lady from the Peabody Hotel … and the same one who laughed and made fun of my freckles and my pigtails as I hid behind my daddy's pant leg in front of that house when I was five!"

The applause from the audience brought me to my feet, and I wobbled like I was drunk from too much whiskey. Like my skin crawled from sadness seeping from my pores. Like my freckles cried out with ugliness. Like my pigtails waved goodbye to the pa who never wanted me in the first place.

The squeaky sound of Willie screaming brought me back to the moment, but the memories lingered inside my head as I shook from the reality of what life gave me. I'd been given a pa who was more lost than I wanted to believe. I wiggled to see what Willie was doing, and realized I'd missed his song, or most of it. I stepped in front of Que, trying to see between the tall hats and shoulders in front of me, and I couldn't see my brother. "What's Willie saying? He's screeching, not singing."

Leroy moved back from the center aisle where he'd swayed and stomped and clapped. "Willie's taking his bandages from his eyes! He's saying, he can see light. That he sees something through the gauze."

"What? Willie can see?"

"I don't know. He's got such a crowd around him now. I can't see him or hear."

I ran through the bodies and made my way up to the front of the church close to the altar, pushing between legs and skirts. I stuck my head between two round hips, and moved a girl out of my way. "Willie? What is it?"

Ms. Jolene held him close to her side, and she knelt next to him, smiling and crying. "Oh, my goodness! This is amazing!" She held the bandages from his head. "It's his eyes! It's a miracle! He can see!"

Everyone started yelling, "Praise God! Thank you, Jesus!"

I charged up to Willie. He kept blinking, and the reverend handed Willie a handkerchief. "Wipe your eyes, son. Tell us what you see!"

"Yes, sir. I will …" He blinked his eyes, and lifted his chin, gazing right into my blue eyes with his chocolate velvety gaze. He touched my face. "Shoelace, I can see you! You're the bestest and prettiest sister. You have spots on your face."

"I do have spots. They're called freckles." I wiped them as if I could wipe away ugly things.

"They make you prettier than …" He looked around at the faces smiling and the people crying. "They make you special like strawberries."

"Do you like strawberries?" I touched his arm.

"I love them. And I love you!"

Grabbing him, I loved on my brother. "I can't believe you can see."

He whispered, "I knew I'd see again, when I had a reason to see."

Weeping, I wrapped myself up in this new great memory and did my best to shake off the ones from my pa. But they lingered like freckles, like spots in my life.

Que reached for me, turning me toward him. "I want you to see how special you are to God. He brought you to Memphis, to bring you back to Memphis. You have come full circle to get your sister and brother back. Since Archie discovered you in Oklahoma when he followed Lizzy Beth, it was a gift to him—to help you find our way home."

I nodded, not sure I could understand all of it so quickly, but somehow part of it made sense. I had my brother. And it was amazing grace and he could now see!

A growl from the back of the church building hollered at everyone. "I want the boy. Give him to me." The man in the suit holding a long gun pointed the barrel at us. "Where's the boy? Give him to me! We're making a trade. You give Boss Crump the papers on the orphanage and return all your research. And we'll give him back!"

The man reached for Willie, yanking on his arm, and he screamed like a broken key on the piano. "No! Don't take me!"

Que ran for Willie, and the man walloped him with the gun. "Get out of the way."

From the floor, Que argued, "He can't leave! The Lord has given him sight!"

With that, the man pointed the barrel of the gun at Que, and the *kaboom-pfft* sent everyone diving behind pews and to the floor. From across the back at the other door, another suit shouted, "Everyone stay inside. No one else needs to get shot!" The two men darted to the side stairs, with Willie screaming, "Shoelace! Come get me!"

I lost my heartbeat as the light shooting through the stained-glass windows gave off the color of death, and Leroy hovered over Que. "No! Not my other son!"

## Drowning in the Wrong Color

"No! Not Que! Not Willie!" My world spun in every direction, and the men charged from the sanctuary while Mr. Reverend shoved the big hats to the side. "Let me pray for Que. Let me get to see the boy!"

Arms reached toward the bodies stacked around him, and prayers tumbled from lips, as the church folks prayed for Que. "Save our boy! Bring him through! Let him live!"

The loud shouts, and quiet whispers rippled from everyone who rallied around Que and Mr. Leroy. Even Ms. Jolene rushed between bodies, and Kissabelle squeezed under arms. Ms. Reverend huddled with Siri and Iris off to the side of the pews, along with some other mothers who cradled crying babies and little kids.

Tears showered down my face and my eyes burned, and my lips hurt from sobbing. "Why does this happen? Why can't I have a life without all of this?"

I wiped my face, and the sting of salt stung my chapped lips. Spinning like a train derailed, I yelled, "God, I need my Willie. Don't let Que die!"

I twirled around, snapping the images of the chaos into yet, another horrible memory. Unable to run, unable to stand, unable to get a breath, I felt my legs wobble like rubber, and I stumbled to a pew. Reaching for the seat, the suffocation of sorrow sent me to the floor, and I crawled under the pew, cradling my knees.

A man's yell brought silence to the church building. "This is not a colored-problem. I'm sorry, Ms. Jolene, but we took you and Willie in to help, but now one of our own has been

217

shot. Not counting Lottie who belonged to both the colored and the white."

Peeking from beneath my cave-pew, I sat up, staring at a man who decided Negro was different than being white. I jumped to my feet. "So, since I'm white, you don't think I matter? Or that my brother matters?" It was like I'd tossed a hundred knives into the hearts of those now staring at me, and trembling, I added, "I have a heart. I bleed. I cry. I have no blood ma and pa anymore. God made me, I can't help my color!"

Mr. Reverend inched his way into the middle of the crowd of men who looked at him for an answer. He reached for me, slipping his brown fingers into my pale-colored hand, lifting me up, pulling me to his side. He placed his arms around my shoulders, and I sobbed. "She's God's child. She may not be of our color, but she is of our God. We cannot be silent about life, or we will die, too."

A man rocking side to side, wrenching his fingers together like they were sweaty, stomped toward Mr. Reverend. I hid behind the reverend, peering into the face of a man whose eyes seemed to hold pain deeper than mine. "Everything was fine before you let Lottie come here with the boy. Look around you, this is not our fight."

Mr. Leroy popped up from the circle of people still praying, charging toward the man. "Look here, this is a heart fight. Not a colored or white fight. It's always the right time to do the right thing."

Tall men and short men gathered with the reverend and I stared into their eyes. A man held his little girl who wore a white lacy dress and she sucked her thumb. Her whimpers lessened when her daddy kissed her cheek. He winked at me, nodding. "It's the right thing for us to do. I cannot bear this burden of hate. We must help this girl get her brother."

The lone man stood against the others. "I can't be a part of this, I'm taking my family and we're leaving until you decide to take care of our own." The quivering sound in the man's voice cut my heart into pieces, his fear something I knew more about than I wished.

Darting from behind the reverend, I ran up to him. "I'm sorry I got in the way. But Que told me God brought me here, so … so I'm not sure how true that is, but I must believe … I have to believe God knows what He's doing."

I whimpered, and shook, and Siri and Iris moved to my side like bookends, each taking a hand. In twin-unison they spoke, "Shoelace is our friend. God gave her to us."

With that the praying people clapped, the stomping shook the floor like a train rumbling down the tracks. Mr. Leroy turned to crawl on the floor toward Que. He jumped up like a rocket. "Praise the Lord! My boy is fine! He hit his head on the pew and the bullet missed him! Those Crump men can't shoot straight! Or maybe, God sent an angel to catch the bullet!"

Running, I dove into the wad of people, fumbling for Que, and crawling like a snail to his side. He leaned on his pa, and gazed up at me. "So, did they get Willie? Tell me no! Tell me he's safe!"

I fell into his chest, weeping like a white-sister on her brown-brother, wrapping my arms around Que. "Willie's gone. They got him. They got him." I whispered in his ear, "But it wasn't the two men from the pond. So, Blake and Blair must be on our side."

Que wrinkled his nose. "Blake and Blair? You know their names?"

Stuttering, I swallowed hard. "No, I don't. I just named them. I have no idea who they really are."

Ms. Jolene touched my face. "Shoelace, it's time for us to do something different. We're causing big problems, and we almost saw another death." She rose to her feet. "Come with me. I'm going to get us some help from my ..."

Kissabelle hollered, "No! You have no one else to help us. We must stay with the reverend. Our restaurant is gone. Your apartment, too. We don't have any choices."

Ms. Jolene hovered, rocking and standing face to face with her sister. "Stop telling me what to do. You leave after Charley's birthday every year, and don't come back until you feel sad on his next birthday. You run, you hide, and you ride the rail. You sleep wherever. You put me through horrible nights worrying about you. Not everything is about you."

I felt like Ms. Jolene was scolding me, like my life was packed in a future like Kissabelle's. Like her ride up and down the tracks could have been mine if I had followed in her footsteps. I could have been her or Tin Can Mahlee, but God let my daddy steal me and He sent me to Memphis, back to Texarkana, then to Wheelock Academy, and off to Jefferson, and back to Memphis. He saved me for this very moment.

Swallowing the salty tears like a drink from my past, I cried, "Ms. Jolene, don't be so hard on Kissabelle. I see her. She just needs a chance to live, to love again."

Kissabelle held me like I was her Charley, and she knelt, weeping with lost tears, those that had probably never fallen along the rail. She embraced me. "Oh, Shoelace, my sister is right. I'm broken beyond repair."

I squeezed her neck. "Beginnings are hard. Endings can be sadder. But we're stuck right here in the middle of this. Will you help us get Willie back?"

She nodded, and the shouts of the others listening to our private talk brought Mr. Reverend into preaching mode. "This is the church that loves to love. It's time we showed our town that we're who we say we are."

Ms. Reverend moved next to her husband. "The love of Christ bled for all. He came to save. To heal. Let's find victory and show our love."

Siri and Iris hummed next to me, their words parting the sea of despair and they sang. "Amazing grace, how sweet the sound that saved a wretch like me, I once was lost but now I'm found, was blind, but now I see…"

The swaying of suits and dresses began like a choir of hope, and Mr. Leroy held Que as they sat in the pew off to the side, and the singing sent chills up my spine. Trying to make sense of the sorrow, I somehow caught a glimpse of a healing taking place inside the church. And it was my healing … a healing to love, a healing to live, a healing so I wouldn't ever run away and ride the rail ever, again!

The man whose fear split the room apart with his ugly words, shuffled toward me, and he put his daughter on the floor, wrapping me up, swinging me around in a circle with my legs out stretched. He sang, weeping, "Amazing grace, how sweet the sound that saved a wretch like me…"

I cried too, and let him love on me.

The man put me down. "I'm sorry. I'm so sorry."

A short time later, dizzy from twirling and from crying, I found myself sitting next to Que, worried and wondering what to do to help Willie. The deacons lingered up front by the choir loft, and most of the mamas had taken their children home.

Officers had come and gone, questioning most of the adults, and talking to Mr. Leroy at length. One had taken notes after talking with Que, and Mr. Reverend had waved his arms in the air, as he explained the kidnapping. The two policemen tried to make it sound like they could solve this horrible thing, but I knew better. If I was sent here by God, I had to do something.

My fidgety fingers and nervous toes wanted to go on a search, but I was going to need Que's help. I whispered, "How's your head? Still got a headache?"

"No, mostly I'm hungry. We've been here for hours. I could use some food."

"Me, too. I'm glad Ms. Jolene and Kissabelle are over there talking to each other. They need each other, don't they?"

Que nodded. "They do. I'm afraid for your Willie though."

"Me, too. That's why I need your help. I need you."

Shaking his head. "I'm not getting involved in something with you. We're leaving this up to the law. And we're going to trust God for the help we need."

"But ... maybe. Maybe you and me are the help Willie needs. Since you work or worked at the orphanage you can take me there. I can ask some questions and see if anyone knows where they might have taken Willie."

Standing up like he might run, he wobbled, and Que sat right back down. "My head isn't so good." He held the back of his noggin. "And I'm not helping you do anything. I'll tell my pa."

I hummed the tune to *Amazing Grace* and started singing, "...was blind but now I see." I leaned close to Que. "Willie can see. He saw me. I saw him. I have to save him."

Que sighed. "I'm not sure I'll live to talk about this. If I get caught, and they don't kill me, my pa will ..."

"We'll be heroes!"

"Really? Is that what you think?"

Clearing my throat, I poured out my hope. "If we save my brother, we will be."

Que took a deep breath, choking on his sentences. "I'll meet you out behind the reverend's house when we get back. We'll take the pickup and cut down the dirt road by the pond. But … we'll need to be quick, and be like ghosts to make this work."

Shouting, I brought everyone's eyes my way. "I'm great at being quiet. I can be a ghost. I can do this!"

Que held his ears with both hands. "This is never going to work!"

## Charley's Hope

"Shoelace, get in the truck!" Que barked at me through the window from inside the cab of Mr. Reverend's idling pickup.

Yelling at him from the back porch, my voice cut through the darkness. "I'm not sure we should do this without telling someone. It seemed like a good idea, like we could do this. Like we should. Like we must. But now, everyone's hearts are tied up like wadded yarn. I'm not sure we …" My brave quest idea from earlier evaporated with each sentence. After hours of listening to the grownups discussing, praying, and worrying, my own doubts surfaced like floating coffins in my veins.

"So, you're having second thoughts? If we're going to find Willie we can't wait. I have a key to the back of the orphanage. We can check and see if he's there."

"I'm not having second thoughts, I'm trying not to be like my old self. I'm good at causing more trouble. This might not be what I should do. And wouldn't Willie leave? Or try to run away?"

"You don't understand. There's a third floor where certain kids get locked inside closets. Or they get tied to beds."

"No! They wouldn't do that to him." I stomped down the wooden steps. "How did you work at the orphanage knowing such things were happening to those kids?"

"I didn't know anything at the beginning, but then I saw hungry girls and boys who were sad. Many of them cried. Or stopped talking. Or got sick and even died."

"Died? How could they let that happen?"

"For the money. Georgia Tann is getting rich! She's evil!"

"But if you saw how they treated them, couldn't you do something?"

"I tried. I even reported her to Boss Crump. That was before I knew they were in this together. He runs everything. I didn't know about him then. Then one of Ms. Tann's men struck me in the face with a strap one night. Said it was a warning." Que rubbed his cheek. "The man said I'd be next to disappear. So, I watched and listened. I started taking the kids extra food from the restaurant. Pa would bake batches of biscuits for me to take to them. I prayed for the children on every floor and at every turn—even those who cowered from me."

"But you stayed … even after you found out."

"I know. That's when me and my pa started talking with Jolene and Lottie and even Archie, before he followed after Lizzy Beth so he could bring her back to Willie."

"Talking? Just talking?"

"Not just talking. Pa helped me sneak babies out, one at a time. We've returned dozens and dozens this last year."

"You helped save some?"

"We have tried. The men watch too closely. It's hard."

"How can this end if all the bad people are in charge?"

"Not everyone is bad. Just some. We'll get Georgia Tann. And that Judge Kelly. You'll see."

"I hope you're right. I'm so confused and scared. I don't know what to think. I just want to go home. I want to wake up from this nightmare. I want … want my Willie." My heart ached with a longing to save and rescue my brother. "I want to be with my Willie."

"Then get in the truck. Let's see what we can do. If we stay here, we'll never have a chance to get Willie. Besides, we've been gathering up their secrets while pretending to do our jobs. They must have found out about Lottie from someone, so I don't know who's talking or ratting on us. But we haven't much time. If we're going, we need to go now."

"But, Ms. Jolene and Kissabelle are bickering and yelling upstairs. They have the reverend and Ms. Reverend pacing, and Leroy trying to calm them. Kissabelle's threatening to leave before Lottie's funeral, and Ms. Jolene's taking the blame for Willie's disappearance."

Que added, "It's not a good time for any of us. We've lost so much. It's time to get a part of our souls back."

I marched to the door of the pickup, stomping down weeds and whispering my case through the opened window. "But Ms. Jolene's ready to get her papers and trade them for Willie. And Kissabelle's threatening to burn them papers up, to get rid of the evidence. She said it's a waste of time to think of getting Willie back, that babies go away and never come home."

Que sighed. "Get in the truck. And stop stalling. Kissabelle's afraid. She's watched Charley get snatched up. She's leaving before sunrise anyway. She told Ms. Reverend at supper, and I heard her say it's for the best. Besides, she always leaves after Charley's birthday."

I climbed inside the truck after pulling open the heavy door. "I can't let that happen to Willie. He must come home with me. He must come home. We have to find him!" My will to run fought with my will to save, and I hopped into the truck, ready to do the right thing at the right moment—even if it felt wrong.

Chugging around the barn, Que jerked the truck into gear, and I held onto the door handle and the dash. "Are you sure you can drive?"

"Some say I'm a pretty good driver. I practice whenever I'm out here." Que held onto the steering wheel. "We'll go out the back road around the barn that follows the tracks. We'll be at the orphanage in no time."

"Don't you need to turn on the headlights? I can't see a thing."

"Yeah! That would be a good idea."

\*\*

My head hurt from gritting my teeth, and my knees knocked together. "Are you sure we should go inside?" I whispered as the truck rolled to a stop in front of a brick house with a porch light on. The yellow light made the bushes eerie in the darkness, and the frogs croaked a funeral song. "Is this the orphanage? It looks like a big ole house."

I glanced through my open window and stared at the three-story brick, noticing dozens of trees surrounding the yard like guards to keep us away. The shrubs laced the bottom of the kid-prison and circled the porch with short and tall shrubs, with stickers on rose bushes.

Que joined me on the curb. "Yes, the house was turned into an orphanage. It's a giant of a place, bigger than any house on the street with woods behind it. Some say there are kids buried back behind the garage. Come on."

"Kids buried?" I shook with fear, unsure if this great idea meant I'd end up in a shallow grave.

Tugging on my sleeve, Que growled, "Come on. Follow me around the back. Ms. Twig will be asleep in the room next to the kitchen. If I wake her, I'll tell her I forgot my wallet. She's older than anybody, and still walking, even if she's bent over a bit. She forgets who she is when darkness comes. She'll believe anything I say to her."

Backing up, I wobbled and started to run back to the truck. "What about Georgia Tann's men? Do any of them stay here?"

"No, just some house moms are here at night. Maybe two or three, counting Ms. Twig. It's close to midnight. Everyone will be asleep."

The snapping of branches swung at me with a whipping sound as we parted the bushes, making our own path to the back of the house. I stepped behind Que. "Maybe this isn't such a good idea. I think someone is watching us."

"We're fine. Stop worrying. I know my way around here."

"Then, why are we hiding?"

Whispering, Que added, "Well, just to be safe, I figured we might not need to announce we're here. You never know who might be out late on a Sunday night in these parts. These bushes are thick. They keep us out of the light."

*Snap. Snap.*

"Ouch! You keep letting those branches swat at me." I wiped my face where the sting of the limb hit my nose. "You just said none of her men will be here. I think you're scared, too."

"If I told you the men come around to check on things, would you be following me right now?"

"Wait? So, we're not alone?"

*"Shhh!* We won't be if you keep talking so loud."

I reached for his shirttail. "Keep me close. I don't want to get left behind."

"Here we are. I've got it." *Click-click.* "The door's open now. Let me get a light turned on in this kitchen."

In seconds, I scuffled inside the spotless kitchen and found myself staring at two suits. "Que, we have company." I lost myself in the earthquake of panic shaking my entire body, and

228

my chest pounded with shivers of short breaths. Running out the back door seemed possible, but my feet wouldn't move.

The man with a curl of hair on his forehead spoke. "Well, if it isn't the little girl from the hospital. Did you ever find your snakes?" His grin told me he was mocking me, but his stance reminded me he was big enough to end my life.

Swallowing the dry air, I flared my nostrils and put my hands on my hips. "I didn't have any real snakes. You two were the snakes." I smarted off as if I could get away with saying anything I wanted, since I was about to die.

Que slugged me. "Stop it. You need to learn how to stop being rude." Que nodded at the men. "Hi, I'm the janitor. I'm not sure we've met." He stuck out his hand to shake theirs.

The man in the other suit laughed. "It's kind of late for mopping up the past, isn't it?"

"You're right. I'm here to get my wallet. I left it here earlier."

The curly-haired man circled behind me, touching my pigtail. "And are you in charge of sweeping?"

Que shook his head. "No, she's staying with Reverend Roberts out at the farm. But I guess you already know that since … since I saw you both at the farm yesterday at the trees." Que called them out, and waited with his hands on his hips, matching my stance.

I added, "And we both saw them at the hospital, too."

*Creak. Creak.*

A wrinkled woman skinnier than a broom peeked into the kitchen from the side room. "I heard noises. It's late. We got problems?"

The first suit assured her. "No, Ms. Twig. We're good. Just locking up for the night."

She twisted her head, her top lip quivering. "Well hello there, Que. We've missed you the last few days. I had to take out my own trash."

"Yes, ma'am. Sorry. I should be back soon."

"Goodnight, then! A woman my age needs her beauty sleep." She closed the door, and seemed unalarmed by our presence. The two suits motioned for us to sit at the table in the middle of the kitchen.

Obeying them, I pulled out a chair, unable to swallow since my throat kept sticking together like a balloon without air. Que plopped down next to me, folding his hands, not saying a word, but his foot tapped the linoleum.

The four of us stared at each other for thirteen heartbeats, and I couldn't stand the quiet anymore. "Blake, what are you doing here? And Mr. Blair? Why are you both here so late? Are you still following us?"

Que squinted his eyes and cocked his head, glancing at me with a look that pierced me. "So, you do know their names?"

Nodding, I responded, "I met them when I went to Georgia Tann's hospital room. They were guarding her. But they … chased me and told me something …"

"What? Told you something?" Que quizzed me, turning to look right into my eyes. "So what did they say?"

"It's a secret. You don't need to know."

Que slapped the table. "Stop this, Shoelace. This isn't a game."

Blake waved his arm, ordering us. "Both of you need to keep it down." He sat down across from me while Blair took a seat across from Que. Blake placed his hands out flat on the table like he was counting his fingers. "Que, we're … we're investigators. We're about to break this case, and we're not hired killers. Yes, we work for Ms. Tann and Boss Crump, but it's not who we are … we're cops!"

Que sighed like he was about to sail around the room like a balloon letting out its last bit of air. "So, you're not going to kill us?"

I whispered into his ear, jumping up from my seat. "See, you are scared."

Pushing me, he scolded me. "Silly hobo girl who thinks she's got all the answers. Well, you don't. You don't."

"What makes you think I'm a hobo girl? I have a home now."

"You did ride into town in a boxcar didn't you? Always a hobo, always without a home."

"That's not true. I have Ms. Susan and Mr. Boyd. And Lizzy Beth. I have a bed, too."

Que argued, "You have that wild streak. That's hard to let go of. You'll grow up to be like Kissabelle."

"I will not. I am changing. I have a new heart. Jesus told me that, or Pastor Cody did." I rubbed my eyes. "I am not the same me."

Blair rocked in his chair, shaking his head. "You two. Stop this, we're here to keep you both safe. We know they're onto your little secret mission. Or that of Lottie's and Archie, and of course, Ms. Jolene, too."

Shouting, I gave Que my what for. "I knew it! We're all gonna die." My little-girl panic part of me leaked out like a broken faucet spewing water.

The rocking man sighed. "My own little girl was snatched up from my wife after she gave birth. We're searching for her, too. We're on the same side with you. But you can't let anyone know who we really are, it will blow our cover."

My tears surprised me and soaked my face. "But do you know who the other men were at the church? Or where they took my brother, Willie?"

Blake asked, "Oh, the blind boy?"

I smiled, remembering his miracle. "No, he can see now. He can see. But he did used to wear that bandage around his head. He has black hair, and dark brown skin. He's almost five."

Que shook his head. "They know who you're talking about, they're just letting you ramble."

Blair swallowed, and the knot in his neck wiggled with each breath he took in-between his words. "They have him at Ms. Tann's private house. He's being guarded in the attic."

Weeping, I cried, "But I need him. How can we get him?"

Blake rose to his feet, sighing, "I'm not sure. Tomorrow they'll give Ms. Jolene a deadline on returning her paperwork. So, if you know where she keeps it, you might get her motivated to trade with them."

Que took a long breath. "But how will we know if we'll get him back? Ms. Jolene's sister, Kissabelle is warning her to burn the papers, to destroy them."

Blake ran his hand through his hair. "She can't do that. It would affect our case, too. We need every piece of evidence we can find."

I yelled, "This is not a case. It's about my brother."

Blair assured me. "I know how you feel. My daughter will be six months old next week. I've never even held her. Never. She came up missing from the nursery at the hospital. Rumor has it, Georgia Tann took her."

I felt a pain like a knife cutting at my heart. Sighing, I pleaded, "Then help me hold my brother. Please, help me."

My tears flooded down my face, and my shoulders hurt from shaking. "I just want my brother back. He needs me."

Blake patted my arm. "Tell Crystal Belle to save the papers." He rubbed his chin. "And tell her that we know where her son is living. It's not over for her. That's the best we can do for right now. And we'll work on getting Willie for you."

I jumped to my feet. "What? You know where Charley is? Can you promise to get my Willie for me?"

Que scratched his neck and then his ear. "Not every story ends happy. They can't keep all of their promises."

I countered, "But God keeps His. Maybe He'll do this for Lizzy Beth since she's Willie's twin."

Blake nodded. "I'll give you two the address if you'll see to it we get those papers."

Que rubbed his eyes. "So, you really aren't going to kill us?" He asked the same questions again, as if he wasn't so brave after all.

Blake answered, "We're trying to help end this, trying to save the children."

Que's hand went to his chest like saying the pledge. "Kissabelle will be shocked! Charley's alive! He'd be in the seventh or eighth grade." Que's voice rose, "Kissabelle has to see him! We have to tell her!"

I screamed, "But … what if she's left town already?"
*Creak. Creak.*

Ms. Twig peeked into the kitchen, shuffled her feet across the floor, and pulled open a drawer by the sink. Spinning in her slippers, she pointed the long object at the four of us. "I've heard everything. Don't move. I've called for help."

Blake scooted up to Ms. Twig. "Now, what could you hear?"

She hollered, "Get back. You won't be the first person I've shot. Or the last!"

*Pam Kumpe*

A small figure moved into the doorway to her left, a shadow of a girl with long blonde hair wearing a white gown. "I'm thirsty. Can I have a drink of water?" She rubbed her eyes, and whimpered, "I want my mama."

## Shoes for Life

Blake charged Ms. Twig, reaching for … for the rolling pin. "Now you know that's not a gun, and you've never shot anyone. Remember, you forget things."

Ms. Twig giggled an old lady snort. "You remember the things I never do, and I remember the things I do in my head but they're not real."

Agreeing with her, Blake placed the pin on the counter. "Take care of our little one there. She's wandered downstairs."

Taking a glass from the cabinet, Ms. Twig swished water from the faucet into the crystal. "Come along sweetie. Let's get you back to bed."

The girl ran toward me, hugging me with a sister's grip. "I'm scared. There's too many girls in my room. We're all afraid of that lady with the glasses. She yells at us when she comes. She keeps saying my ma and pa are gone too, but I know they're not. I know they are looking for me."

Glancing at Que, I didn't know what to do, except hold her. "I'm sorry. My pa's gone, too. And my ma." Sitting in the chair, I let her cry as she hovered close to me, shaking and whimpering. I glanced at Blair whose eyes watered, and he shook his head, biting his lip.

Ms. Twig scooted the girl away, tearing her from my side. "Come along. Back to bed. Take a drink, and I'll tuck you back in your bed." Ms. Twig nodded like she was talking in her head before talking out loud. "These good men are doing plenty to help you find your parents."

Whispering to Que, I caught what she said about Blake and Blair. "So does she know they're the good guys?"

Que leaned toward me, whispering, "She may, but hopefully she forgets enough that no one will listen to her."

Blake plopped to his chair and the four of us stared at each other for what felt like hours. I watched the big clock on the wall behind their heads; it ticked for like three minutes. The longest minutes ever. The time now one in the morning.

Yawning, I figured we needed to go, especially if Ms. Twig did make a phone call. "She called someone. We probably need to go back to the reverend's house."

Que folded his arms, the keys to the pickup dangling between his fingers. "We need to get back. But how will we ever get to Willie? No one can get inside of Georgia Tann's house. She has men guarding the front, the alley, and even at each end of her road on Stonewall."

Blair spoke up, "She's known for taking children to her home for a few days at a time. No one will suspect a thing."

I shouted before I could keep my words inside my mouth. "What? No one will suspect a thing? Willie will have no idea what's going on. He'll be crying and now that he sees, he'll be scared." I grabbed my neck. "He won't understand. Que, you have to take me there."

Que nodded. "We'll go in good time. But right now we need to leave this place. The truck's parked out front. We're sitting ducks."

Blake and Blair stepped to the back porch with us, and Blake grabbed Que by the arm. "I forgot to give you the address for Charley." He rushed inside, slamming the screen, and returned out of breath, passing Que a piece of paper. "Here's the address. It's near the river on the other side of Beale, north a few blocks. I'm not sure he knows he's adopted. I just know we need to save the rest of these children.

We need to stop the baby stealing and kidnapping of our children."

Blair agreed. "We'll see how we can help you with Willie, too. We do have access to Ms. Tann's home. As long as we keep our cover intact."

Que stuck the paper inside his pants pocket. "Thanks. I know Ms. Lottie would love to see this end. As my pa would…"

**

Racing up the stairs a couple of feet, I twisted my body to look down at Que in the shadow of the light coming from a lamp in the parlor. "I'll go check Ms. Jolene's bedroom. She's in there. You'll see."

Que shook his arms like a wild turkey. "She's gone, I tell you. She's gone. I have a feeling."

"You can't go by a feeling." I frowned at the teen who reminded me of Crush when we hit heads over stuff.

"You can go by feelings when you see her do this year after year. You know, Ms. Jolene almost gets used to her being here, then she's gone."

Frozen in my memory of how Tin Can Mahlee fought to settle down, I wondered how my life might have become if my steps hadn't mattered in this journey to a new family with a brother and a sister. Sighing, I couldn't get my mind off Willie, but helping Kissabelle helped make sense of some of these past few days.

Cracking the door to the room where I'd slept with Iris and Siri, I saw them wrapped up, tied like a knot with their arms, sound asleep. I pulled the door closed, and moved to the rooms across from theirs, not sure which door to open. Sneaking a peek inside the first door, I found Mr. Reverend snoring, and Ms. Reverend whistling with her nose along with him. Sighing, I came to the next room, cracked the door and there on the bed was Ms. Jolene, all alone. No Kissabelle.

Stepping inside, I looked for Kissabelle's satchel, and saw the broken china doll on the floor and a few pennies sparkled at me as if to say she'd packed and headed to the tracks.

Charging on my tiptoes I ran for Que, bouncing down the stairs and plunging right into him as he rounded the staircase. Keeping my voice low, I shook my head like a girl stuck on a bridge overtaken by a rushing river. "She's gone. She is really gone."

"I knew it. But maybe we can catch her. Maybe my hunch is right. Maybe the Lord will keep her close and she'll be at the cemetery waiting for the next train—and we can stop her from leaving!"

## Less-Than-Desirables

"Are you sure this is where she might come? Why the Elmwood Cemetery?" I leaned up to the dash, the blue cast of the late-night fog caught the moon's glow and everything seemed gray.

Que let the pickup slide to a stop on the small arched bridge leading over the railroad tracks. "She rides in here, and she rides out here."

We creaked our doors open in unison like Iris and Siri might, using twin moves, and shuffled to the edge of the bridge wall, casting our gaze into darkness toward a pit of endless goodbyes. I hollered, knocking the silence into splinters of noise. "Kissabelle, wait! We need to tell you something. We have good news!"

Que shoved me, belting commands. "Shoelace, it's not like those woods over there don't have the less-than-desirables living in the shadows. Be quiet."

Shoving him back, I gave him my what-for. "I used to live there a couple years ago. Am I a less-than-desirable? My pa left me and Tin Can Mahlee there with Peg Leg and White Beard while he took care of stuff in Memphis. I learned to read in those woods. I learned to throw rocks and studied my alphabet with Skip on the tracks, too." My tears welled up, and my longing for the old life clashed with my longing for my new life.

Storming off from Que, my memories for the past seven years flashed before me like a thousand tombstones, and my feet kicked into a run for my life. Shouting to the blue angels in front of buried bodies, I called to anything and anyone. "I am not a less-than-desirable. I am me!" I pounded my chest with both hands. "I'm Annie Grace Kree. I matter! I am made by God. He wants me! He called me to life. I am not the same hobo girl I was two years ago. I am new!"

Tumbling to a group of markers and stones, I beat the grass with my hands as if I might let the past toss me into the boxcar of escapes from living. I found myself staring up at a tall tombstone that shot toward the moon like a rocket. As high as two stories up. "Who is buried here? I bet he's not a less-than-desirable."

A beam of light cut through the shadows and lit up the tombstone rocket. The shoes next to me told me it was Que, and I rose to my feet, sobbing and wiping my eyes. "Leave me alone. You keep reminding me who I was. And I don't like it."

Que held the flashlight, and his free arm reached for my shoulder. "I don't know much about you. If the past reminds you of how far you've come, let that be a good thing."

"What do you mean?" I sniffled, leaning on the rocket marker.

"Sometimes I can come on a little strong with my words. My life has gone through hard times, too. And by many, I'm the wrong color and that makes me a less-than-desirable. I'm sorry. I didn't know you lived there, I only know a small bit about you. I shouldn't have said what I did."

Sighing, I sucked in enough fog to cloud my thoughts. "I'm the little version of Kissabelle. I'm the little version of a lost person, except I'm not lost anymore. I've been found, and Pastor Cody told me about Jesus and how He guides us. How He speaks to us in our Bibles. How He changes us. I'm changing, and being a less-than-desirable isn't about where I lived or will live. It's about ..." I felt hope rising in me from somewhere around my PF Flyers. "… it's about who we are on the inside. Pastor Cody said it's about our hearts."

Que nodded, kneeling next to me as I sat on the damp grass. "You're right. I know God is still working on me, and He's started something good in me. I'm going to believe in that truth. I'm unfinished."

Smirking in the darkness, I blurted, "Yeah! You're an unfinished mouth!"

Que nudged me. "You're one to talk."

\*\*

"You could have sent the angels down and brought my boy back to me. You could have let him stay. You could have stopped this, but you didn't." The cry of a woman wailing nearby brought us both to our feet.

I spun around and bumped into the rocket marker. "Who's buried here?"

Que remarked, "No one. Not yet anyhow. It's for Boss Crump. He bought it and had the marker set, so it would stand taller than most. But the pigeons leave their droppings, and I'm not sure he'll like that."

The cry of the whispered whine and yell, mixed with sobs brought us to the road winding through the cemetery. I froze, stopping and listening. "Which way is that coming from?"

"I'm not sure. It's like a dozen different voices are crying to the dead."

"Could it be … Kissabelle?"

The woman let out a scream. "Prove me wrong, God. Bring him back! I can't say goodbye this time. I need to know what happened, need to see my boy even if it's in a dream. I can't carry the worry or the burden or the sorrow anymore."

I marched down the pebbled road. "It's her. Listen."

Que pulled on my arm. "This way. Over to our left."

We hurried toward the painful wails as if the storm of hurt and sadness was swallowing up our Kissabelle. I called to her, "We're here. We have good news about your Charley."

Que pulled me back to a halt. "Can you just wait? Blurting this out might cause her to run."

Not caring, I yelled, "Kissabelle. We met Blake and Blair. They work for Boss Crump. But they don't. They guard Georgia Tann. But they don't. They're on the trail. They're cops!"

Que knocked me to the ground with a shove like a big brother who might want to make his point clearer. "What in the world are you doing? One second you sound like a girl who has some wisdom, then you turn back into a toddler. Good grief, keep some of what you know to yourself."

Spitting dirt from my mouth, I jumped to my feet. "Stop shoving me!" I plowed into Que with a full-out leap, body slamming him to the ground.

Pushing me off, he pinned me on my back. "Stop it! You're so much trouble! You remind me of my little brother!" With that he let go of me, sighed, and whispered, "I'm sorry. I think I'm a lot like you. I can't control too much right now. I keep falling into not-so-good reactions." He sat back on the ground, dropping the flashlight, and the beam of light shot across the grass toward an angel guarding a tombstone.

I glanced at the angel, and sitting on top of the coffin-out-of-the-ground casing, I saw the boots of ... of Kissabelle. She was sitting cross-legged, talking to the angel who appeared to stand next to her listening. Tapping Que, I pointed at her. "There's Kissabelle. She's with an angel."

Que picked up the flashlight, turning it off, letting us linger in the eerie night. He switched it back on, letting the light guide our steps, and we inched our way closer and closer to Kissabelle. Que explained, "That's the Snowden angel, and the angel weeps over the tomb, much like Kissabelle does for her Charley."

I argued, "Then we need to tell her about Charley. You have the address. We can take her there. We can let her see him."

"And then what? Charley has lived there all his life. He has a good family."

"How do you know they're good? He might be with less-than-desirables."

"Well, I have seen him. He hangs out on the corner of Beale Street by A. Schwab's General Store. There's a bunch of my friends who play in a jug band. They use a kazoo, a washtub for bass, and jugs. One has a broken guitar with a couple of strings. They love to mimic the sounds coming from the stages up and down the street." Que hummed a tune of notes. "And Charley's in love with the Blues."

I whispered, "He loves music? Can he play?"

"I've seen him buzz his lips on the jugs a few times. But most of my friends …" Que stopped explaining, staring into the dark.

"But what? Tell me."

"I just realized that my schoolmates don't treat Charley like he fits. He's a little too white for some of them. But he keeps coming back. He doesn't notice they're making fun of him."

"That's horrible. Your friends are downright heathens." I stomped on a flower beside a marker, repeating my rant. "Downright horrible."

Que shown the light in my eyes. "Stop your fits. We're here to get Kissabelle. We need to talk her into coming back to the reverend's house, so he can let her know about Charley."

243

I pushed the flashlight aside. "Don't shine that in my face."

"I had to get your attention. And you calling my friends heathens wasn't too nice, either."

"Well, that's what my Grandma Elsie would call me when I was in trouble, when I disobeyed, when I didn't listen to her."

Coughing, Que laughed, "Then you must have heard that word a lot."

Giggling, we found ourselves stepping within a dozen feet from the weeping angel, but Kissabelle was gone. "Wait! Where'd she go?"

*Chug-a-lug. Chug-a-lug.*

The rumble from the tracks behind us told me the answer. "No! She's going to hop a train. She can't go!"

## When Goodbyes Become Hello

Charging to the truck, across the bridge, down the ravine, and under a fence, I bolted to the tracks. I followed the padding sound of feet galloping like a horse charging alongside the boxcars thundering on the tracks with a clap of booming clacks. "Kissabelle, wait for me! I need to tell you about your Charley."

The moon must have known my need for light as a blue haze of an early sunrise switched to a yellow glow. "Morning? It's morning!" Stopping, I looked back to the bridge where Que waved his arms at me as if he thought I'd listen to him and come back. Running, I barreled ahead, catching a glimpse of Kissabelle as she grabbed a rung on the ladder of the boxcar up ahead.

"Geronimo!" I yelled at the train, at the roar of the wheels clicking and clacking near my feet. From inside the boxcar, Kissabelle leaned her head out, gazing at me. She motioned for me to not jump. Motioned with flailing arms and a twisted look on her face.

I reached for the rung, dragged my foot on the ground, and fumbled with my grip. My hand slipped, my face slicing into the rocks at my feet. Rolling, I landed to the side of the tracks, my face wet with cuts, my nose bleeding, and my heart breaking. "Kissabelle! Come back!"

I curled into a ball, my knees skinned, my overalls ripped, and my entire body aching from the toss of the boxcar.

Whispering to my daddy who had fallen from the coal car two years ago, I remembered how I'd fallen time and again, and how Tin Can Mahlee rescued me from the cuts, doctoring me, and caring for me—while my daddy did what daddies who are broken do. Nothing!

Weeping, I listened as the rumble of the train headed toward the river, and how Kissabelle rode out of my life and I held the answer. I wondered if my grandma had felt this way when my daddy stole me from her grasp.

"Shoelace? My gosh! Are you alive?"

Switching from one side to the other, my cheek by my ear burned and the blood ran to my lips. "Que, she left us. She needs to know about Charley! She needs to know."

Que wrapped me up in his arms, and I lost myself in the sorrow of losing my grandma when her heart gave out. I lost myself in the days and nights when my daddy never showed up, when he must have got stuck with me when Georgia Tann rejected me. When my Tin Can Mahlee couldn't be a real mama, because her life was injured with wounds like Kissabelle's wounds.

Sobbing, I wished for the nightmare of goodbyes to leave. For the sadness to lift the fog and let sunlight ride in for the day.

Que lifted me into the pickup. "Let me look. Let me see your face." He wiped my skin with a handkerchief, and I touched the cloth. He smiled. "Yes, it's from Archie. He's known for having them, known for wiping away our tears."

I wobbled and gained my strength, my fear worse than my cuts. "I'm not hurt too much. I've never fallen when I've tried to hop a train before—at least, not without having someone to catch me. Or help me back up."

Que whimpered, "I thought you were dead. You're our messenger of hope who rode into our town, braver than the wind, with courage exploding from your heart."

246

I cried, "I don't have any courage. I only have … sorrow right now."

"Me, too. We must go back to the reverend's farm. They'll know we're gone. And we'll be in for a lashing."

I glanced out the side of the truck, beyond Que's shoulder. "Will we ever see Kissabelle again?"

"I'm not sure, but I saw her bag beside the weeping angel. She left it behind. She must have run from us and forgotten it. Are you able to ride back to the grave, so I can get it?"

Nodding, I sighed and wiped blood on my sleeve. "It's just a little blood. I don't think I'll even need stitches." Licking my lips, the bloody sweat and the morning worry collided, and Que moved to the driver's seat of the pickup.

Bouncing to the gravesite, we rode to the angel in silence. Que parked the truck, sliding from the seat. "I'll get her bag."

I closed my eyes, the world sinking like coffins falling into graves where mamas lost their babies, and babies lost the mamas. And to a place where other girls like me lost their daddy too, but knew that God was guiding just the same. But it gets so confusing in the in-between.

Scratching my neck, I sat up, the pain in my leg piercing my skin like a jab of a nail sticking in the bone. Placing my hand on my leg, I rubbed the spot, and glanced down to see the spike going through my pant leg like a needle being threaded to let the blood leak from my soul.

I leaned my head out the pickup window. "Que, I'm in … in big trouble. I think I'm hurt worse than I said."

Que kept his back to me, staring at something, frozen like a boy-angel; he was speaking to someone or something. "Come with us. I see you remembered your bag. I see you jumped from the train to come for it." He clutched the giant satchel. "And what is so important in here?"

I focused my gaze on the not-so-angel woman on the other side of the monument, the one where the angel hovered with its tears. "Oh, my goodness, it's Kissabelle."

I hobbled from the truck, and limped to them, their arguing going back and forth, and neither of them saw me. I tumbled a few feet across the grassy patch to their side, and collapsed next to a tombstone with the name Gil T. Kree etched on the front of the marble. The date was November of 1945, when he died. "No way! Not my daddy! It couldn't be."

From behind me, Que rushed to my side. "What are you doing? You should have stayed in the truck."

From the other side of the tombstone, where I pointed at the name, Kissabelle knelt, sighing. Her words were like a breeze of goodbyes ending with hello, with hope. "This is your pa's grave. Jolene had it put here when they found his body. She loved him for as long as she knew him. She saw the man he could have been, and hoped he'd become the man … the pa you needed."

Whimpering, I let out a gasp. "My daddy's buried here? He's not stuck in the mud at the Indian burial grounds or worse, caught in the rapids of a waterfall downstream in the Mississippi?"

Kissabelle moved toward me, embracing me with her long and rough arms. "Yes, his body was found on the shore, and sweet girl, your pa lived a wounded life. He held the invisible scars of his own pa beating him and not treating him with love. He didn't know how to love you."

I cried, "How do you know? He never told me about getting beaten as boy."

"No, but he told my sister. And she told me. And now, I'm telling you. When life crushes your spirit, it's hard to find the strength to fight, it's hard to live, to love anyone. You go into

248

survival mode, and you make choices that keep you trapped. You hurt the ones you should love most."

I gazed up at Que who was now crying, and then to Kissabelle who wept with him, with me. "So, Kissabelle, are you trapped like my pa was? I know how to let you find freedom to live, but you'll need to be strong. You'll need …" I reached for the ache in my leg, and lost myself in the blood coming from my mouth, and went … away for a second. I was still awake, weak, confused, but not.

Que gathered me up again, and my eyes cracked open, and Kissabelle walked alongside us to the truck. "I can be strong, but I'm not used to being anything for anyone for very long."

I whispered, "This won't take long. But you need to see this."

Que argued, "First we need to take you to the hospital."

I shook my head. "Not yet. Take us to Winchester Street. I have to show Kissabelle what the Lord has done with … with her Charley."

Kissabelle let out a puzzled sound, a blubbering mess of words. "Did you just say my … my Charley?"

*Pam Kumpe*

## Muddy Water of Choices

"What in the world? Girl, you've got a railroad tie in the leg of your overalls. It's got you twisted like your knee's broken but, you're ..." she yanked on the nail, tearing my pants.

Screaming, I kicked my leg like it was brand new as Que spun the truck around in the road outside the cemetery entrance. "I'm not hurt, except for the scratches. The nail got twisted in my clothes, and made me limp. I thought I might lose my leg."

Que laughed. "Talk about being a scaredy cat, but I'm actually glad you're better than I first thought." He held the steering wheel, the morning sun moving higher in the sky as if to light our way.

Scooting closer to the door, I wiggled in the seat, and my arm brushed up against the side of Kissabelle's leg. I put my shoes on top of her giant satchel, using it for a step stool. "What are you carrying? Your satchel is packed!"

"Never you mind. It's my belongings, and they don't belong to you." Kissabelle placed one of her boots on the bag with my feet. "Nothing I have is nothing you need."

"Well, I know something about Charley that you need." My mouth thought out loud for me, and I felt my mind tell me to be nicer. "I'm sorry. Que and me. Well, we heard something about your son."

Que gurgled, coughing. "Let me tell her. We were at the orphanage last night looking for Willie. It seems he's at

250

Georgia Tann's house, but we learned something that you do need to know—especially before you hop a train and leave."

"What could it be? Did you hear that he's dead?"

I spouted off, "No, we have an address for him. He lives here. And Que knows him."

Que defended himself. "I know what he looks like, and I've watched him play the guitar with some of the boys on Beale Street. He plays the jugs, too. He loves music."

Kissabelle jumped from her seat hitting her head on the cab of the pickup. "Ouch!" She rubbed her noggin. "What? You know him? Why didn't you tell me? I can't believe you'd keep this from me!"

Que raised his voice. "Stop and listen. I didn't know that was him. Until last night, when I saw the address. But … but he doesn't go by Charley."

"You have his address?" Kissabelle screamed.

I joined in with my louder than regular pitch. "That's why I said we need to go to Winchester Street. He lives in an apartment there, and Que …" I pointed at him. "Que, tell her more."

Que inhaled. "I've made trades with him. He loves to fish. And I love to eat fish. I've gone with some of the guys when he's caught himself a tubful."

I pursed my lips. "What? You didn't tell me that part." I shook my head. "I hate fish. What in the world would you give him for some nasty ole fish?"

Que smiled. "I traded him my marbles from when I was a kid. He has a younger brother, collects stuff for his brother to look for in treasure hunts. His brother is … is around five. He thinks slower than most of us. Talks only a little. And he's the cutest little blond boy who loves to hunt for stuff. He thinks he's a pirate finding gold."

I wiped my nose, my arms burning from the scrapes on them. "Gosh! You didn't tell me any of this last night. You know him pretty good, and his brother!"

"I do. He's a guy who makes friends because he's kind to others. He doesn't care who he meets, he makes a friend."

Kissabelle sniffled. "But you said he's not Charley? What is his name then?"

Que cleared his throat. "He's called …"

Kalunk! Kalunk!

We jerked forward when the truck hit the holes in the dirt road, and Que swerved, hitting the soft spot on the ground. The tire sunk in a low spot, like we'd hit quicksand. I leaned out the window. "It's a swampy over here, and something's leaking from under that house and flooding the road."

Que put the truck in park and jumped from his seat, and Kissabelle slid out behind him. I opened my door, and stomped into the muddy water. "You're stuck. What are we going to do?"

Que motioned for me to stand on the bumper. "Both of you get on the front and weigh the truck down. I'll put her in reverse and get some traction to get this wheel out."

Kissabelle blocked Que from getting back into the seat of the pickup. "First, tell me my son's new name."

Que sighed. "You're not going to like it."

She pushed him. "Tell me my boy's name."

Que yelled, "It's Foster Featherly."

"Foster Featherly?! What a sissy of a name! Who names their son that? Who ruins a kid's life by giving him a name everyone makes fun of?"

Wrinkling my nose, I agreed with Kissabelle. "That's a horrible name. Poor kid."

Que smiled. "That's why we call him Shelby after the county. It makes him sound like he's bigger than life, like Memphis."

Kissabelle cupped her face. "I can live with Shelby, but not Foster Featherly!"

In two steps, she joined me on the bumper, and Que spun mud from beneath the truck, and we tumbled to the ground, splattering mud on each other. Laughing, I wiped her face with my hand. "You're a mess!"

Kissabelle hopped to her feet. "Stop it. We don't have time to play. I need to find Charley, I mean Shelby."

The three of us scooted into the pickup, and my muddy PF Flyers left marks of mud swirls along the canvas bag holding Kissabelle's life inside. "Sorry, I've got mud all over me now."

Que hollered, "No! Look up there at the railroad crossing. It's a car inching into the road. Hold on. I'm turning right here, since the car is up there on the left at the next block. Then we'll go up the alley, sit for a minute, and cut back this way."

I snarled, "Every dark car doesn't belong to Crump or Georgia Tann, does it?"

"No, but not every black car is out this early on Monday morning, barely moving, inching like a snail."

Kissabelle pointed as we drove by a tall house with pillars. "There's another black car." She shot her arm in front of my nose. "There, it's parked in that driveway."

Shaking my head, I corrected, "I think that car lives there."

Que quieted the both of us. "Stop it! This is not a game. I keep telling you that, Shoelace!"

"I didn't say anything about this being a game. You need to quit bossing me. I'm not good with bossing. I can come up swinging at you. So maybe you need to stop treating me like I'm some little girl."

Kissabelle scolded me, "Don't talk to my Que like that! He's one of the wisest of all of us."

Folding my arms, I sat back in the seat pouting. "Fine! I'll just sit here. It's not like we're looking for Willie anyway."

Que leaned forward looking around Kissabelle. "We will look for him. I promise. It's time for us to go back to the farm. We need to get my pa and Reverend Roberts. We need the people from my church to come together. We can surround Georgia Tann's house late tonight and get your brother. You'll see. We can form a march for his freedom!"

Rocking, I felt my heart beat in my toes. "Do you think we can do that? Will they help us?"

"Freedom is driving us all right now."

Kissabelle changed the subject. "So aren't you going to pull back on the road? We've been idling in this alley forever."

Que nodded. "Yes, we're almost to Winchester Street. I'll park up from his apartment. And then … are you just going to knock on the door?"

Kissabelle blasted her lips like she got lost in her words. "I'm going to get him. I'm stealing him from them. I'm taking my boy and we're leaving town together."

Que skidded to a stop, jerking my head with a pop. He gripped the steering wheel hard, his hands tightening. "Kissabelle, you can't just take him. He's lived with this family for all of his life."

"But he's my family. What about me?"

Que turned to her. "But they have given him a home. You don't even stay in one place for long."

"I can stay. I can get a home. I can be his mama."

254

I felt my life repeating itself, their talk of Kissabelle being a mama for her boy reminded me how I had longed for Tin Can Mahlee to be my mama, too. But somehow, no matter how hard she tried, she failed. No matter what she wanted to do, she did something else. She was broken from the past, and the past wouldn't heal.

Gazing at Kissabelle, my heart hurt for her because as much as she wanted to take Shelby, she needed to leave him behind, to show her love for him. I sighed with two long inhales. "What do you think he will want? He doesn't even know you."

Kissabelle argued, "He can get to know me. I have missed his teething. I have missed his first steps. I have missed his first day of school. I have missed his … his life."

Que brought his thoughts into our talk. "But, Kissabelle, he doesn't know you. Really, Shelby laughs, plays music, and fishes. Stealing him will cause him to lose his smile, and his music will fade. You can see him, but you need to promise not to take him. His pa works as a teacher at the high school, and his ma sews for the neighbors and bakes pies for the Peabody Hotel."

I rolled my eyes. "So when were you going to tell me you knew Shelby like this? You act like you hang out with him."

Que made a check mark sign in the air. "Yes, Shoelace! I do know him. We come from different worlds, but he doesn't mind letting me inside his. He's one of my best friends. We just came from different sides of the tracks."

Kissabelle held her ears. "I'm Charley's ma. I am his ma." She rattled on. "I can have him. I can take him. I never had a say in his being taken from me."

Que shook his head so fast, I thought he'd get dizzy. "This isn't going to work. I knew we didn't need to tell you. It's only going to make this worse."

Kissabelle shouted, "Stop the truck. Stop it now. I'm getting out. I'm leaving you both. I don't need anyone to tell me what to do about my own son. Give me the apartment number. Tell me!"

Que pulled to the side of the road, and we rolled to the corner in front of a group of red brick apartments. "Kissabelle, you can't just go and take a teenage boy from all he's known."

I cracked my door open, and she pushed me from the truck. "I can do what I want, when I want, and how I want. Give me my bag."

I moved away from Kissabelle whose arms waved like Tin Can Mahlee's used to when she went into her crazy stunts. I touched her arm. "Please, be the ma Charley deserves. Please!"

Kissabelle paused, slinging her bag over her back. "I have to do this. He's my boy!"

Que called from the driver's seat. "Both of you, duck behind that car. There's a black car up ahead. I'm going to lead them away from here. I'll be right back."

I knelt behind the blue sedan, and Kissabelle paraded up the street like she was invincible. She shouted, "I'll knock on every door until I find my Charley."

## The Answer in the Window

Charging up behind her, I cried out, "Stop! You don't just run into your boy and ruin his life."

Swerving with her bag, she slammed into my shoulder. "Ruin his life? What are you saying? I'm his mama!"

"But, he doesn't know you are … you're not dressed like a mama. You live in places he's never gone. You smell like someone who needs a bath. You live in old clothes. And walk down streets alone at night. You ride in boxcars!"

Halting in her tracks, Kissabelle glanced at her worn-out boots with the laces untied and bent down, tying her shoes. Mumbling she countered me, "I took a bath Saturday."

"You know what I mean." I kicked the dirt, unable to know how or what would not hurt her heart too much, but somehow, I knew Charley needed a warning before she crashed into his world.

Kissabelle knocked some of the caked mud from her unraveling pants' hem, and scooted her boots on the ground to get the bottoms clean. "I'm not too cleaned up, am I?" She smoothed her hand over the wrinkles in her brown shirt, standing up taller. She blinked her eyes, and the tears let loose down her cheeks. "But if he's near, I need to see him. I can't, not see my Charley. I thought he was gone forever. Now I need him even more."

*Chug-a-blab. Chug-a-blab.*

To our side, Que coasted to a stop in front of a white house with green shutters, with a white picket fence. He rolled to the curb, slamming his fist on the steering wheel, his head shaking like a mad teenager.

Running to him, I jumped on the side step of the passenger door. "What's wrong? I thought you were leading that car away …" I glanced up the road. "Where did the black car go?"

Que spouted, "The driver crawled through the intersection up there, and he drove on, up toward the next block. And now I'm out of gas. We've run aground."

"Why didn't you check the gas gauge? And this isn't a boat, we're on solid ground. Trucks don't run aground."

"Well, this one did!" Peering at me with angry eyes, Que puckered his lips as if he trapped ugly words from lashing at me. "If those are Crump's men then we're in for it."

"But why would they even care what we're doing? Or me, for that matter? We don't have what they want anyway. It's Ms. Jolene who has the papers they're after, those we can trade for Willie!" The leftover sorrow that I'd tucked away at not having time for chasing my brother slipped up my throat like acid burning. Plopping to the ground like a caked piece of mud, I cried, "Willie! Will I ever see you again?"

Kissabelle bounded up to me, sitting on the ground with me. We were like two lost puppies in need of hope, in need of answers, in need of rest. In need of family. She wiped my hair from my face. "I forget that your sadness is in Willie, and mine is in Charley. You want your brother. And I want my son."

For a few seconds, Kissabelle rocked with me on the pebbles in the road, sighing and staring at the apartment building across the road. I stared at her and then back at the spot where curtains blew from the breeze of an open window.

Que joined us, kneeling, softening his words. "I'm going to use someone's phone. I'd use Shelby's phone, but I'm afraid you two might rush him, and we'd have a nightmare loose on Winchester Street."

Kissabelle sobbed, a flood of icky and snotty sounds coming from her nose. "I can't let him see me like this. But I would ... would love to know what Charley looks like, to see him smile." She let go of me, and yanked her bag to her knees, clutching it.

Que placed his hand under her chin, tilting her head up. "Will you stay here if I go use a phone? We need to call Reverend Roberts. We need to let him know his truck's not stolen, and where we are ..."

Kissabelle nodded. "I'll sit right here. I'll sit right here."

"You promise?"

"I can promise to promise."

"But does that mean you won't knock on the doors? Or run after me?"

"It means I'll be right here. I'll stay put."

Que jogged up the sidewalk path toward the main door of the apartments, and jumped every other concrete step until he disappeared inside, to what might have been a hallway.

My heart nearly jumped from my chest, and I grabbed the handle on the pickup, and stood to my feet. I held onto the pickup as if I needed to hold onto something solid. "Oh my! I bet Que's headed to Charley's apartment. He knows them, so he'll go there. I'm sure of it." My over-thinking exploded from my head and out my mouth, and landed in the morning air, much louder than I had first said it in my brain.

Kissabelle rose to her feet, her hand on her neck, and she grasped the handle of the pickup too, as if she was using it for a magnet to keep her from following Que. "I need to see him. I need to see my Charley!" She charged ahead, scrambling to run in her clunky boots, and lost her footing, tumbling to the grass by the end of the building. Her bag rolled like a log, landing up next to a shrub. She crawled to it, sighing.

"Charley? It's me! It's your mama." She announced this at the apartment wall, her voice growing shriller with each shout.

A woman stuck her head through one of the opened windows. "Hey, this is a good neighborhood. We don't let less-than-desirables over here. Be on your way. The mission is back down that way on Poplar Street. You can get breakfast there." The woman with rollers in her hair motioned her hands like she was herding off a wild animal from the yard.

Frozen, I shook my head, not saying a word, but praying for a miracle that might let Charley not have scars from this encounter. One that might let this end better than the onslaught of chaos that was happening or about to happen—and this time, it wasn't my fault.

The front door to the apartment building flew open, and a boy with wavy brown hair, carrying a fishing pole pounced down the stairs to the curb. He held a Prince Albert tobacco can in his hand. "I've got me a bunch of worms. I'm sure the fish are biting."

Staring at his can, I remembered how I used to write poems and hide them away inside the old tobacco can at grandma's manor. Then for a split second a poem rolled off my lips, *A boy was taken, and life went to shaking. The mama is here. She's filled with fear. How this will end, is anything but clear.*

The woman with rollers came back to the window, and Kissabelle slid around the end of the brick wall, out of her view. I moved to the side of the road leaning on a tree, to hide in plain sight, to listen. The woman bellowed with a joyful tune in her voice. "Son, what about your chores?"

"I'll get to them, ma. My new friend's back in town. His parents are looking for work. He's sure they'll move here before Christmas. He's a singer. And he loves to fish like me.

I think they'll move in our apartments too, when they decide on jobs."

"But, you have your own job to take care of here. You didn't make your bed. Or take out the trash."

"Oh, but ma! It's summer! Can't I do it later?"

She waved both her hands in the air like she was leading the band, like the chorus was her favorite part of a song. Her smile never left, her words sounded soft but firm, and her eyes sparkled when she spoke to her son. "But what will your pa say when he gets home? He's teaching those summer school classes to pay for those braces you need, so we need to do our part."

The boy dropped his can, and a patch of dirt along with squirming things wiggled in the grass. "My worms!" He gathered up the worms and pushed them into the can.

"Son! I'm talking to you. Focus. What will your pa say when he gets in?"

The fisherman boy kicked at a clump of dirt. His black PF Flyers made me look down at my stained red ones. Wishing someone wanted me to do chores, I remembered how Mr. Boyd did use kindness when I first moved in with them. But since I broke every rule when I moved in with them, his tone shifted to that of a guard, whenever he dealt with me. As did Ms. Susan's words, since I disobeyed her on purpose.

The call from the window brought me back to eavesdropping, and Kissabelle inched from around the corner of the apartments. She stared with a gaze that made her look like a bull ready to attack, like she wondered if this was her son.

The woman yelled, "Hey lady! Get on down the road. This isn't your kind of neighborhood. We're family here. Go on now. Be gone."

The boy ran up to the window, looking up. "Ma, she's probably hungry. Why don't you give her those biscuits on the table from breakfast? We have plenty."

"Sorry son, I get nervous around strangers." The woman left the window, returning with a paper sack. "Miss, come here. I've got some biscuits for you. I put an apple in the sack, too. I'm sorry for being abrupt with you. Raising a boy can make you lose your patience sometimes."

Kissabelle reached up for the sack and it tumbled to the lawn. The boy picked it up for her. "Here you go, ma'am. My mama makes the best biscuits this side of the Mississippi. The best pies, too."

The woman corrected her son. "Now, Shelby! You know I only make the best pies, not the best biscuits."

Sniffling, Kissabelle nodded, and fumbled to hold onto the sack. "Your name's Shelby?"

"Yes, do you know me?"

"I think I do. You remind me of my ... of my own son."

"What happened? Is he gone? Was he sick?"

Coughing and slobbering, Kissabelle wiped her face. "He is gone ... but seeing you makes him found."

The woman in the window interrupted, noticing Shelby was trying to inch away, to sneak off. "Now Shelby! What will your pa say when he gets home and your chores aren't finished?"

"Oh ma! He'll say, 'that's the finest catch of fish ever.'"

Laughing, she waved him on. "Be back by two. No later, ya hear?"

Kissabelle rushed toward her son and hugged him like she'd squeeze his love into her heart. "I have missed you! I have missed you! I can't believe it's you!"

Scrambling from her grasp, Charley hollered, "Lady, I'm not yours to hold. I have a ma. Mama, you might need to call the police after all, this hobo is wacko."

"I'm not. I just thought you looked so much like my son." She held her arms close to her chest in a crisscross. "I'm sorry. I'm sorry." She fumbled for her balance, and rushed to her bag. "I'll be gone now. I'll go. I must go. Or I'll have to do what I can't do. I can't do it. Or I'll ruin everything."

Hurrying to her side, I reached for her hand. "Come on, Mama Belle. We have to get to the tracks."

Charley marched away from us, shaking his head, and turned back to his mama. "I'll be back by noon, because Elvis has to leave for home with his parents on the train. Thanks, Ma!" He ripped from the yard like a bullet sent from the barrel of a gun, and raced up the hill, rounding the corner.

Kissabelle never moved, barely was breathing, but every so often her shoulders rose and fell, like a seesaw on a park at the playground. Her gasps were long, her breaths deep.

Whispering to her, I reminded her, "He's happy. You can tell."

Kissabelle pointed at the hill, screaming a whisper in my nose. "That was my Charley! Did you see him? He's beautiful!" With that, she tumbled to the ground and unsnapped her satchel, dumping her bag. I glared at the contents. "What were you thinking? We're going to be in so much trouble!"

The woman in the window called to us. "Are you two leaving, or do I need to call the police?"

*Pam Kumpe*

## Leaving Charley, Loving Charley

I popped off, dancing around the items littered on the grass. "We're leaving. She's lost and I'm trying to help her find her way to … to the train station."

The woman urged us. "Did she lose something?"

Kissabelle jumped to her feet, holding a pair of white baby shoes. "I'm not lost. I had to find these." She moved to the window, holding them up for the woman to see.

"Who's are those?"

"They were for my son, Charley, but someone stole him."

I marched up, grabbing the shoes. "Kissabelle, you can't do this."

Snatching them from my fingers, Kissabelle mumbled, "I have to tell her. She must know who I am."

The woman leaned closer. "Who are you?"

*Creak. Kaplunk.*

We all three glanced to the front door leading inside the apartments, and Que pounded from the steps, running faster than I wished. He raced up. "We're in big trouble. Reverend Roberts and my pa, and Ms. Jolene are on their way. They know we're gone. And they said …"

The woman shouted, "Que? What are you up to? Are these your friends?"

"Yes, I know them. We're on our way …"

I bumped into him. "We're on our way to the train station."

Que stumbled, pushing me away. "Stop it, Shoelace. This is Ms. Featherly. She's my friend."

264

"What are you doing here? Shelby just left to go fishing with the new boy, Elvis. They shouldn't be too far up the road."

"Ma'am, I used your neighbor's phone. I had to call Reverend Roberts." He spun around. "His old truck ran out of gas."

She leaned out the window. "You drive?"

"I'm learning, ma'am. I haven't gotten the part down about putting in gasoline though." He grinned a fake smile, and I rushed to gather up loose bills floating across the yard.

Kissabelle offered the shoes again. "Ms. Featherly, I want to give you these."

"Miss, I don't need them. My son is thirteen."

"He's not your ..."

Que stepped up and put his fingers over Kissabelle's mouth. "Not now! You will make things worse."

She shoved his hand. "Stop it! That lady took my boy!"

Ms. Featherly argued, "Que, she's crazy. I'm calling the police."

"No, please. She's hit a hard patch."

Kissabelle bent down, gathering up the birthday shoes she's collected all these years. "My boy needs his loafers. No, he needs new church shoes." She rambled and stuttered, and slobbered and cried.

I finished chasing down the money, and held a stack of it close to my chest. "Que, she's taken Ms. Jolene's money."

Que knocked the shoes from Kissabelle's hands. "You stole Ms. Jolene's cash? How could you? You know your sister's restaurant burned and her apartment. What kind of person does that?"

Ms. Featherly now stood in the grass next to me, her rollers loosening, her curls dangling. She shook her head. "What is going on here? Wait, I've heard about Jolene. She lost her place in the fire Friday night. Everyone is saying it's arson." She put her finger on Kissabelle's chest. "Was it you? Who are you?"

Kissabelle jumped back. "Don't touch me. I'm Jolene's sister. I'm out of town, mostly. And you should know, I'm Shelby's real ma! But he used to be my Charley! But someone snatched him up!"

"No way! He's my son!" The growl in Ms. Featherly's tone scared me, and I stepped behind Que.

Que unblocked my being safe, and placed himself between Ms. Featherly and Kissabelle, and they frowned at each other like boxers who were ready to land a left punch to get what they believed to be theirs. They taunted each other with the same words. "He's my son! He's not yours!"

Tossing the money inside the bag, I grimaced, ready to give my two cents, but I saw a folder with a stack of papers inches thick, with string around it. It was the same folder Ms. Jolene had on the table with the reverend, when they whispered about baby stealing and the orphanage. I reached for the folder. "What is this?"

Kissabelle yelled, "Leave that in the bag. It's only causing sadness. No one really cares. It won't change a thing. It got Lottie killed!"

I marched up to her, tossing the folder to the ground. "Kissabelle, you can't keep talking to Ms. Featherly like you're crazy. Or to me like that, either."

She frowned at me for mouthing, "You're just a kid. I don't listen to little girls."

"I'm twelve. Do you hear me?" I put my hand on my hips. "Besides you act like Ms. Featherly isn't important or doesn't matter. She's had Charley since he was a baby! She's raised him! She's fed him! She's held him! She's laughed with him! She's cried with him! And tucked him in bed."

Ms. Featherly added, "And prayed with him …"

"But that's not my fault! He was taken!" Kissabelle screamed, holding her head like she couldn't stand hearing me talk.

I grabbed her arms, pulling her hands down. "This is real. Georgia Tann stole your baby boy, but this mama had no way of knowing. And she seems like a mama I might like."

Ms. Featherly squirmed, wiping her hands with her apron, her eyes full of tears. "I've heard the rumors. I've heard them. Could it be true? We adopted Shelby when he was hours old. We were told his mama died giving birth. And yes, it was with Georgia Tann and her adoption agency."

Kissabelle collapsed to the grass, curling into a ball. "I have to go now. I am dead. I can't stay. I must go. I'm not here. I'm not alive. I am …"

Que bent down, and I did too, but Kissabelle came up swinging, her fist jamming into my jaw. Screaming, I flew backwards. "Ouch! Whoa!" Holding my face, I found myself on top of the shoes, and I wept like a baby at how ugly this became. I crawled to Kissabelle. "You have to do the right thing for Charley. The right thing is to let him live and smile and not ever feel your fist in his jaw."

She inched on her knees toward her bag. "I'm gone! I must leave! I'll hurt him. I'll ruin him!"

Ms. Featherly rocked me in her arms, after she checked my teeth, after she noticed my gums were bleeding. She blotted my mouth with her apron. "Dear God, what shall I do? I love my Shelby."

Que stormed to Kissabelle. "This is exactly what we warned you about, and now you've gone and set a fire with your mouth. Only ashes will remain if you interfere with Charley's new life."

Ms. Featherly responded, "His name is Foster Featherly, and his life isn't new. He loves his nickname, Shelby. And he's been ours since the beginning of his first breaths. I didn't know he was taken, honestly." She sobbed the biggest tears ever, the marble-sized drops of pain rolled down, dripping on her blue blouse.

Kissabelle rose, twirled, and stomped. "I'm leaving. I'll not be back except for his birthday. I'll leave a present for him if ... if I might. I get him shoes every year. Can I keep on doing that?" She groaned, "I had a marker put at Elmwood Cemetery and that's where I leave them, because the day he was born was the day I died."

Ms. Featherly shuffled up to Kissabelle, holding out her hands. "My sweet woman. Your hands have cracks and callouses, and your wrinkles make you seem older, worn. But I see your green eyes, and I know your heart beats for what is right. Your spirit is stronger than the stones that crashed in on you. I pray that through Jolene you'll keep up to date on ... Shelby ... Charley. And we'll watch for the shoes every June. I'll even let her know what size you'll need to get."

Kissabelle fell into Ms. Featherly's arms, whispering, "He's beautiful, isn't he? I bet he's smart, too."

"Yes, he's the smartest boy in his class. I'm sure he got that from you. Did you notice he has your green eyes?"

Weeping, the two mamas held each other, and I longed for Ms. Susan, who is my newest and bestest mama ever. She wants me. She loves me. She'll be with me in the future when I cry. When I laugh. When I fall. Or when I get taller. And she'll buy me shoes every year, too. And she'll read my book, the one about my life—the one where I became a messenger of hope after ashes left soot on my PF Flyers.

Que reached for my hand, and I licked the salty tears coming down my face. He almost whined, "Look! Over there! It's a black car. It's got to be Boss Crump's men."

Shrugging him off, I shook my head. "No, that's not them. That's Reverend Roberts."

He turned my head. "No, over there. That black car."

I twisted his face the other way. "No, over there."

Kissabelle hollered, "Inside! We need to get off the street, and now!"

We scrambled for the shoes, for the papers, for the few stray bills floating on the grass. Chasing after Ms. Featherly, we tumbled inside her apartment—the one with dozens and dozens of photographs on the wall behind the sofa, of her son. Photographs of Kissabelle's flesh and blood. Ms. Featherly locked the door, shaking her head. "What in the world is going on?"

Que rushed to the opened window, twisting the knob as the window closed. "Boss Crump is working with Ms. Tann, and my job at the orphanage has gotten me involved in a case that has put me against them. They're crooks, steal people's money, and sell babies they have no right to."

Kissabelle wailed, "Look at these! He's the prettiest baby ever!"

*Knock. Knock. Knock*

Ms. Featherly froze, her eyes grew big, and she whispered, "What shall I do?"

Scuffling sounds came from the hall, and the knob on the front door to her apartment jiggled. "Anybody inside? Que? Shoelace? Are you there?"

## When the Party Leaves

"Quedellous, are you inside? We saw you!" The hollering from the other side of the door told me exactly who was looking for us.

"Que, it's your pa! See, I told you. It's Mr. Reverend, too!" I barreled to the door, unlocked the knob, and twisted it, but before I could get my hand off, the door rammed into me. "Whoa!" Jumping back, I barked, "You could have let me open the …"

Standing face to face with Mr. Blake, he glared at me, uttering, "We need to go."

Que pushed me aside. "What do you want? I heard my pa, that was his voice."

Blake motioned. "It's fine. They're all here. Come inside Reverend Roberts. You too, Leroy."

Ms. Featherly slid to a big-armed chair, perching herself behind the back of the high-backed arch. "What is going on here? This is my apartment!"

Mr. Reverend scooted across the wood floor and extended his hand, his suit out of place for a Monday morning. "Ma'am, we're here to retrieve Leroy's son, and this one, too." He pointed to me. "This is Annie Grace and she must come with us."

Ms. Featherly mumbled, "I think she should stay with her people." She pointed to Kissabelle who hadn't stopped absorbing the pictures of Charley on the wall, with him in a stroller, on a blanket, the photos of him crawling and walking. "Isn't she her mother?"

Kissabelle switched from a stone face lost in time stare to looking at me. "She's not my daughter. I have one son. One. And he's ... he's perfect."

I walked up to Ms. Featherly. "I'm just passing through town. I'm staying ... staying with the reverend."

Ms. Featherly argued, "I'm not so sure about this."

Leroy moved next to Que, "Son, tell her that we know Shoelace, and she's been our company for the past week."

Que waved both arms as if he was directing traffic. "Her name's Annie Grace. She uses a nickname, like Foster does. You know how we call him "Shelby"? Well, everyone who is friends with Annie Grace, they call her Shoelace."

Smiling, I inched up next to him. "So, you think I'm your friend now?"

Frowning, he grumbled, "We're working on it. So, don't mess this up."

Ms. Featherly piped in, "I'm not sure what's happening, I'm going to call my husband. Maybe I should phone for the police to clear this up."

Mr. Blake, who looked like he was wearing the same brown suit from the weekend, reached inside his pocket, pulling out a wallet. He flipped the folded leather apart. "I'm an officer of the law, ma'am. We're involved in a serious matter. Hiding this girl from her own kind has been of utmost importance. She's involved in a case of historical magnitude. She's changing the lives of many."

Squinting my eyes, I shook my head and whispered to Que. "What is he doing? Am I that important?"

"Yes, you are to God. He is using you. Even if you tend to get loud and distracted. So, hush, Blake's making a way for us to leave without causing any more of a disturbance."

Ms. Featherly held the wallet and glanced at the identification. "Are you sure?" She turned to me. "Are you safe?"

Grinning, I latched my arms around the reverend. "Yes, ma'am. I'm safe. We ran out of gas in the pickup outside. Or Que did, and I saw this poor woman who seemed lost." I pointed to Kissabelle.

She muttered, "I'm not lost. I'm on my way. I came to see my son, and now ..." Kissabelle sighed. "Now, I have to go. I have to leave."

Ms. Featherly inched toward her front door. "Then I expect you'll all be on your way. I do have to get to work. My pies won't bake themselves this morning."

Kissabelle lugged her bag, stopping at the hallway, rushing back to Ms. Featherly. "Can I leave the shoes?"

"The shoes?"

"Yes, I have thirteen pair. I've bought them for Charley's birthdays. May I ... can I ... give them to him for his birthday? You don't have to say who or what or even why. Maybe you could put them on a shelf in his room."

Ms. Featherly stepped back, rubbing her chin. "I'm not sure about that, he'll ask questions."

I looked at Mr. Reverend and Leroy, whispering, "Charley is ... he is Foster Featherly. He's friends with Que and plays in street bands on Beale. They call him Shelby. But he's also ... also Charley. Tell them, Blake. Tell them how you found him."

Before anyone could move or speak or help change Kissabelle's mind, she ripped into her bag. "One, two, three ... little tiny shoes. Four, five, six ... little boy loafers. Seven, eight, nine, ten ... PF Flyers and loafers. Eleven, twelve ... big boy's shoes." She clutched the last pair of shoes. "These are for last week's birthday. I think he'll like these black Converse."

Talking under my breath, I shrugged, "Who wears Converse? PF Flyers are the best."

Ms. Featherly shook her head, standing in front of the pile of shoes. "But, I don't know. I don't know if …"

Kissabelle hugged Ms. Featherly. "This is the best present for me, to know he's alive! You have no idea!" With that, Kissabelle reached into her giant bag. "Shoelace, here's Ms. Jolene's papers," and she shoved them into my arms.

"You took all of her research?"

"I figured I'd learn about Charley. But …"

Que placed his hand on her shoulder. "But God sent Shoelace to send you to him, instead." He smiled, a teenage smirk that made me glad I was credited with something good for a change, instead of horrible-bad things.

Kissabelle dug into her bag again, rummaging and stacking the money into her clasped hands while Blake ushered us. "We need to go."

She didn't listen and piled the money into the reverend's pockets on his jacket, and then handed him a wad from the bottom of the bag. "This is Jolene's money from her china doll. Give it to her. She's going to need it to build her restaurant back."

The stacking, the shoving, the shuffling, and the sorting unfolded with questions coming from each of us. But Kissabelle ignored us, closed her bag, and charged from the hallway, only to turn back right before she opened the door to the front yard. "I'll see you all this side of the Mississippi River, someday down the tracks."

Leroy rushed toward her. "Wait! You don't have to go."

"I must go. I know one thing. It's boxcars and living for the next rumble that will take me to the only life I know. Besides, God gave Charley a better mama than me—"

Standing like a statue, I had no words for her, and then Blake broke the silence. "We need to get back to the farm. There's something we need to do. And it can't wait. I hope we're not too late."

## Cake for Whom?

Sitting in the back of the reverend's car next to Que, we whispered back and forth. I leaned over to him. "So, your pa's gonna punish you for taking the truck, huh?"

"Yes, and for risking your life, too."

"I was not in danger, was I?"

"Well, I haven't driven much. After this morning, now I'll never get to drive."

"I wonder what the rush is to get us to the farm. Do you think Blake knows something bad? Or could it be good news? Whatever it is, we're following him down side streets and going way too fast."

"He knows something. I could tell by how he looked at you."

"Do you think it's horrible? Like, is Willie …" I gulped, unable to finish that question or icky thought.

"I'm sure he's fine. It's probably about Crump's men."

Shaking my head. "Haven't you noticed, Mr. Reverend's car is exactly like Blake's car. Same everything."

"Yeah, I've noticed."

"You can't tell a good guy from a bad in a car."

Que rolled his eyes. "No kidding."

The dust from the long dirt road leading up the farm house smothered the car with sooty sand, and the windows were caked with dirt. As we pulled into the driveway, I yelled, "I see a bunch of people on the porch. A whole bunch of people. Your people!" I touched Mr. Leroy on the shoulder. "What's going on?"

"We're having a party!" He turned to us, smiling like a secret lurked inside his throat.

Que and me leaned forward staring through the front glass of the car, in between Mr. Reverend and Mr. Leroy. Que asked the question I wanted to. "What? Whose party? And now? We need to find Willie and get busy about it!"

Leroy twisted his head. "You told me you spent the night snooping at the orphanage and stalking Kissabelle at the cemetery and then bothering poor Ms. Featherly, which I know was for good reason—and now you're telling me to get busy searching for Willie?"

Mr. Reverend sighed. "Let them off the hook. Tell them about last night. The part they missed."

I smarted off, "Tell us! What is going on?"

Mr. Leroy explained, "Our deacons and the men from the church paid a visit to Georgia Tann's house in the wee hours. One of our officers phoned and let us know he got a tip where Willie was ..."

I blurted out, "I bet it was Mr. Blake or Mr. Blair." Coughing, I asked, "Where is Mr. Blair? He's usually with …"

Mr. Reverend mixed up his words with mine. "Our men surrounded the home, took a few rifles and shotguns for protection, and I carried my Bible. I knocked on the door, and two of the suits that were guarding the boy bolted to the front porch, knocking me on my back and my Bible flew open."

"No way! You went after Willie?"

"Yes, and then Blake and Blair were with us. It seems they'd left the two of you and came upon our little meeting on Stonewall Street."

"And what happened?"

Mr. Leroy cut in. "It went down fast. One of the men charged us, and Blair pulled his pistol, but the man from the porch shot first and …"

"No! Is he … is he alive?"

"No, sweetie, but he got off a round and shot both men. They were the only two guards at the house, and with Ms. Tann in the hospital, the other ladies inside gave him up without a word."

Mr. Reverend parked the car behind Mr. Blake's car. "The men died at the hospital, and Mr. Blair lost his life, too. It crushes me. His wife has gone through so much. This town needs the Lord. We must do more to win souls and save folks for Christ."

Wiping the tears from my eyes, I had to ask the next question. "So, where is Willie?"

Together, Mr. Reverend and Mr. Leroy spoke, "He's inside."

I grabbed the handle on the car door, opening it. "Is he really?"

Mr. Leroy smiled. "Yes, he's not hurt. A little scared, but he's calmed down this morning. He rested with Jolene since we brought him back."

Mr. Reverend opened his door, and the scream of joy and fun and laughter and shouting pierced through my sadness. Mr. Reverend took my hand. "We're having a party before you all leave. Mr. Boyd is here. He's fine; the doctor released him. And Mr. Marion Kane, too. We picked up Archie, but he's not moving so fast, so watch the hugging."

My heart beat faster than I could run, and the men from the church and their families clapped as I charged up the steps, and into the parlor. My arms ached to embrace Willie, but I saw Mr. Marion first and yelled, "I love you! I'm so glad you're here. I'm so happy you're not dead."

Then I charged to Mr. Boyd who sat next to him on the sofa. I screamed lost words that I never thought I'd say, "Daddy! Daddy! You're not hurt too much, are you?"

He held me close. "I'll never hurt too much to hold you. I just got grazed by the bullet. I received a few stiches in my leg, and I'm good."

Mr. Marion patted my head. "He has forty stitches! But he'll heal. And I just got a little slice on my arm … mostly it's my heart rate they were worried about."

From behind me, I heard the sweetest little sound. "Shoelace? It's me! I can still see you!"

Twirling around, I hopped like a rabbit toward … toward my Willie! "It's you! You're alive! I'm sorry this is happening. We're going home! You'll go with me, too! And I'll never leave or go anywhere! Ever!"

Willie cried, "The bad men won't hurt me, will they? They held my arms and squeezed them, but they won't come again to take me. Will they?"

"No, baby brother! No!"

Ms. Reverend scooted up along with Ms. Jolene, who was weeping and smiling. She held the two of us as if we were sacred to her. "Willie, you'll go and have a home in Texas now. And you'll have Shoelace and get to meet your twin sister, Lizzy Beth."

He glanced up at her. "Will you come see me? I need to see you, too. I like seeing people."

She sighed. "I'll come often, and I'll stay as long as I can."

Willie hugged me, and ran to Jolene. "I love you! I wish Ms. Lottie was here."

Jolene sniffled. "I think she is honey. I think she is …"

Iris and Siri joined in the hugging and wrapped their arms around me, and I glanced at their shoes. Iris, wearing her white PF Flyers, announced, "We're having cake! Mama baked it this time. It's for Willie! And it's a party for you too, Shoelace! You are our new sister."

Siri laughed, glancing at her brown arm. "But you're a little pale, though."

Willie looked at his arm. "I am pale, too. I match Shoelace."

I held him close. "Well, you do have that Choctaw blood in you, and you got the black hair and darker skin than me. But you do match me. We belong to each other!"

Blake moved into the middle of the room. "We need to make the party quick. We need to get these balloons out of here, too. Crump's men will be here anytime, I'm sure of it. I hate to break things up, but … the police will be coming here to question Reverend Roberts about last night, too. We need to have this place in order."

Ms. Reverend touched his arm. "I'm sorry to hear about your partner, Blair. This whole thing is a horrible crime and it's taking lives. We must put a stop to this, but the Lord is giving us this time for cake. I'll get you a piece."

Willie held my hand. "I'm never letting go. I'm never letting go."

Mr. Boyd reached for my hand and for Willie's hand. "And I'm never letting go of either of you! Lizzy Beth will be thrilled. I can't wait to see Ms. Susan's face!"

*Kabam.*

The man who loved on me yesterday at the church meeting stormed into the room, and the screen door bounced with a slapping flop-flop. "We have company. Three black cars! Three! They're coming down the driveway!"

## Slingshot of Hope

Blake marched to the window looking through the pane. "It's my people. Not to worry! I've called for them before Crump and his men catch wind of our taking Willie. Which I'm sure he's heard, but that's why we need to move … and move now."

Rushing up beside him, I gawked, trying to see past the bodies scrambling and now holding guns. "Look, they don't know it's not Crump's men. They're ready to shoot!"

"You're right!" He raced through the door, pushing between bodies and arms, and I joined him as if my feet felt glued to this march of hope.

Pushing myself between the legs and arms, I jumped from the porch and hurried to the yard. I climbed on the top of Blake's car, balancing myself in the wind, my feet pressing dents in the shiny hood. "Stop! Everybody stop! Put your guns down! These are Blake's friends! They're here to help us! They're here to …"

*Kaplunk!*

The thud and the sting on my forehead sent my hand to the burn, and the sticky goo oozing from my brow ran down my face. Glancing at my fingers, the blood coated my hand like death, like horror, like anger rising faster than hope in Memphis.

Wobbling, I knelt on the hood, and then someone pounded onto the hood, a suit—a suit of hope, a voice speaking for God. "Friends! Friends! Stop this now! The anger must stop. The killing, too." Reverend Roberts clutched me to his side, and from the other side of the car Archie reached up to hand me a handkerchief.

The cars skidded to a stop on the other side of us, and three drivers popped from the cars. It was as if slow motion life stalled like a breeze caught in a bottle and the lid trapped the movement.

Wiping my head with the cloth, I found myself remembering the lopsided grins in the boxcar last week. The three drivers skipped toward us, and then a fat man who had a piece of straw in his mouth showed himself, sliding from the passenger side of the first car.

He called to me, and danced a sidestep in front of the other three men. "If it isn't our little friend from the tracks."

Swallowing hard, I swayed like I might faint, and Mr. Reverend hung onto me, keeping me from tumbling off the car. I probed, "What? Who are you four? I remember you from the other day when … when I first met Kissabelle!"

The round one spoke, "Yes, she's full of information. She helps us track down leads up and down the rail."

Blake stepped next to them. "These are my men. They're undercover, too. They ride the tracks and follow the families who come to Memphis buying babies, and they see where they go. They ride in and they ride out. They hide out, too."

The fat one tossed his straw to the ground. "Nice to meet you, little hero girl!"

"I'm not a hero. I'm just a girl who wants to go home."

"And that's why we're here. We'll put you in a car with Willie. We'll put Mr. Boyd in another. And Marion Kane in another car. We'll take three paths to the train station. It's time to send you on your way."

Swallowing in the air sent from heaven, I wiggled to the front of the hood, finding courage to speak to the people who lingered with guns and sticks.

Mr. Reverend whispered, "Are you strong enough to stand?"

"I am, thanks to you and these people!"

"Then share from your heart. This is your time."

Holding my head, I saw Willie on the porch with Ms. Jolene, and he cried, but Mr. Boyd smiled and put his hand to his heart and whispered in the wind. "I love you, my daughter."

I sucked in the fear lingering in my throat, summoning the Annie Grace Kree courage. "Who threw the rock that hit me in the head?"

My question dropped to the dusty ground like a grain of sand lost in the millions of others. Silence fell. And no one answered. I balanced myself and went on, "My Grandma Elsie met me one night in the front yard at her manor in Texarkana. I had disobeyed her and snuck outside, and I figured she'd paddle me and banish me to my room forever."

Mr. Reverend tapped me on the back. "Go on, child. Speak from your heart. We need to be reminded that we're all God's children. We all have hearts—they get lost and tucked away when life spirals though."

I licked my lips. "What do you think happened when I saw her standing on the front porch?"

More silence. Even the birds stopped tweeting, and the sun beat down like a fire, and the sweat poured down the faces of everyone glaring at me. The small colored boy not much older than Willie shuffled forward, and the slingshot in his hand hung at his side. "I am the one. I hit you with the rock. I did it."

I slid off the hood, and knelt in front of the boy, wrapping my arms around his small quivering frame. "I forgive you. I do. We all want to silence the pain, and it gets hard to breathe.

282

We might react with more pain. With more hurt. Even anger. And I can't live like that anymore. So, I forgive you."

The boy slithered from my embrace, running back from me, and hurried into his mother's arms, where she carried him off from the crowd.

Mr. Reverend took control of the whispering, and I crumpled to the ground like a broken blade of grass. Around my neck, arms slid and comforted me. I saw Willie. I saw Iris. I saw Siri. I saw a girl. I saw a boy. The children had come around me and held me, and loved me. I found myself speaking to my birth daddy one last time, whispering to myself, "Daddy! I wanted to be yours. But I am so thankful that you loved me as best you could. I forgive you for not being more, but I'm so happy God is the more I need—He's given me life."

Weeping like a baby stolen back from the baby stealer of life, the one that kept me on the rail, kept me running and hiding like Tin Can Mahlee, like Kissabelle, I heard the reverend say what lived inside my soul.

I rose up taller, as did the children. As did the grownups. As did Blake. And his four men, except for the short round man. He was crying. As did Ms. Reverend who was now singing, "Amazing grace, how sweet the sound…"

The little boy who had held the slingshot burst between all the others. "I have this for you. It's a wet cloth to wipe your head. I'm sorry." The boy blubbered his words, and his mama placed her hand on his shoulder, nodding and weeping with him.

She glanced at me. "We're all sorry."

Mr. Reverend added, "Remember, we are the church who loves to love. May we never forget this, and may we do small things for the Lord, in a great way."

Blake interrupted, "We must go now! It's time! You need to say your goodbyes!"

Mr. Marion walked up, slowly, and purposed. "Does anyone know what happened to my car? I left it at the church."

Archie answered, "I think the police impounded it."

Before I could let Mr. Marion know Archie had also sold his old pickup truck, Ms. Reverend bellowed from the porch, pointing. "Up there! By the road! I see a man! He's watching us!"

Blake ushered us. "Shoelace, get your things. We're leaving, and we're leaving now!"

Mr. Reverend ordered, "Take the back road behind the barn, but cut between the trees with the yellow mark. It's about a hundred feet behind the pond. You'll miss the main highway this way, and it'll take you straight to the train station."

Archie grabbed me by the neck. "Go get your life, Annie Grace. My place is here. I'll keep up Lottie's race. We'll stop Georgia Tann, you'll see."

My arms collapsed around the neck of the sweetest man alive. The one who rode into my life, to save it! "I'll never forget you!"

"Same here. You're not easy to forget!"

Ms. Reverend handed me my satchel. "Go on. God speed, my child!"

Iris and Siri waved to me from the porch, and all the people who held guns and sticks now lined up along the dirt road behind the old farm house—the one I may never get to see again. I held onto my brother. "We'll be home before you know it."

Willie huffed, "So is Texas big? And will I like it?"

Smiling, I assured him, "Yes! It's huge. And you'll love it in Jefferson. Timmons and Tak are about your age. They'll love you!"

He placed his head on my shoulder. "I hope so."

The fat man sitting in the passenger seat glanced over his shoulder. "We'll have you to the train in no time."

Nodding, I sighed. "I'm used to riding in boxcars. But having a seat will be nice—especially since I'll be sitting with Willie, Mr. Boyd, and with Marion Kane."

## When Smiles Return

*Click. Clack. Click. Clack.*

Switching the light on and off, I shot the beam from the flashlight onto my church dresses and onto Lizzy Beth's clothes. They are lined in a perfect row and face the same way, and our shoes were perfect until I sat on them.

*Click. Clack. Click. Clack.*

The dreamcatcher drawn on the closet wall by Lizzy Beth was still there, but now there's a monster next to it. Willie calls it the Memphis Monster and used her crayons to sketch it with Lizzy Beth on the second day. He fit right in, and was so happy to be here. As for Ms. Susan, she cried and smiled and hugged, and we had so much company. It was like a reunion at our house.

Willie went to the doctor who said there's nothing wrong with his eyes. Said he's not sure there ever was anything wrong. He can see for miles. And he's smarter than Lizzy Beth, if that's possible.

But the two of them together are double trouble, and they get in more trouble than me these days. Daddy Boyd had a carpenter build a bedroom for me behind the kitchen, and added a small hallway for me. I have a bed in the shape of a boxcar too, and a dresser with my poetry papers on top. I have mountains painted on my walls and clouds on my ceiling.

We've been home for three weeks now, and so far, Willie hasn't slept in his room, which was the sewing room. He's sleeping with Lizzy Beth, afraid to be alone. I haven't slept in my bed yet, either. I crawl right in between them and snuggle, holding them close.

The nightmares keep rushing in after dark, and I see the masked man from Texarkana sometimes in my sleep, and then sometimes I see the face of the woman in glasses who stole babies. But mostly I see Taddy, and Tin Can Mahlee, and Pastor Cody, and Skip, and Silas, and Molasses Jones, and Baby Hope. And always … always my grandma rescues me right before I wake up.

Archie called from Memphis and he told Mama and Daddy the orphanage case is about to crash in on Georgia Tann, and that she's dying of cancer, too. I try to pray for her that Jesus saves her, but I have to pray to mean it, because it's hard. I do mean it, but she's hurt so many. And her life has become ugly. But Jesus could make it pretty, at least for her, on the inside of her heart.

*Click. Clack. Click. Clack.*

"Stop flashing the light in my eyes!" Lizzy Beth shoved me from the left, while Willie laughed on my right. She grabbed the flashlight, shooting the beam upward to the ceiling above the rack of clothes. She announced, "Remember, we're hiding from ma and pa inside the closet, and they'll never think to find us here."

Giggling, I kicked the door open which we never latch. "They'll never think to look in here? They know this is where we go every time!"

Willie shot to the bed, the afternoon sun shooting through the window, and he bounced on the mattress, clapping his hands. "What is their surprise? They told us it's a surprise. Is a surprise a good thing?"

Lizzy Beth crawled up from the floor, joining her brother. Her long hair flopped up and down, and her pink shirt made her skin so bronze looking, and they jumped together. Even

Willie's black hair and its curls were like her hair. They favored each other like matching socks. I glanced at my pale skin and my blonde hair. I'm sort of like an extra sock.

Lizzy Beth yakked, "I heard them say we're getting a puppy."

I spouted, "You did not. We're not getting a dog." I sat on the bed, going up and down in little swaying motions as they pounced in jumps with screaming. I emphasized my statement: "We make too big of a mess for Mama Susan to let us have a dog. She's a clean person. She lines up everything. Labels it, too. We have to take our shoes off to come inside."

Willie fell to the bed in a swoosh, landing on his back. "So, does she think we're too messy? Will she keep me? Or will I have to go somewhere else if I make a bad mess?"

Lizzy Beth fell onto her brother, slobbering sister words at him. "You and me will be here forever! Forever! We're theirs! They love us!"

I assured them both. "They've adopted you. And they've adopted me. We belong to them. They will never get rid of us. We are loved beyond our messes!"

The door to the bedroom swung open, and Mama Susan carried a chocolate cake in her hands. "We have the best news! Come to the parlor. Let's have a picnic on the coffee table."

Daddy Boyd peeked over her shoulder. "Yes, come. We can't wait to tell you."

Rushing from the bed, Willie and Lizzy Beth raced each other into the front room, sliding in their socks. I charged past them like lightning, belting my questions. "So, what's the surprise?"

Mama Susan smiled. "All three of you sit there on the sofa."

288

Like labels on a shelf, the three of us organized ourselves on the edge of the sofa. I begged, "Tell us. Tell us what the surprise is."

Daddy Boyd sliced the cake. "It's about this cake. Sort of." He placed slivers of cake onto saucers, and moved them to the side as he cut a slice for all five of us.

Willie grinned. "So, are we getting cake every day?"

Lizzy Beth laughed. "No! We only get cake on special days."

Willie nodded. "Every day I get to stay with you," he touched Lizzy Beth's cheek. "And every day I have you, Shoelace is … is my special day."

I hugged Willie. "You are my special. You are right. We should get cake every day!" I leaned over and hugged Lizzy Beth. "And you are, too! I have two specials!"

Mama Susan and Daddy Boyd knelt across from us, and turned to each other. Mama looked at Daddy with glistening eyes. "Shall I tell them?"

Together the three of us screamed, "Tell us!"

Mama Susan explained, "Shoelace, the manor in Texarkana that your grandma owned, it's now ours! We bought it!"

Willie shook his head. "So what's a manor?"

She went on, "It's a house that people go to when they travel or if they need a temporary place to rest."

Willie blinked, looking at me. "That's the surprise? We get a house?"

Daddy Boyd laughed. "Sort of. That's a surprise for Shoelace. We wanted the manor to be hers when she's grown. We'll staff it with a housekeeper and have it fixed up. And rent out rooms."

Sighing, I found my memories of the past two years flying through my head like a flashlight of shooting beams. I stuttered, "Thank you! My grandma Elsie loved that place."

Lizzy Beth groaned. "So what's my surprise? What's Willie's surprise? That's not our house."

Mama Susan hurried to the kitchen, returning with a brown, wiggly, long-eared puppy that squirmed from her hands. "Catch him! He's wild."

Lizzy Beth rushed to him, as did Willie, and Daddy Boyd announced, "We thought you two would like to have a puppy!"

Laughing and running and chasing consumed the twins, and they circled in and out of rooms as I sat back on the sofa. Every couple of minutes, the four paws scurried around the table, and the puppy twisted and jumped and yapped.

Mama Susan moved to sit with me. "I thought you'd be proud we bought the manor for you. But I can see you're troubled." She stroked my hair. "You're my daughter, and nothing will change that, but I had hoped to do this for you— to bring joy to your heart. Someday you may want to move there when you're grown. You never know where life will take you."

"I am happy, I suppose. But so much took place there. So much death. And Taddy was my best friend, and he doesn't even like me now."

"But he and his mama live here now. In Jefferson. He'll come around."

Sighing, I vented, "I'll never forget how Tin Can Mahlee sat in the corner of the parlor the night we saw the killer. Or how I saw the Phantom through the window."

"But remember how much she loved you. That's the memory to hold onto."

"I am trying, but I can't forget how Skip died after I saw him playing Grandma's piano at the funeral for my pa, and how I met Skip there. But he's dead, too."

"But there's life in the walls … you came from there. You're very much alive. You're the reason Willie and Lizzy Beth have each other." She turned from consoling me. "Boyd, catch that puppy for them. He's scratching up my floor."

Chuckling, Daddy Boyd gobbled down another bite of cake. "You're the one who said a puppy wouldn't drive you crazy. He's been here for less than a day, and you want me to chase after him. He's not my puppy."

"Boyd! Please! Maybe he should be a yard dog."

I giggled under my breath, then shouted, "Oh, my gosh! He took some cake from the coffee table, and he's tracking chocolate on the floor!" I jumped from the sofa. "Here, let me get him. I think his name should be …"

Willie raced by me. "His name should be Lottie."

Yelling at his blur of a body when Willie disappeared into the dining room, I countered, "His name can't be Lottie. He's a boy."

Mama Susan stood next to me, wiping frosting from her shoe. "He's a girl. And Lottie would fit him-her-nicely."

The chase after the puppy reminded me how I've chased so many things in the past two years: how I found and lost things, and how every step mattered—which brought me to this family, to this street where I live across from a library, which I love.

To where I live near Crush and his brothers, how Toby, the preacher in training lives here and teaches me scriptures. To where my first best friend now lives. Who isn't my friend right now but he will be. To where I'll need to climb a tree at Taddy's house to toss rocks at his window so we can start over. To where I have my own room. To where I have a brother and a sister. To where I have a mama and a daddy. To where I can find hope when nightmares come at night.

Ms. Susan flew by. "I'll catch this dog if it's the last thing I do…" Her words ended, as she slid across the hallway entrance on the rug, clasping the puppy.

*Ar-roof. Ar-roof.*

The puppy squealed, and Lizzy Beth and Willie squealed and chased the magic rug-ride down the hall, following Mama Susan. Their giggles grew louder than the whistle on a train rumbling into town.

I watched their hugging and yelled, "Yuck! That dog is licking Mama in the face!

She hollered, "Stop that! Oh, I hate puppy breath!"

Daddy Boyd touched my arm. "I have a surprise for you. It's something I found at your grandma's house when we made the trip to buy the manor. In her room, under the bed, I found a locket."

A twisted my face. "A locket?"

"Yes, and inside … well …" He reached inside his pants pocket. "Here, take a peek."

I clutched the locket, running to Lizzy Beth's bedroom, tumbling into the closet, where I hid from things and figured things out. Opening the locket, I sat in the darkness, unable to let the light in, and then like a rocket of noise and chaos, Willie and Lizzy Beth opened the closet door.

Lizzy Beth yelled, "Come on. We're taking Lottie outside. She piddled on the floor and Mama isn't happy." They ran off and she hollered, "Hurry up. Come with us."

"I'll be right there." I held the locket, peering through the tears. "No way! How did my grandma get that picture?"

Daddy Boyd came to me, shuffling in his loafers, kneeling on his knees. "I had hoped that you might want it. I didn't mean to make you sad."

"Sad? This is the best!" I hopped to my feet, hugging his neck, and showed him the photo. "This is me! Me! And I'm smiling and eating birthday cake at the manor! It was my first birthday cake ever. And my grandma baked it for me! Oh, I love chocolate cake! And I loved my grandma! Thank you so much!"

Daddy Boyd whispered, "May all your birthdays be filled with cake and smiles and love … and always with hope!"

Mama Susan bellowed from the back of the house. "What was I thinking? I have cake on the floor! I have dog pee on the floor! I have a mess bigger than messy!"

Daddy looked at me. "We better go help your mama out! Or we'll be living in the back yard with the puppy!"

I placed the locket in my overalls pocket, tapping the spot. "Cake! What a great surprise! A puppy! Not such a great surprise! A locket! The best!"

## The Brown Shoes Clue

Talking to God in the dark, I rattled on, "You could have saved my grandma. You could have made my daddy stop running. You could have given me a mama who lived when I was born. You've done things like this before. My Bible tells me so. You have power. When I cower down and hide, you should come and get me."

I took a deep breath. "You've sent angels to folks, too. You've sent a slingshot to a boy to kill a giant. You've parted seas. You've built a big boat and saved a family. You've saved a man after his brothers threw him in a pit. You called one man after your own heart to write lots of verses. Why can't you call life back to those who left me?"

I kicked the floor, growling and scowling, trying to figure out the stuff I couldn't figure out. "God, even now, I want you to prove me wrong that this hole from saying all these goodbyes, that they'll make me stronger."

I whined, and waited for God to answer, but again—He left me with silence.

"So, God! My nightmares shout at me like ghosts and call me to dark places. I want to run away late at night. I want to keep my sight on You, too. I want to stay here."

I paused like I do every night, and God refused to answer. He just let me do all the talking. "I know I'm scared. I want to pray. I want to live with Ms. Susan and Mr. Boyd. I love my brother, Willie, and my sister, Lizzy Beth. I love their puppy. I'm just alone in this home with a rope of fear tied to my waist when I sleep, and I end up in this closet. God, I need to find a way. So, I can stay!"

A wiggling something moved to my left, clicking on a flashlight, not my flashlight, but one she held. I glared at Mama Susan. "What are you doing in here? This is my place to pray!"

Ms. Susan whispered, hugging my neck. I jumped and hit my head on the monster-drawn wall. "Ouch!"

She hushed me, "Quiet now, you'll wake the children."

"Oh my! You scared me to death."

"Well, I was here first, waiting for you. You see, I come in to check on the three of you each night, then I find your spot empty. You're in here with the door closed, and it's breaking my heart. I don't want you to be alone. So tonight, I came in here early, and prayed for God to send you into my arms."

Weeping, I placed my head on her chest. "Mama Susan, I do love it here, it's just I need to see my grandma's manor one more time, to believe and to see, to talk to her before you fill it up with strangers who eat from her kitchen and sleep in her beds."

"I will take you. I have the keys to the car. Let's go now. It's nearly sunrise anyway. I'll let Boyd know: besides it's Saturday. I'm off from the cafe, and he's taking the twins fishing in the bayou with Timmons and Tak."

Nodding, I slipped on my old ratty PF Flyers for one last ride, for one last walk. "I'm ready."

"So, you're wearing your shoes and pajama gown?"

"Oh, maybe I'll put my overalls on."

"I'll wait for you out back, and we'll stop for breakfast along the way—just us." Ms. Susan tiptoed from the bedroom, and I grabbed a shirt from the drawer and ... pushed the locket beneath the folded clothes for safekeeping. "I'll keep that forever!"

\*\*

Pulling up to the manor, I noticed the tree beside Taddy's old apartment, and leaned up against the glass, peering from my side of the car. "That's where Taddy lived, on the second floor."

"I know, and he was blessed to have you."

"He might disagree."

Ms. Susan parked the car on 4th Street between the manor and the apartments. She stared at the backyard. "We've got to fix those screens, and paint that wood, and put a new roof on the carriage house. I think we'll make an apartment in there, maybe a writer's study for you."

Smiling, I stepped from the car, and pushed the gate open, moving across the weeded grass with straw-like stalks, the brown and dry crunch beneath my shoes, popping. "Oh, look over there! That's where I planted peanuts! They've grown wild and died!"

Sighing, I saw old dry things at every turn. Dry ground. Dead grass. Dead peanut bushes. Even the shrubs by the manor needed water. I glanced at Ms. Susan who rolled up the garden hose.

I marched up to her. "I soaked Taddy and made mud puddles out here with that hose. My grandma yelled at me that day."

Ms. Susan giggled, "Well, you can bet I would, too. I'm sort of a cleaning nut. I like it polished. I like it scrubbed. I like shiny."

Nodding, I moved to the screen on the back door. "Do you think it's locked?"

"Yes, I have the key. Let me open it for you." Ms. Susan reached inside her pocket of her sundress, and slipped the key into the lock. "There, the door's open. I'll wait out here for now. You go inside and see what you see. And say what you need to say."

I moved inside without answering, letting the screen bounce behind me on the frame. Calling lower than a whisper, I called to my grandma. "I'm home from school. Grandma, where are you?"

Charging into the parlor, I came to the sofa, the chairs, and the tables; all were covered with white sheets. I ran my hand along the edge of the back of a chair, and peered at the wooden floor where I'd spilled a glass of tea when I first moved in with Grandma. "I'll get the mop. I'm sorry. I didn't mean to make such a mess."

Running to the kitchen, I searched for the mop and found the ice box wide open, and nothing inside. "I didn't mean to leave it open. Sorry, Grandma!"

The mop was gone. The food was gone. Only some soap powders sat in the window by the sink. And the new stove sat lonely in the corner.

Climbing the stairs, I came to my bedroom and pushed the door open. "Grandma, can you help me make my bed? Your scratchy quilts came from Memphis, did you know that?"

I moved to the balcony by my room, opening the glass-paned door, letting the summer heat beat in on me. It felt like death. Like suffocation. Like nothingness. "I shouldn't have come here. I can't do this. I can't say goodbye."

*Meow. Meow. Meow.*

"What? Is that? No! It can't be. It's Rainbow! My cat! You're still alive? Where have you been? I can't believe it's you!" I reached for the furriest and grayest cat ever, and plopped to the floor by the rail, cuddling my old friend. "Where have you been?"

*Meow. Meow. Meow. Meow.*

I rubbed her neck and under her chin, my finger catching something. "What's this? You have a collar now?" Puzzled, I glanced through the bars on the balcony up and down the street.

*Meow. Meow. Purr. Purr.*

"What's this tag say? Oh goodness, they've gone and changed your name."

*Kaboom. Kaboom.*

The noise from downstairs brought me to my feet. "I'm up here, Mama Susan. I've found my old cat."

I marched to the top of the stairs, and peeking at the name on the tag, screamed, "No! That's your name! Who would do that?"

A scuffle from the parlor brought me to a stop. "Mama Susan, I said I'm upstairs." Glancing down the steps, the brown loafers and the ironed slacks told me I had company. I moved closer, but the person marched into the kitchen.

Holding my cat, I lingered on the stairs, unable to go up, unable to go down. I sat down, waiting to hear Mama Susan call for me or speak to the man who probably wanted a room.

I kissed Rainbow's noggin, whispering, "I'm taking you home with me. You're mine!" I glanced at the tag which read, *Phantom.* Tossing the collar to the bottom of the stairs, the clunk against the wall brought the stomping closer.

I rose. I froze. And Rainbow scampered down the steps with a paw-dance, and the brown shoes came into view, along with the slacks, the jacket and the face. The man reached for Rainbow. "Well, there you are, Phantom."

Charging with two giant jumps toward him, I shouted, "Phantom? That's not my cat's name."

"Well, she moved in with me and I named her." The man's voice shrilled like a ghost from my past. "I've moved back to Texarkana, and I rented Priscilla's and Taddy's old apartment. And took in your cat. I got my old job back at the *Texarkana Gazette*, too. Seems there's some new leads about the Phantom Killer. A guy named Doodie is a prime suspect. But he's not being looked at ... so I'm here to do some investigating."

Frowning at Ernie, I pursed my lips, spitting in my mouth, only to scream at him. "You left Tin Can Mahlee and broke her heart when you moved to Florida. You're horrible!" I grabbed my cat. "And her name is Rainbow."

"Not anymore! She's my cat! You were gone! Besides, she tends to sneak out at night, and Doodie's taken a liking to her. I may need to let him have her."

Storming past him, I rounded into the kitchen, running, and spun around, expecting Ernie, the reporter to follow me, but I was alone. "Ernie? Where'd you go? Ernie?" Peeking into the parlor, Rainbow rolled around on the floor next to the staircase, purring. "Ernie?"

*Kaplunk-ta-plunk.*

The screen slammed behind me, and Mama Susan stormed up to me. "I saw a man leave the front porch of the manor. Who was he? Did he hurt you? What's he doing in the manor?"

I raced past her, out the back porch and jumped the picket fence, galloping across the street. Climbing the tree beside Taddy's old apartment, I searched inside the apartment by staring through the window.

I spoke to the tree. "I don't trust Ernie. Why is he really back?" On the bed a newspaper clipping revealed a headline: "Couple Murdered on Lover's Lane". I glanced at the paper. It was a Florida newspaper, and I nearly fell to the ground. "What? A couple died there, too?"

Fumbling for my grip on the branch, I leaned in. "Ernie's got newspaper clippings of all the Phantom Killer stories taped on the wall too, and photos of all the people who were attacked and hurt, and who died. But wait, that's me! Why would he have a picture of me?"

"Get down from that tree!" Mama Susan hollered like a sergeant sent to rescue me. "We're here to say goodbye to your grandma. What are you doing?"

Swallowing hard, I whispered to God. "So this is why you brought me back to Texarkana. I'm a 'vestigator, and I'm going to solve the case of the Phantom Killer!"

*Unwavering Hope*

### *Discussion Guide*

1.  Kissabelle (Crystal Belle) suffered from losing Charley
    to a kidnapping, and lost her way. She fought for each
    step, but ran from the sorrow. Have you ever felt like
    life has kidnapped your joy? Have you ever taken the
    path of running from life?
2.  Jolene loved Shoelace's daddy with eyes that saw him
    differently than that of a hobo or drunk or wayward
    man. She also saw her sister, Lottie, with eyes of love,
    even though her own daddy was unfaithful to her
    mother. Have you faced family matters that didn't
    come together with perfection or good news? Can you
    love with eyes like Christ?
3.  Reverend Roberts held his position as a father to Iris
    and Siri with authority. He was firm, disciplined, and
    caring. He was respected by his congregation and truth
    rose up in him. Does truth rise up in you?
4.  Ms. Reverend was an example of a virtuous woman.
    She walked with firmness and discipline too, but
    allowed her twins to make mistakes and to live with
    security, to have fun. Is your walk one of virtue?
5.  Leroy became a single father after losing his wife to a
    shooting, not counting that his younger son, Riley, got
    shot. What can we glean from Leroy's walk?
6.  Que was a teen on the verge of becoming a man. His
    world was skewed, but he worked on figuring out how
    to live when a person's skin color mattered to others.
    He was confident but fragile, and longed for a normal
    life. Has anyone ever judged you unfairly?
7.  Blake and Blair, two undercover cops, were in a
    pursuit to catch the Baby Stealer, and their jobs put

them in constant danger to do the right thing for future children in Memphis. Have you ever had to take a stand when others walk away?

8. Willie found sight when he was ready to see. He was innocent, and yet, he suffered. Has brokenness caused you to lose your sight on what matters?

9. Mr. Man at the church who didn't want to help Shoelace is like many of us—if we're honest. He found himself with blinders on, those who let the color of skin determine his answer. Have you ever fought to keep the blinders off? What can you learn from this man?

10. Georgia Tann's life became one of horrid secrets and of hurting children. She used the courts, doctors, and judges to make money while selling stolen babies. How can we love such a horrible person? Do you find it hard to get past a person's sin? Do you pray and share the Gospel with people who are lost—anyway?

11. Shoelace discovered that every step she'd taken since birth, since the day her daddy kidnapped her—brought her to the place where she could reunite her half-sister, Lizzy Beth, with her twin brother, Willie. Yes, every step mattered. Even the kidnapping mattered. Do you question the chapters in your own life? What can you gain from the lessons Shoelace learned?

*Search me, God, and know my heart; test me and know my anxious thoughts. See if there is any offensive way in me, and lead me in the way everlasting.*
*Psalm 139: 23-24*

The Harahan Bridge / The Mississippi River

Annie Grace Kree Chronicles Series

# 1 Untied Shoelace
# 2 Unknown Soul
# 3 Rescue of Undaunted Spirit
# 4 Unwanted Sidekick
#5 Unwavering Hope
#6 Unshackled Courage / Coming 2018

Other Books by Pam Kumpe

See You in the Funny Papers
A Scoop of Inspiration
Things I Learned in Jail
In the Lick of Time
A Goat with a Tote
My View from the Bridge
My View from the Street
My View from the Heart / Coming Christmas 2017

www.pamkumpe.com

*Leave comments on my Facebook page.*
*I'd love to hear from you!*

www.ingramcontent.com/pod-product-compliance
Lightning Source LLC
Chambersburg PA
CBHW020411260626
47156CB00007B/2337